A FOOT IN EACH WORLD

A FOOT IN EACH WORLD

Essays and Articles by
LEANITA McCLAIN

Edited and with an Introduction by

CLARENCE PAGE

NORTHWESTERN UNIVERSITY PRESS
EVANSTON, ILLINOIS

Northwestern University Press, Evanston, Illinois 60201

© 1986 by the Estate of Leanita McClain

All rights reserved. Published 1986
Printed in the United States of America

Library of Congress Cataloging-in-Publication Data

McClain, Leanita , 1951–1984.
   A foot in each world.

     1. Afro-Americans—Illinois—Chicago—Social
conditions.   2. Chicago (Ill.)—Social conditions.
3. Chicago (Ill.)—Race relations.   I. Page,
Clarence, 1947–   . II. Title.
F548.9.N4M33   1986   305.8′96073′077311   86–23510
ISBN 0–8101–0741–4
ISBN 0–8101–0742–2 (pbk.)

To Lloyd and Elizabeth McClain

Contents

CRIME AND PUNISHMENT

HOME AND FAMILY

SCHOOLS

Introduction

Milestones . . .
DIED. Leanita McClain, 32, sensitive, idealistic columnist for the Chicago *Tribune* and the first black member of the paper's editorial board, whose emotionally charged commentary reflected the tensions of the city's racially polarized politics; by her own hand (an overdose of pills), after bouts of depression brought on at least in part, friends said, by the strain of being a role model and by the furor resulting from an article she wrote for the Washington *Post* last summer titled "How Chicago Taught Me to Hate Whites," which prompted the city council to consider demanding an apology; in Chicago.

— *Time,* June 11, 1984

This book was the idea of several people at once. There were members of her family, people with whom she worked at the *Chicago Tribune*, her personal friends, at least one official of Chicago Mayor Harold Washington's office, and me. But the real impetus for this project was Edward Bassett, dean of the Medill School of Journalism at Northwestern University, who suggested it to Jack Fuller, who, as the *Tribune*'s editorial-page editor, was McClain's supervisor and friend. Knowing I was similarly interested, Fuller passed the suggestion on to me and the project was born.

We all agreed that media reports like the one illustrated above introduced many people to Leanita when it was too late for them to see her work for themselves. And those who had seen at least some of her work knew little of the person behind the often controversial words. Many of those who were stirred by McClain's writing had a way of lavishing praise and hero worship on her at a faster pace than she was willing to accept it.

Warm, witty and influential, Leanita McClain was also alienated, frustrated and, as she confided to those who were close to her, nervous about her own success.

Although she began her professional career in 1973, it was not until she wrote a provocative "My Turn" opinion column published by *Newsweek* in October 1980 that the public could read her personal views. In that first column, "The Middle-Class Black's Burden," she described her frustrations as an upwardly mobile black professional whose success came at the terrible cost of alienation from her own people. Few writers in the years that followed the racial advances of the 1960s have dealt so bluntly with the issue of what constitutes having "sold out," or how blackness should be defined—or whether it should be defined. "Whites won't believe I remain culturally different," she wrote. "Blacks won't believe I remain culturally the same."

Of course, there is nothing new or uniquely American about successful blacks receiving abuse from black militants. Algerian philosopher Franz Fanon, for example, chided the black bourgeoisie of French colonies. McClain provided a rare case of the bourgeoisie speaking back. "I have a foot in each world," she wrote, "but I cannot fool myself about either. I can see the transparent deceptions of some whites and the bitter hopelessness of some blacks. I know how tenuous my grip on one way of life is, and how strangling the grip of the other way of life can be." She concludes that whites should avoid trading in old stereotypes about poor blacks for new stereotypes about successful ones. At the same time, she notes, blacks should find encouragement in the success stories of some as an affirmation that the American Dream can work. "Inasmuch as we all suffer for every one left behind," she concludes, "we all gain for every one who conquers the hurdle." Interestingly, this sentence probably describes as well as any McClain's personal struggle to find cheer in her own success while so many with whom she had grown up were left behind in what she liked to call "the old country."

"Leanita McClain's life was an inspiration for young black professional women," wrote Bebe Moore Campbell in a postmortem in the December 1984 issue of *Savvy* magazine. "Her death is a grim reminder of how much we all have yet to learn." Campbell, in an article titled appropriately "To Be Black, Gifted, and Alone," used McClain as an example, albeit an extreme one, of the unique stress faced by black professional women in a workplace as unaccustomed to them as they are to it. "Leanita McClain finally laid her burden down and escaped the narrow alley located between pain and desire to another place. Her unanswered question continues to haunt her sisters. 'I have made it, but where?' "

She was the first black member of the *Chicago Tribune*'s editorial board and the newspaper's second black staff columnist in its 137-year history. Two months before she died she was named one of America's ten most outstanding career women by *Glamour* magazine. She had also received the Peter Lisagor Award from the Chicago chapter of Sigma Delta Chi, the Society of Professional Journalists; the 1983 Kizzy Award as an outstanding black female role model in Chicago, and in that same year the top award for commentary from the Chicago Association of Black Journalists.

Not that any of this made her happy. "Everyone is so nice to me," she said sadly as she looked at her awards in her living room during one of my last visits with her. "But why am I not happy?" It was a plaintive plea for help which no one—not her family, friends or psychiatrists—could answer.

"Interviews and some of her remarkably revealing childhood writings make clear that McClain's struggle to resolve grave personal identity problems was compounded by the unusual stresses faced by blacks who undertake the long journey from a childhood in the ghetto to jobs in white-dominated professions," concluded reporter Kevin Klose in a profile for the *Washington Post* after interviewing three dozen people, including her relatives, coworkers and psychologist. "These racial pioneers may possess special reservoirs of eloquence, as did McClain. But they must withstand enormous strains of isolation that whites seldom encounter in achieving similar success."

"She got all the stresses on all levels of blackness," black Harvard psychiatrist Alvin Poussaint told Klose. "There is guilt about feeling she had certain advantages because she's light-skinned, the apprehension that maybe other blacks would not accept her because she's light-skinned, the old self-doubts: 'Am I really thinking black, or are my experiences different because I'm light-skinned? How effective am I? Can I speak for my brothers and sisters?' "

Neither Klose nor Poussaint knew Leanita during her life, but they probably came about as close as anyone—and closer than most of those who speculated publicly about her death—to uncovering the demons that tormented her soul. Even her family and friends could say only that they knew the part of her that she chose to reveal.

"Lea was quite an accomplished actress, you know," said James Yuenger, a *Tribune* reporter and longtime friend, in his eulogy at her funeral. "Beneath that public person who was so pretty and gay and successful, there was a constant, ultimately deadly thread of uncertainty and self-doubt.

"But she knew—and refused to keep quiet about it—that despite the transitions taking place in this country, racism remains alive, and she did not mask the depth of her rage at injustice and mulish misunderstanding. When she spoke out, when she spoke the truth, it disturbed a lot of people who had thought they knew her. She was subjected to meanness and hypocrisy—and she knew who the hypocrites are."

Of course, there was more to Leanita than the race question, which columnist George Will calls "America's perennial problem." Yet the race question seemed to invade every aspect of her life, even from her birth.

She was born on Chicago's South Side in Provident Hospital, which she would seldom disclose without noting with pride how a black surgeon once performed the world's first open heart surgery in this black-owned hospital. She was the youngest of three daughters born to Lloyd McClain, a factory worker, and his wife Elizabeth. She grew up in the sprawling Ida B. Wells public housing project, a complex coincidentally named for a heroic black female journalist. Asked in later years why she thought she had been able to "make it" economically while so many of her fellow housing project residents did not, she would attribute it to her family. She would often single out something she had that remains too rare in project households, a loyal father.

Leanita and her two older sisters, Leatrice and Anita (from which Leanita's name was derived), went to public schools at a time when strict dress codes were observed, gangs and drugs were not yet a plague and it was not as difficult as it would be in later years for a couple of struggling parents to protect their little girls from the dangers of life in the projects. Her marks were good enough for her teachers to promote her a full grade ahead of her peers. Her mother would later recall that she expressed concern to a school official about Leanita's ability to keep up with older students. The official assured her that the school could advance Leanita two additional years and she would still keep up.

It was in high school that she began to write poetry, which she would keep in cardboard folders, hidden from public view.

> I should like to die in winter
> When my blood upon the snow
> Will leave a clue to those who pass
> Of my brief, futile life.

The garnet stain like a Rorschaht [*sic*] test
Will lead each to his conclusion.
"Too much, too soon," one will say.
"Too little, too late," will say another.

And none will learn the truth of the matter.
My secret will melt with the snow.
But the spot will run red each winter hence.
Though I be rotted below.

That sensitive young woman was only two years old when the United States Supreme Court declared that school segregation was wrong, that separate by its very nature was not equal. Hers was the baby boom generation that grew up with boycotts, sit-ins, riots, police brutality, assassinations, attempted assassinations, the Civil Rights Act, the Voting Rights Act, Vietnam, and Watergate. In her family's small two-bedroom apartment, she watched the televised coverage of Chicago police clashing downtown with demonstrators at the Democratic National Convention in the summer of 1968. She would recall later with cynical irony that she was not surprised to see police wielding clubs on young people, only that the young people were mostly middle-class whites. Her sisters became public school teachers, a profession Leanita considered until one day while attending classes at Chicago State University (the same former teachers' college that both of her sisters had attended) she was notified that her oldest sister, Leatrice, had walked into the crossfire of a gang feud and had caught a load of buckshot in an arm. Fortunately Leatrice was not permanently injured, but the incident soured Leanita on the idea.

College introduced her to class consciousness in a big way, she would later recall. At Chicago State the boys from the better-off neighborhoods would suddenly withdraw their requests for dates when they found out she lived in a housing project. She reacted by regarding her poor background as a badge of honor. Low income does not mean low breeding, she would point out. In fact, she found a certain nobility in the poor and their struggle to survive. "Poverty snob" was the label she made up for herself. McClain would later tell friends that it was one of her instructors at Chicago State who suggested she apply to the Medill School of Journalism at Northwestern University. She did and was awarded a full scholarship.

Although she graduated with high grades and met students and faculty who would become lifelong friends, she hated graduate school. It was her first time away from home, and she felt quite out of place in the suburban campus among students from families far wealthier than any she had ever known. And, though the scholarships and money saved from summer jobs covered her big expenses, she sometimes went for days with nothing but eggs in her refrigerator just to avoid asking her parents for help.

In the spring of 1973, during her final quarter of graduate school, she was hired as an intern by the *Chicago Tribune*, which, after she graduated, hired her as a full-time general assignment reporter. She covered such diverse assignments as a circus parade (in which she rode an elephant) and the aftermath of the assassination of Dr. King's mother in Atlanta. But she was a reporter for less than two years before she moved to the copy desk. Although she never failed to perform with excellence, the life of a reporter ran counter to her inclinations. She loved to write and edit but hated most aspects of daily news reporting, particularly the need to prod and cajole total strangers into revealing intimate details of their lives. The copy desk suited her shyness.

She performed well and her supervisors were no less eager than her public school teachers to promote her ahead of her peers. Soon she was promoted to the picture desk and then to the Perspective department.

She accepted each advancement with fear that she would not be able to do the job well enough to meet her own demanding standards of excellence. And each time she took the new position within a month she began complaining that the job was too easy.

Besides a job, the *Tribune* unintentionally put her within heavy breathing room of a husband, a fact that should not, as James Thurber once wrote of his own marriage, get "lost in the shuffle of these reminiscences." You could not call ours a love at first sight. But I clearly remember how I was stricken immediately by the cute, sandy-haired, green-eyed and freckled young black woman I saw trying to find her way around the *Tribune* news room on her first day at work. We became friends and our infrequent dates turned within weeks into a warm romantic relationship. We were married on May 28, 1974, a little more than a year after she came to the newspaper.

It was a marriage cast in the American Dream. We hosted integrated parties. We vacationed in the Caribbean, Europe and Acapulco. We played racquetball and jogged in the park. Among coworkers, we were known good-naturedly as "the golden couple," the very embodiment of black success. But I do not think anything concerned Leanita more than the plight of her race, of the poor and of black women. She had difficulty resolving that with our own young urban professional life. Among our mostly white neighbors in Chicago's trendy Belmont Harbor area, rising condominium fees and the quest for good imported wines were the biggest social concerns.

Lea felt that young black professionals were, as a group, more socially concerned than their white peers. None of us is free until we are all free, Leanita would say. Yet black professionals were themselves the object of criticism from black activists who charged they had forgotten "where they came from." Leanita resented that and, after much thought, decided her feelings might provide grist for what was fast becoming the greatest of the few remaining national soap boxes for freelance opinion, *Newsweek*'s "My Turn" column.

"I am a member of the black middle class who has had it with being patted on the head by white hands and slapped in the face by black hands for my success," she wrote in her blunt manifesto.

I had doubts that *Newsweek* would find room for an essay so personal—or that the magazine's mostly white editors would even understand it. But, in fact, it was just the sort of from-the-heart expository prose for which the "My Turn" section editors hungered. Ten days after she dropped her unsolicited essay into the mail, she was called by a *Newsweek* editor who wanted to arrange for a photograph. The column had been accepted.

Reaction was immediate and strong. Phone calls streamed in, mostly from other black middle-class women who wanted to say, "Right on, sister," or words to that effect. More than one hundred pieces of mail streamed in from as far away as South Africa, where a Cape Town newspaper had reprinted the column, editing out, interestingly enough, a line that referred to how her dilemma was not unique to the United States. Some critics, almost all of them white, wrote in to advise her to stop complaining and be happy with what she had. She began to receive invitations to California and Washington, D.C., to speak on one aspect or another of the changing agenda of black America. She also was invited by James D. Squires, the *Chicago Tribune*'s newly installed editor-in-chief, to write columns for the newspaper, perhaps with potential for national syndication. The emerging class of black professional baby boomers needed a voice, and Leanita McClain was becoming that voice.

More promotions came—assistant Perspective section editor, Perspective section editor, occasional columnist, weekly columnist, editorial board and twice-weekly columnist.

"This place had never given this kind of opportunity to a woman or a minority," Squires would tell the *Washington Post*. "And I wanted to give it to one with a good chance to succeed." She was a "young superstar," he said.

* * *

Our marriage fell apart. As our careers blossomed, we grew apart more than I realized at the time. It was not until one day when Leanita said she wanted a divorce because she needed to find peace for her restless, troubled spirit in her own time and place, that I realized our marriage was in trouble. We tried for almost two years to hold it together, then decided to part as friends.

In the summer of 1983 her bitter account in the *Washington Post* (headlined "How Chicago Taught Me to Hate Whites") of how betrayed she felt by whites she had thought to be more reasonable touched off a flurry of controversy, locally and nationally.

Many will say in retrospect that the anguish Leanita expressed in the *Post* piece was a reflection of her own personal anguish. Perhaps. Most people had no idea that she had already made an attempt at suicide one night, not long after she moved out of our household. Or that she was seeing a psychoanalyst sporadically. Or that she constantly lamented to me and other close friends that life for her no longer had much meaning.

They found Leanita's body on Tuesday, May 29, 1984, lying as though she were asleep in a second-floor bedroom in the three-story, four-bedroom house she had bought and in which she lived alone in Hyde Park, a racially integrated island in Chicago's South Side ghetto stabilized by the presence of the University of Chicago. A stack of sealed and labeled suicide notes was neatly arranged on a nightstand. She overdosed on drugs prescribed to ease her depression.

It was precisely ten years and one day after our wedding day.

"Have you ever lived in a 9-room prison constructed of your own hopes?" she asked in what she sarcastically labeled her "Generic Suicide Note."

"It is not recommended.

"Happiness is a private club that will not let me enter.

"As my dreams will never come true, I choose to have them in perpetual sleep," she wrote.

Then, a reference to one of her teen poems: "I had always hoped to die in winter, but it will be cold enough soon for me."

I could imagine her awash in her final bout of depression on that particular Memorial Day, a dreary day with rainy skies, high winds and unusually cold temperatures that ruined picnic plans throughout the Chicago area and left countless families caged in their homes on the washed-out holiday, snapping irritably at each other. For Leanita, it was a perfect day to self-destruct. "And now I take my leave," she wrote.

* * *

When I think of Leanita's emotional troubles, other sensitive artists like photographer Diane Arbus or the poets Sylvia Plath and Anne Sexton come to mind. Arthur Miller once wrote of fellow playwright August Strindberg that "Strindberg not only suffered what by most definitions would be madness but managed it like a conductor managing an orchestra. It makes his suffering no less real and painful to say that it was always being turned over and over by the bloody fingers of his mind."

So it was with Leanita. Material comfort and worldly honors could not lighten the burden she placed upon herself, a cross she felt she had to bear for her people. From her vantage point, it became difficult to distinguish between the world's problems and her own. But through the magnifying glass of her own troubled soul she brought important issues into focus so that the rest of us could see a little more clearly.

The works on the following pages were selected as a sample of her work at its best. We categorized her writings into her most often expressed areas of interest and arranged her columns chronologically to make it easier to observe changes in her development as a young columnist and to follow such historical events as the continuing factional fights in Chicago's city council. Their value is more than historical. McClain was concerned with more than the maneuverings of a few local political players. Her accounts focus on the nature of power and how prejudice can be used in the fight to get it or keep it.

Clarence Page

The following untitled poem was originally composed, according to her notes, on March 15, 1963, when Leanita McClain was eleven years old.

WHAT BECOMES OF THE LONELY?
What will become of me?
Shall I burn in flames of fire,
Or drown within the sea?
WHAT BECOMES OF THE LONELY?
What will become of me?
Shall I pick the flower of life
Or be stung by its bee?
WHAT DOES BECOME OF THE
    LONELY?
What will become of me?

Why doesn't someone tell me,
Why won't they let ME see?
What does become of the lonely?
What will become of me—
The door of happiness is locked,
Doesn't someone have the key?
I have yet to find,
I have yet to see.
WHAT BECOMES OF THE LONELY?
WHAT WILL BECOME OF ME?

The following poem was not dated but must have been written during Leanita McClain's later working years after she moved to the city's mostly white, upper-class North Side lakefront and became a regular rider of the Number 151 bus. "Fourth pres." and "holy game" apparently refer to the Fourth Presbyterian Church and Holy Name Cathedral downtown.

of a sun. morn.

On the 151
Here they come
On their way to fourth pres.
Or holy game
Wonder what these monied folk,
Or think-they're-monied folk,
Pray for.
Peace in our time?
For most of them, time will run out next
    week.

All the rich little old ladies
And their nurses
They look at you, thinking
"Won't you let a poor little old lady sit
    down"

My thoughts answer back
"Tell that to my grandmother who died
    scrubbing your floors"
We all settle in for the ride.

They all think theniggerbusdrivers are crazy
Because they sing to themselves
Or because they say things that they couldn't
    have said
Only yesterday
"I can't understand you, young man," they
    whine
"Twenty-five cents on Sunday," he says a
    third time
"I'm sorry . . ."
"A quoter, a quoter"
Oh, a quar-ter
It lingers in the air
The niggerbusdriver and I exchange smirks
Cause we know all black folks are crazy

The following untitled poem was dated May 1, 1973, when Leanita McClain was twenty-one years old.

why do I need a husband, mama?
when I can have everyone else's
traipsing thru the fields of nonchalance
I stop at intervals to turn a stone
and find a man.
I hold the stone to my breast,
a much needed rest for us both.
O, miserable men of lovely, nagging wives
Always their eyes look homeward.

RACE

McClain's racial consciousness found its way into just about everything she wrote. Of all the attributes that make us what we are, McClain felt none is more important than race in determining our chances to succeed in life. The emotional language that often enriched her views of urban politics, for example, came in part because of her profound disappointment over the way Chicago treated its first black mayor, compared to his white predecessors.

But she wrote numerous columns that explored in an intriguing way the question of race itself, how we view it and how it affects us. When we were in Europe and Africa, she quotes James Baldwin, there were no "white people" or "black people." After blacks came to America, it was not sufficient for both groups to simply call each other white or black. Her painfully ironic column about the light-skinned California political candidate who called himself black only to have his blackness challenged by a darker-hued political opponent says volumes about the inherent contradictions of America's racial standards. And, while many social scientists come forth with observations that class is outpacing race as a determinant of one's life chances, McClain constantly reminds us that race at all class levels remains too important a determinant to be casually put aside.

Newsweek, *October 13, 1980*

The middle-class black's burden

I am a member of the black middle class who has had it with being patted on the head by white hands and slapped in the face by black hands for my success.

Here's a discovery that too many people still find startling: when given equal opportunities at white-collar pencil pushing, blacks want the same things from life that everyone else wants. These include the proverbial dream house, two cars, an above-average school and a vacation for the kids at Disneyland. We may, in fact, want these things more than other Americans because most of us have been denied them so long.

Meanwhile, a considerable number of the folks we left behind in the "old country," commonly called the ghetto, and the militants we left behind in their antiquated ideology can't berate middle-class blacks enough for "forgetting where we came from." We have forsaken the revolution, we are told, we have sold out. We are Oreos, they say, black on the outside, white within.

The truth is, we have not forgotten; we would not dare. We are simply fighting on different fronts and are no less war weary, and possibly more heartbroken, for we know the black and white worlds can meld, that there can be a better world.

It is impossible for me to forget where I came from as long as I am prey to the jive hustler who does not hesitate to exploit my childhood friendship. I am reminded, too, when I go back to the old neighborhood in fear—and have my purse snatched—and when I sit down to a business lunch and have an old classmate wait on my table. I recall the girl I played dolls with who now rears five children on welfare, the boy from church who is in prison for murder, the pal found dead of a drug overdose in the alley where we once played tag.

My life abounds in incongruities. Fresh from a vacation in Paris, I may, a week later, be on the milk-run Trailways bus in Deep South backcountry attending the funeral of an ancient uncle whose world stretched only 50 miles and who never learned to read. Sometimes when I wait at the bus stop with my attaché case, I meet my aunt getting off the bus with other cleaning ladies on their way to do my neighbors' floors.

But I am not ashamed. Black progress has surpassed our greatest expectations; we never even saw much hope for it, and the achievement has taken us by surprise.

In my heart, however, there is no safe distance from the wretched past of my ancestors or the purposeless present of some of my contemporaries; I fear such a fate can reclaim me. I am not comfortably middle class; I am uncomfortably middle class.

I have made it, but where? Racism still dogs my people. There are still communities in which crosses are burned on the lawns of black families who have the money and grit to move in.

What a hollow victory we have won when my sister, dressed in her designer everything, is driven to the rear door of the luxury high rise in which she lives because the cab driver, noting only her skin color, assumes she is the maid, or the nanny, or the cook, but certainly not the lady of any house at this address.

I have heard the immigrants' bootstrap tales, the simplistic reproach of "why can't you people be like us." I have fulfilled the entry requirements of the American middle class, yet I am left, at times, feeling unwelcome and stereotyped. I have overcome the problems of food, clothing and shelter, but I have not overcome my old nemesis, prejudice. Life is easier, being black is not.

I am burdened daily with showing whites that blacks are people. I am, in the old vernacular, a credit to my race. I am my brothers' keeper, and my sisters', though many of them have abandoned me because they think that I have abandoned them.

I run a gauntlet between two worlds, and I am cursed and blessed by both. I travel, observe and take part in both; I can also be used by both. I am a rope in a tug of war. If I am a token in my downtown office, so am I at my cousin's church tea. I assuage white guilt. I disprove black inadequacy and prove to my parents' generation that their patience was indeed a virtue.

I have a foot in each world, but I cannot fool myself about either. I can see the transparent deceptions of some whites and the bitter hopelessness of some blacks. I know how tenuous my grip on one way of life is, and how strangling the grip of the other way of life can be.

Many whites have lulled themselves into thinking that race relations are just grand because they were the first on their block to discuss crab grass with the new black family. Yet too few blacks and whites in this country send their children to school together, entertain each other or call each other friend. Blacks and whites dining out together draw stares. Many of my coworkers see no black faces from the time the train pulls out Friday evening until they meet me at the coffee machine Monday morning. I remain a novelty.

Some of my "liberal" white acquaintances pat me on the head, hinting that I am a freak, that my success is less a matter of talent than of luck and affirmative action. I may live among them, but it is difficult to live with them. How can they be sincere about respecting me, yet hold my fellows in contempt? And if I am silent when they attempt to sever me from my own, how can I live with myself?

Whites won't believe I remain culturally different; blacks won't believe I remain culturally the same.

I need only look in a mirror to know my true allegiance, and I am painfully aware that, even with my off-white trappings, I am prejudged by my color.

As for the envy of my own people, am I to give up my career, my standard of living, to pacify them and set my conscience at ease? No. I have worked for these amenities and deserve them, though I can never enjoy them without feeling guilty.

These comforts do not make me less black, nor oblivious to the woe in which many of my people are drowning. As long as we are denigrated as a group, no one of us has made it. Inasmuch as we all suffer for every one left behind, we all gain for every one who conquers the hurdle. ■

August 9, 1981

When blacks journey abroad, green is beautiful

In Morocco a few years ago, Chicago optometrist Dr. Charles Payne found himself the only black in a group of tourists, not an unusual circumstance for the globe-hopping doctor.

Enraptured by the historic splendor of a fortress, he was jolted from his reverie when a native rushed through the crowd to confront him.

"Brother! Brother! They have captured you!" the excited Moroccan exclaimed. Apparently, Payne says, his would-be emancipator's study of United States history had stopped short of Abraham Lincoln and the Civil War.

Many black travelers bring home such priceless souvenirs—tales of the innocence abroad about U.S. race relations, of cases of mistaken identity, or of our own misapprehensions about being accepted.

Once, taken for Italian by a hotel desk clerk in Moscow, I was struck by the wondrous realization that for once my skin color held no clue to my ancestry. Instead, it has proven a curiosity, an attraction of sorts, among foreigners, rather than a signal to withdraw, as is often the case in my own backyard.

Whites may grow up looking Greek or Irish or Polish, but with rare exceptions the experience of blacks has been that, whatever our nationality or heritage, we are simply black. So thoroughly have we understood this fact of life, so insistent are we all, black and white, in reinforcing it daily, that for a black—even one who is green-eyed and freckled, as I am—to be taken for Italian is one for the books. Even when it happens in the Soviet Union.

Such stories bring to mind the perhaps apocryphal tale of the black man who affected a British accent, majestic robes and dazzling headdress to travel in the Old South. Posing as an African prince, he slept in the finest suites in the finest hotels and consumed the most lavish meals in the most discriminating restaurants. Wherever he went, he received the highest courtesies from unsuspecting whites, who never noticed the laughter in his eyes.

Because blacks are accustomed to the disquieting stares of rubes when we so much as venture to a remote shopping mall at home, we automatically pack our guard as carefully as our Michelin Guide when we go abroad. It usually turns out to be excess baggage. Most of us soon learn that in the eyes of foreigners we are Americans first—meaning bigger feet, bigger appetites and bigger pocketbooks—and blacks second.

On the other hand, according to Lethonee Jones, a member of the social work faculty at Western Michigan University in Kalamazoo, foreigners often have been mistaken for a Sudanese in Egypt, an American Indian in Turkey, and "some kind of African" in Denmark. In Jordan, she was pressed to stop being coy and speak Arabic. In East Africa, everyone thought she was a Ghanaian from West Africa. In West Africa, she says, "You just keep quiet and blend in."

Even when blacks fit into the epidermal rainbow, as we do in the Caribbean, Latin America or Africa, we may be "culturally" conspicuous. As one cordial Tanzanian professor put it most succinctly to my journalist husband, "You are a separate tribe."

When *turistos* of our tribe stroll through Mexico's marketplaces, savvy vendors hawking the standard onyx chess sets, giant sequined sombreros and silver jewelry change their accents: "Hey, soul brother. Hey, soul sister," comes the hustle. They know that ultimately all Americans come in only one color—green.

Amusing as such experiences can be, they aren't always pleasant.

Strolling in Toledo during her visit to Spain, a young black schoolteacher was immobilized when a little girl ran up, pointing and calling out to her mother, "Negrina! Negrina!" No translation was needed. In Spain, one forgives a child who may never have seen a black person, but a black Army officer had a similar experience in North Dakota. The world is smaller than we think.

Utility executive Donald Duster, a former state economic development director who has toured 30 countries, was pulled aside and briefly questioned as he deplaned in Tel Aviv. Dressed in his grubbies and hiding behind his Foster Grants, he came to realize he may have looked a little too much like an Arab. Duster's most trying experiences, however, have been traveling by air, seated among white American passengers. Their mouths gape, he says, at the thought that a black person other than a sports star or musician is actually setting out to see the world, or—imagine that!—can afford to travel.

Another irony that black travelers have observed is that people who wouldn't want you living next door at home suddenly become good friends when they need you, and you them, to, say, decipher the Paris Metro.

Racial sensitivity makes blacks keenly aware when they find themselves the "only one" in a crowd. A curious camaraderie thus develops among blacks traveling abroad. On the seemingly mile-long moving sidewalks in Charles de Gaulle Airport in Paris, my husband and I impulsively waved to a black couple who were being conveyed in the opposite direction. Just as naturally and spontaneously, they returned the greeting with ready understanding.

Even at home, many blacks won't travel to out-of-the-way places for fear of there not being "any black folks there." It wasn't so long ago that we traveled by this instinct, carrying a list of places that catered to "coloreds" and knowing there would be a relative waiting at the bus terminal with timetable nervously in hand.

Such memories die hard. Lethonee Jones, who describes herself as a "citizen of the world," sees a provincialism in black people that still limits their travel to "safe" places, particularly the Caribbean.

Indeed, before jetting to Australia, I was warned by my father, among other elders, that "they don't like our kind there." He went so far as to suggest that I act the part of maid to my white Australian traveling companion.

"Come now, they don't like our kind anywhere," I said, only half in jest, and settled in for the 20-hour flight from Chicago.

My fears lasted only as long as it took me to hit the streets of downtown Sydney, where the clamor and bustle was dotted with dark-skinned Fijians and even a brother clad in a dashiki [ah, shades of the sixties] and carrying a monstrous "box" that blared the latest pop.

There were so few stares during our four weeks' travel in Sydney, Canberra, Melbourne and Brisbane that in time I stopped looking for them. My companion, 20 years removed from her homeland and easily as apprehensive as I had been, gladly discarded her worries, too.

On occasion, a black traveler may be less conscious of the racial difference than white companions.

An official of the Chicago Council on Foreign Relations tells of a black woman in China whose appearance halted bicycle traffic in Peking. As the Chinese braked and stared, the woman's concerned companions sought to set her at ease. The newly awakened Chinese, they suggested, had never seen a black person before. But the woman noticed something familiar about those stares. "It's these," she suddenly asserted, pointing to her blouse. It wasn't her blackness, but her more than ample bosom that had the tiny Chinese aghast.

Black hair, naturally, is another point of foreign intrigue. A black woman who arrived in Greece was stopped by security agents who frisked her mammoth Afro in search of a knife. On a grimy, jampacked bus in Lima and again at a party in Australia, strangers who pawed my hair were not, I was sure, observing a local greeting custom.

Because I ordinarily wear my hair straight but travel with an Afro for convenience, I've spent some tense moments in immigration trying to explain that the woman in the passport photo and I were one and the same.

In Denmark one summer, Jones and her 11-year-old daughter, both Afro-coiffed, were subjected to stares everywhere. Her daughter felt so threatened by the attention that she asked if she could walk behind her mother. Her fears were allayed one morning when one gawker finally burst with, "Your hair—it's so beautiful!"

This is not to say that the United States has a monopoly on prejudice based on skin color. The abuses of black GIs abroad, and of the offspring some leave behind, are legend. In England, East and West Indians alike charge that they are victims of a frightening hate campaign by "skinheads, Pakibashers," and other fascist thugs.

Even American blacks are the occasional victims of such local biases until they brandish the great equalizer, the U.S. passport and its promise of dollars.

Businessman Duster is certain he was tailed once in South Africa, and, American or no, he stood helpless at a curb waiting for a taxi licensed to carry blacks.

One couple still recall quite bitterly the disrespect they were subjected to in Portugal. The natives were more than friendly, however, upon learning that they were American and not among the wave of Angolan refugees.

Apart from the tribulations black travelers encounter abroad, we sense that we are truly a breed apart when we encounter otherwise hospitable foreigners who fail entirely to understand the empathy black Americans feel for other people of color.

As black Americans struggle to form a global bond based on a common heritage of oppression, others set us apart. White South Africans fail to see the irony when they invite black Americans to a dinner that a black South African would be worthy only to serve.

The Aussie who wants to talk American politics and to joke about who really drives on the wrong side of the road finds it difficult to make a connection between the black experience in America and his own dismal record with the aborigines.

The embraces I exchanged with a group of aborigines on first meeting them took my white Australian acquaintances by surprise. The aborigines, about a dozen of them, had been camped out in tents for about four months in a land-rights protest atop Capitol hill in Canberra.

It was an old-fashioned sit-in, complete with soul handshakes all around, and I felt right at home. ■

August 31, 1981

The insidious new racism

Shortly after McClain became Perspective editor she wrote the first of what were then billed as "occasional columns."

In light of the line that would close her suicide note years later ("I will never live long enough to see my people free anyway"), the final paragraph of this column is poignantly prophetic.

Thank you, Pierre de Vise.

The controversial, oft-quoted urbanologist/demographic crystal ball gazer was infinitely quotable when he charged recently that white politicians deliberately try to undermine the political potency of black officials by putting them in charge of public agencies that are virtually unsalvageable, "sinking ships." He cited as victims Eugene Barnes of the CTA,* schools Supt. Ruth Love, and Dr. James Haughton of the defunct Health and Hospitals Governing Commission that ran Cook County Hospital.

The ultimate ulterior motive for this, de Vise theorized, is to make certain blacks will be blocked in any bid for the mayor's office.

In a paper delivered before the Conference on Public Policy for Equal Opportunity and Affirmative Action at the O'Hare Marriott Hotel, de Vise said, "By appointing blacks to preside over failing agencies, white politicians and bureaucrats can achieve two goals. First, they can blame failures, not on abandonment by the white middle class (where the blame belongs), but on the supposed greed and incompetence of black officials and workers. Second, they can additionally undermine public re-

---

*Chicago Transit Authority

spect and confidence in black officials, thereby reducing and retarding the chances of a successful black mayoral candidate in the years ahead."

Can white politicos really be so cleverly conspiratorial? Probably so with power at stake, even in those cases where the black community clamors for certain offices.

De Vise said nothing that is new to black people. But a few hosannas went up anyway that a white person actually said what blacks long have believed. His statement was a godsend in much the same way as former HEW Secretary Joseph Califano's announcement a few years back that racism remained the No. 1 social ill in America. Black people knew that, too.

Had a black person made either of these charges, they would have been dismissed with an, "Oh, no, not that racism gripe again."

Yes, I'm afraid so, that racism gripe again. Granted, it has been sounded so often without cause that even black people get tired of it, but it is far from licked.

As pervasive as it is, racism is nearly impossible to prove. And now it has taken on a new guise. De Vise provides perfect examples of this new, sophisticated racism.

Under the new racism, it's OK to let a black woman run the public schools because the students are 80 percent minority now and, besides, the people who hold the purse strings are white. Leave Eugene Barnes to sink or swim. He's an easy mark; it doesn't matter that education and mass transit are major headaches nationwide. And what of Cook County Hospital? It's just for poor people anyway. Who cares about these agencies as long as large numbers of whites aren't affected? And yet these black officials must be held accountable.

The tactic has been applied selectively on a broader scale to whole cities such as Gary and Detroit. So a black is elected as mayor; let's pull out and leave no economic base, then point fingers.

The new racism says, all right, it was wrong all those years to have separate drinking fountains and to reduce blacks to menial labor. So take this job, but don't get promoted.

The new racism says, OK the law gives blacks the right to live anywhere, but it still doesn't want them next door, even if it's $700,000 digs in Oak Brook (as in the recent discrimination case won by black businessman William Phillips).

How does it differ from the old racism?

The old racism wouldn't let blacks into some stores; the new racism assumes that any black person, no matter how well dressed, in a store is probably there to steal, not to buy. The old racism didn't want to educate blacks; the new racism still marvels that some black people actually read books on the bus. The old racism didn't have to address black people; the new racism is left speechless when a black, approached condescendingly, has an eloquent comeback.

The new racism still cannot handle black people who are as intelligent, diligent, thoughtful, kind or living as comfortably as whites. The new racism still doesn't accept blacks as full partners in politics, in business, in community life.

The new subtle racism may well revert to the old overt racism.

"Oh, no, not that racism gripe again!"

It took hundreds of years to build it, another hundred even to dent it, and I fear I will not live to see it demolished. ■

November 29, 1982

The racial truth of politics

Now that the 1983 campaign for mayor is on with a solid black candidate in the running, the volume is being alternately turned up and down on the topic of race, which has never exactly been whispered about in most quarters of the city.

It is disquieting that so much energy has been channeled to this subject instead of the more important matters of the financial condition of the city, schools and housing, or even the innocuous topic of ethnic festivals. Instead of deploring race as a factor, it may be time to face the music and dance: It always has been a factor. Everyone of every hue in this city may at last have to tackle the black-white issue and realize that it is not so black and white. Racism is a two-way street.

The black side has its historic points for debate. One cannot be a full-fledged black here without adhering to the beliefs that (1) Riverview* was shut down because "we" started to be more prevalent; (2) the shape the Loop is in has less to do with the lousy economy than with the fact that "they" wrote it off, headed for North Michigan Avenue and decided to let "us" have it, and (3) no one in power cares about the public schools because only "our" children attend them.

---

*An amusement park that opened in 1904 in an all-white section of Chicago's north side and grew to legendary popularity. It closed in 1967, shortly after it became a popular attraction for blacks from Chicago's south and west sides. Many people, including Miss McClain, suspected a connection.

Likewise, no white person here worth his salt would dispute the beliefs that (1) when "those people" move in, it's time to move out; (2) don't ride the "L" or go downtown after dark, because, well you know . . . ; and (3) "they" are taking the best jobs and getting all the social program money and soon they're going to take over and the city is going to go down the tubes. (On that last point, little do whites know that some blacks are looking over their shoulders at the burgeoning Hispanic population, which is expected to outdistance blacks in a decade, and thinking, if not saying, the same thing. By the way, Hispanics will always be more palatable to whites than blacks, despite similar problems.)

These points are prickly because, though they are not statements of fact, they are statements of fact about perceptions. The truth hurts. Everyone may be trying to downgrade racial innuendo in the mayor's race but that does not invalidate it as a problem. It can't be wished away.

U.S. Rep. Harold Washington, a candidate who just happens to be black, says he wants to be everyone's candidate and has addressed taxes and other problems that make no racial distinction (except to those immovable objects on both sides who believe "those people" are keeping us from getting anything). But at the same time he has exhorted the true believers that it is "our turn."

Mayor Jane Byrne, who has no more bridges to burn with the black community, is trying to construct a new one based on social programs in her new budget. Yet speaking before a black church congregation, she said: "I will not let race become a campaign issue; that would be a step backward."

State's Atty. Richard M. Daley is assured of some sympathy votes because of the memory of his dad, who at least spoke to blacks, though often in a different tone and language than he spoke to whites. He has taken on Michael Scott, one of the black school board members replaced by Mayor Byrne, as a deputy in his campaign.

With Aldermen Edward Burke (14th) and Roman Pucinski (41st) and whoever else has the urge putting in their names for a contingency "great white hope" just in case Washington takes the primary, it's time to acknowledge that race is going to be an issue whether anyone wants it to be or not. Accept this for the ugliness that it is, and stop all the false piety about how we are a decent enough people to rise above it. Chicago ain't ready for reform—not yet. But if we start now, we might be ready next time. Why keep up the pretense? Don't try to sweep it aside; deal with it. To solve the problem, we must first define it. This mayoral campaign may provide the best chance.

All those years of being called the most segregated city in the nation haven't been undeserved. Neighborhood boundaries in this town weren't made up by the cartographers. There are real, frightening reasons behind this racial standoff—and imaginary but more frightening ones—to be dealt with. It's a shame, but more shameful to be dishonest about it.

Some simple exercises can start the peace process. Blacks should keep in mind that *every* political maneuver isn't meant to shut them out, but whites should keep in mind that that is too often the case. Whites must stop thinking that *every* black teenager who whisks by on the sidewalk is a thug, and blacks might accept that more than a few whites genuinely understand and sympathize with them. Whites might think deeper about the historic and socioeconomic reasons—not excuses—for black shortcomings and not brush aside a race of people as hopeless and hopelessly all the same, with the exception of a few mutant achievers. Blacks might knock harder at the doors of opportunity and recognize that some will not open without special effort.

These ideas are not so naive as they may sound when one considers maintaining the status quo, and the status quo is the issue here. The crusades being waged on both sides are galling. Blacks are not trying to take over, though some of them may well think this is the big one. Whites can't keep running everything, though many certainly would like to. A pox on both their houses. The point is that this mayoral race, whoever wins, could be the great political emancipator for everyone in this town.

But first everyone has to 'fess up, and everybody has to give—and take. ■

April 23, 1983

Militancy and black women

The rhetoric was sixties, but the subjects were decidedly eighties.

The 100 black women who gathered at a conference of the Milwaukee Black Women's Network symbolized the new militancy. The new militancy is not fist-waving or teeth-clenching or Swahili-speaking, though the Afro hairstyle is still prevalent. Rather, it is business-suited, financially astute and well-spoken, but still with a heavy dose of the old-fashioned, emotional politics of "black is beautiful."

The roomful of confident black females was living proof of Andrew Young's summation of the evolution of the revolution: "In the '60s the problems were social. We addressed those problems: the back of the bus, the lunch counter, the movie theater, the hotel-motel, the right to travel.

In the '70s the problems were essentially political. We addressed those problems with the [election of] thousands of black elected officials. . . . In the 1980s the problems are economic."

Before the women split up for workshops on such topics as effective communication, dressing for success and cable TV ownership, they were roused with a preachy rendition of the old militancy delivered by Marcia Ann Gillespie, former editor of *Essence* magazine and a contributing editor to *Ms*.

"I am a Sojourner Truth feminist," Gillespie intoned, referring to the black woman, a freed slave, who became the darling of the abolitionist lecture circuit in the 1840s.

Gillespie admonished black women not to be afraid of the term "feminist" or to participate in feminist organizations run by women of the "majority culture," which is the new militancy term for the pejorative sixties descriptions of whites. Feminism is a liberation struggle like any other, and blacks are particularly well equipped for it, she said. But black women must be ever mindful that they often will have to split with majority feminists, particularly on Third World issues, said Gillespie, who attended a world conference of women in Europe last year.

In discussing media images of the black female Rochell Bridges of Milwaukee's WISN-TV further evoked sixties *déjà vu*. To enthusiastic and knowing laughs and nods of the head, reminiscent of the old chants of "right on," she outlined the stereotypes black women must break through. They are of Mammy, the strong-as-a-mule character of Hattie McDaniel in "Gone with the Wind"; the Tragic Mulatto, played by Jeanne Crain in "Imitation of Life"; the Hot Mama of blackploitation films; the Innocent Ingenue, *à la* Diahann Carroll's old "Julia" show; and Sapphire, of Amos 'n' Andy fame.

Her point is that black women, like all women, should not be typecast in life or in the media. They are all and none of these. If anything, they most often display the best quality of Sapphire, her strength, Bridges said.

The image conjured by those in attendance supported her point. It would have been an instant education to those who see black women only as welfare queens or sequined-gowned superstars. The upwardly mobile segment is slowly growing. But it is contrasted by the more rapidly growing segment shunted aside under the newfound sociological catch-all, the "feminization of poverty." A Census Bureau report has discovered that median black income actually would have increased to $14,830 from 1970 to 1980 instead of decreasing from $13,325 to $12,674, except for those poorest single female heads of households, which weighted down the figure.

It is this loss by the bulk of blacks just at the time of such strides for a relative few that fuels the new militancy in all quarters of the black community. Particularly susceptible is the black middle class, which whites see, mistake as the norm and then are baffled by its discontent. The new militancy is an anger by those who are being showcased that other blacks are not being given the same chance. Many of the women at the conference were those who took advantage of the chance. They are still capitalizing on the liberal programs of the sixties, on the education they could not otherwise have afforded and the self-assuredness imbued in them because they made it. They want to see the same afforded to others.

The new militancy is being preached by as unlikely a bomb thrower as Naomi Sims, the former model turned one-woman wig and cosmetics business enterprise. In her new book, *All about Success for the Black Woman* (Doubleday), she translates it to the corporate world:

"We [black women] are invariably the losers in the minority sweepstakes that pits us against Black men and white women. At the moment white women are winning hands down; they occupy over 15 percent of all managerial positions. One theory for this is that of the three groups white women 'fit in' the executive structure the best, because they learned from their husbands, fathers and brothers how to manipulate in that world. They only have to be assimilated on one level, that of the job, not also on a social and/or cultural level. . . . In other words, sex is less of a barrier than race, and a corporation wishing to promote up from the ranks or to recruit executives from outside will prefer white women. That leaves us nowhere."

No one would deny that the progress of blacks is real and measurable; the very evidence of it is that a book so titled is on the market. But to those who thought the revolution was over, the sisterhood in Milwaukee was a time to gather reinforcements. ■

May 21, 1983

Portrait of a "living legacy"

To a people robbed of history, the work of photographer James A. J. Van Der Zee is an immense treasure. Van Der Zee, who opened the Guarantee Photo Studio in Harlem in 1916, recorded decades of black America. He died Sunday at 96 just hours after receiving an honorary degree at Howard University.

Van Der Zee was to black portraiture what Ansel Adams is to nature photography. But like most else in black culture he was not well known outside of it. Sadder still is that he is not all that well known to young blacks.

His work is like the remaining volume in a set of lost rare books. One would delight in the entire set, but because so much is missing, what remains is more precious still. The photos of Van Der Zee, though taken primarily in Harlem, represent a picture encyclopedia of the commonality of the black experience over the span of miles. His church women were the church women of every black congregation everywhere. His proper matrons were the aunts and grandmothers of black people everywhere who had no dried and faded treasures of which to boast or to frame.

It is difficult to express the limbo of the black Diaspora to those who can journey back to the ancestral home in County Mayo, or who regularly correspond with an uncle in Krakow, or who finger the lace handkerchief great-great-grandmother stitched on the boat on the way to Ellis Island. Most blacks have neither heirlooms nor language to attest to their origins, substantiate their continuity, for all the enthusiasm stirred by Alex Haley's *Roots*.

Van Der Zee opened his studio at the beginning of the great Harlem Renaissance, the 1920s and 1930s. He was one of the many talented who, while their outpourings were distinguished, remain unusual all the more because they were the first to enjoy a wide public forum.

Black men and women of arts and letters flowed into that New York enclave, magnetized by fame and full of zeal to explain black America to itself and to the wider culture, to enlist in the army of good works that would at last deliver black people. For all of the rowdy good times that ran concurrent to the poetry readings and nightlong philosophical debates, the Harlem Renaissance left an astounding body of black feeling and thought, including the Negro national anthem, "Lift Every Voice and Sing." It did not, however, bridge the cultures or deliver black people, and many black schoolchildren today are lacking in knowledge even of this recent past.

Van Der Zee's archives are significant not because of his "name" clientele, but because of the nobodies he photographed in the everyday joy and struggles of life. He was in the midst of the tumult of the back-to-Africa movement of Marcus Garvey, he shook the prodigious hand of poet Langston Hughes, he jostled the musculature of the Brown Bomber and Jack Johnson into memorable poses. But he also left the vision of the Moorish Zionists (black Jews), a peek inside a hair salon, a high-styling couple in raccoon coats.

Born in Lenox, Mass., in 1886, Van Der Zee began taking photos in 1900. Largely self-taught, he received his only formal training when he worked for a department store portrait taker in Newark, N.J., in 1915. In six months, he opened his own studio. He was a pioneer in the artistry of photography, experimenting with superimposing images and retouching, using glitter to simulate snowflakes or painting a necklace on a bare-necked subject.

Van Der Zee retired in 1969 in unpleasant personal circumstances. But that year the Metropolitan Museum of Art put on an exhibit called "Harlem on My Mind," the title of one of Van Der Zee's collections, which renewed his fortunes. He started to work again in 1980 and was much in demand by such stars as Bill Cosby.

Van Der Zee's third wife, Donna Mussenden, some 60 years his junior, finally cataloged and copyrighted many of his 75,000 works. In February 1980, they were displayed in the Cultural Center here during Black History Month. The artist himself appeared at a reception at Timbuktu, a black-oriented book store on the Near South Side. When Van Der Zee arrived, he was a disconcerting sight at first in a wheelchair, but he was unbelievably robust and jovial at 94 and plunged into autographing.

What was it that compelled those of us in the anxious crowd who confessed to having only recently discovered this "living legacy," as an award from President Jimmy Carter so aptly described him, to seek him out? It was an ignorance of the past, no disgrace to confess to, for ferreting the secrets of black history is a never-ending quest.

There are so many gaps in the chronicles of black America, so little effort to fill them because many educators are themselves deficient in the area. Any proof of the endurability and achievements of black people is snatched up, coveted, exchanged. Such was the allure of Van Der Zee. He had helped to preserve a race of people who were then "invisible," to give it form, to affirm its being, to legitimize its past. ■

July 2, 1983

Grains of truth
in fiction

A new book called *The Negotiations* is subtitled "A novel of tomorrow." But that tomorrow is the not-so-distant year 1987. The first jolt in its plot is that Ronald Reagan is not re-elected in 1984.

The reason is that unemployment improved for whites but not at all for blacks, job riots broke out and the fictional President Dorsey Talbott Davidson, a Democrat, won. (Walter Mondale et al. should remember that this is fiction.)

But that is not the end of it:

"It was shortly after 8 p.m. on Tuesday, Sept. 1. The polls had closed in the most unusual election ever held in the United States of America. Unlike in times past, white Americans had not participated in this election. Only black Americans had been eligible to vote, and they had flocked to the polling places in unprecedented numbers. Later an analysis would reveal that of those black citizens registered to vote, 85 percent had voted. . . . It was a referendum, through a yes or no vote, to ratify or reject the following proposition: The Black American Council is hereby authorized to negotiate with the United States of America for the creation of a separate and independent state, within the continental limits of the United States, for American citizens of African descent."

Black Americans in the book vote 52 percent to 48 percent to secede from the union.

The premise is a fascinating one to ponder on this Fourth of July weekend with many blacks feeling abandoned in the land of the free and the home of the brave.

The book is by Herman Cromwell Gilbert, a South Sider and former assistant to U.S. Rep. Gus Savage. It is the first work from Path Press, a Chicago publishing house that is "re-introducing" itself. Path, the reincarnation of a firm begun in the late sixties, publishes works "by and about Black Americans."

The idea of blacks seceding is improbable, but it has a long tradition in the United States. There have been back-to-Africa and black nationhood movements in the past. The country of Liberia, founded by freed U.S. slaves in 1822, is an example. In the twenties Marcus Garvey had a decrepit boat ready to set sail. The late Elijah Muhammad's vision was a more recent example.

Black anger and political strength might just lead to such a confident rejection of whites. But let's not be alarmist. The book is not a sociology tract, just one writer's fancy.

It is not the make-believe separation plot that makes the book significant, but the sentiments that lead to the vote to secede—sentiments that are genuine and growing.

The disenchantment that fuels the plot did not have to be invented. President Reagan could have been the inspiration for the book with his retreat on affirmative action, cuts in the kinds of social programs that gave the black middle class bootstraps to pull on and proposed tax breaks for private schools that discriminate. The direction the president is taking the nation will not likely lead to separation, but he certainly ought to think about why 26 million blacks aren't traveling with him.

Any one of these notions from the novel is fairly widespread in actuality:

"Black America was really saying . . . that it no longer had confidence in white America."

"The post-civil rights, anti-black mood in the country. . . began under Nixon and intensified under Reagan. . . ."

". . . the government had little respect for blacks in general."

And one downtrodden character, who calls himself "The Man Who Had Never Had a Job," is especially and painfully real. He is nearing 30, a handyman in a tavern who relies for food on the kindness of a mom and pop grocery where he gets rotting fruits and stale lunchmeat.

The character speaks for that here-and-now 25 percent of unemployed black adults and 48 percent of unemployed black teenagers when he says, "I ain't never had a job. Been looking for one for almost 12 years, but I ain't never had a job. Think about it. Me and thousands and thousands of other young men, black and white, but especially black, who want to work but ain't never had a job. And ain't got much chance of getting one."

He signs on to the black homeland idea with a despairing, "Things can't get any worse."

The Black American Council of the novel is a six-member panel representing a cross section of blacks, from nationalists to cautious moderates to old-line integrationists. The council was founded in the winter of 1984 after the job riots were halted by a government crackdown "which had been much more ruthless than that exercised against the Black Panthers and other militant groups more than a decade earlier." Here, too, the facts are stranger than the fiction because many blacks ardently believe police action against them could be fomented by the most minor incident.

Of course there is that 48 percent of black America in the book who votes against separation, including the Congressional Black Caucus, a mysterious Los Angeles multimillionaire who schemes to thwart the idea and a dissenting member of the Black American Council who quits before the negotiations get underway.

President Davidson's antagonistic view of the referendum is that: "If Lincoln was willing to abide the evil of slavery to preserve the Union, then definitely I am willing to abide the lesser evil of inequality for a minority of our citizens to preserve it."

The reader is taken through mass demonstrations; the legal and constitutional obstacles to separation; the obligatory FBI plant within the black council; murders by the authorities and a black militant group; CIA intervention to keep African nations from flirting with the proposed black American nation; and a call for black-white unity from a feminist leader. And there is also a revolutionary platform of social and economic reforms passed at an AFL-CIO convention to correct the past sins of discrimination and entice blacks back into the fold. These include a Marshall Plan for urban renewal, a national health plan, full employment, a reduction to a 30-hour work week and nationalization of the utilities.

Author Gilbert has perhaps taken genuine sentiments to an implausible conclusion. One can quarrel with his plot, but not with his perception of those sentiments. ∎

Washington Post, *July 24, 1983*

How Chicago taught
me to hate whites

One Sunday in July 1983, readers of the Washington Post *were greeted by a startling headline in the newspaper's outlook section: "How Chicago Taught Me to Hate Whites." The author was Leanita McClain and, while the* Post *editors offered the view as a personal account of the intense emotions stirred up by an election whose volatility had drawn national attention, the piece kicked up a controversy of its own in Chicago. That it had been published in an out-of-town newspaper only caused more of a fuss among Chicagoans who feel defensive enough about the city's reputation as one of the nation's most segregated. McClain's account gave fuel to the city's detractors by describing with characteristic eloquence how she was yanked out of her middle-class comfort by the bitter racial animosity that emerged during the city's 1983 general election campaign.*

Incumbent Mayor Jane Byrne and State's Attorney Richard M. Daley, son of the late Mayor Richard J. Daley, were the clear favorites in the race until Harold Washington, a black congressman from the city's South Side, galvanized black voters and forged a coalition with reform-minded whites and Hispanics to win a plurality in the Democratic primary election. His unexpected victory led to a revolt in white precincts that gave the entire campaign an ugly tinge of racial animosity. The Republican challenger, former State Rep. Bernard Epton, had been such a long shot before the primary that even Republican leaders donated to his campaign with great reluctance. But after Washington became the Democratic nominee, Epton became the "great white hope," spurring defections by white Democrats unlike anything ever seen in Chicago history. McClain's observations on the mean spirit that emerged out of the city's precincts during that turbulent time would have been provocative enough in a local journal. In the Post, *it was dirty laundry hung out for all the world to see in the leading newspaper of the nation's capital.*

She would fill three cardboard boxes with the mail that poured in to the Post *and the* Tribune *in response to the piece. A number of whites predictably said she was painting with too broad of a brush, that many whites supported Washington and were crucial to his victories in the primary and general elections. Some blacks chided her for being naive if she was so surprised by the behavior of white bigots.*

Ald. Aloysius Majerczyk introduced a resolution in city council calling on McClain to "apologize to the people of this great city" and for the Tribune *to reprimand her. City Hall watchers got a laugh out of that. Majerczyk represents one of the least racially tolerant areas in Chicago. It was in his part of town that the Rev. Martin Luther King Jr. was hit with a brick during a civil rights march in the 1960s, prompting King to remark that Chicago had more hateful and violent crowds than any he had seen in Alabama or Mississippi. Majerczyk's resolution was sent to committee without debate.*

John Madigan, a local white radio commentator, was sufficiently enraged to broadcast three commentaries in five workdays castigating McClain. Later in the month he broadcast a fourth and, following her death, a fifth. Ignoring most of what she had to say, he latched on to her descriptions of how she had been "turned into a hate-filled spewer of invective" and sometimes "feel[s] like machine-gunning every white face on the bus." Madigan, a devoted defender of the late Mayor Daley, said Tribune *editors should be no less outraged by McClain's words than they were over Daley's "shoot to kill" order against rioters in the 1960s. Overlooked, of course, was how McClain meant the words in a figurative sense while Daley's order was indeed an official command.*

But there also was a revealingly large amount of supportive mail and phone calls. As happened in response to her Newsweek *column, a number of blacks thanked her for expressing thoughts they wanted to express but for which they could not find the words. "I like her anger," said one black woman. So did a few sympathetic whites.*

Though the commentary describes the turbulent atmosphere surrounding the 1983 elections as seen through one woman's eyes, it speaks volumes about the frustrations felt by black Americans over the resiliency of America's racial caste system. While McClain in her own mind might have done everything right in trying to succeed and be accepted by white America, she, like other blacks, was told in no uncertain terms that blacks who aspire to high office will be fought no less vigorously than they were in Dr. King's day.

"Now I know," she wrote, "solving the racial problem will take more than living, marrying and going to school together and all of those other laudable but naive goals I defend. This episode made even these first steps seem so far from reach."

Interestingly, one also detects in her writing a sense of guilt for the way her position of prominence was letting white people off the hook, freeing them from sharing her profound sense of obligation to the black masses. Interestingly, McClain did not like the headline. She thought it overstated her case. But, in fairness to the headline writer, her commentary concludes, without equivocation, that

*the racially tense atmosphere surrounding the campaign that led up to Chicago's
electing its first black mayor in 1983 did teach her "that I can hate." It is toward
this emphatic statement that the mood of the piece builds. Perhaps Leanita was
surprised by the heat of her own anger.*

*"I really didn't think Chicago was ready to deal with the issue again so soon,"
she explained to Neil Tesser, one of her Northwestern University classmates who,
as a columnist for the Chicago weekly* Reader *newspaper, wondered why she chose
an out-of-town medium to express her rage. "I wanted to explain the Chicago psychology to an outside audience, such as* Esquire, *but then the time element was
getting away from me: it would have had whiskers on it by the time it appeared in a
national magazine. So I started thinking of a newspaper that would have a national audience." Through it all, her supervisors at the* Tribune *defended her, even
though they, too, were more than a little surprised to find that the piece that appeared in print was more volatile than the last draft she had shown them as a courtesy.*

*"I don't agree with her characterization of how whites felt at the election of
Harold Washington,"* Tribune *Editor James Squires told the* Reader. *"I know
many who were very happy. But Leanita's willingness and eloquence in saying it
was a positive stroke. It shows us how far we still have to go in race relations."*

Throughout the controversy, McClain stood by her words.

*"Yes," McClain said, "the article is a representation of the inner workings of
a black mind; but it could have been one of any number of professions. I just happen to be a woman working at the Chicago* Tribune. *But there were so many black
people—schoolteachers, movie ushers—who could have come up with the same
emotions and hurts."*

Chicago—I'd be a liar if I did not admit to my own hellish confusion.
How has a purebred moderate like me—the first black editorial writer for
the *Chicago Tribune*—turned into a hate-filled spewer of invective in such
little time?

Even today, the vicious, psychotic events leading up to and following
Harold Washington's election as the first black mayor of Chicago leave
me torn as never before. I've become a two-headed, two-hearted creature.
The sides are in continual conflict, by turns pitying, then vilifying the other, sometimes with little reason, never with tranquility.

In one day my mind has sped from the naive thought that everything
would be all right in the world if people would just intermarry, to the naive
thought that we should establish a black homeland where we would never
have to see a white face again.

The campaign was a race war. So is the continuing feud between Harold Washington and the white aldermen usurping his authority. Even
black and white secretaries in City Hall are not speaking to each other. But
why am *I* so readily doubting and shutting out whites I thought of as
friends?

I am not one of those, despite a comfortable life, who have forgotten my origins. It is just that I had not been so rudely reminded of them in so long.

Through 10 years working my way to my present position at the *Tribune*, I have resided in a "gentrified," predominantly white, North Side lakefront liberal neighborhood where high rents are the chief social measure. In neither place have I forgotten the understood but unspoken fact of my "difference"—my blackness.

Yet I have been unprepared for the silence with which my white colleagues greeted Washington's nomination. I've been crushed by their inability to share the excitement of one of "us" making it into power. I've built walls against whites who I once thought of as my lunch and vacation friends. And I've wrapped myself in rage as this sick, twisted city besieged the newspaper with letters wishing acts of filth by "black baboons" on the daughters of its employees. Just because it endorsed this black man.

An evilness still possesses this town and it continues to weigh down my heart. During my morning ritual in the bathroom mirror, my radio tuned to the news-talk station that is as much a part of my routine as shaping my eyebrows, I've heard the voice of this evil. In what would become a standard "bigot-on-the-street" interview, the voice was going on about "the blacks." "The blacks" this, "the blacks" that, "the blacks, the blacks, the blacks." My eyes fogged, but not from the bathroom steam.

"*The* blacks." It is the article that offends. The words are held out like a foul-smelling sock transported two-fingered at the end of an outstretched arm to the hamper while the nose is pinched shut.

"The blacks." It would make me feel like machine-gunning every white face on the bus. Why couldn't these people just say "blacks," letting it roll from the tongue?

"The blacks." These people were talking about *me*, as I stood in my bathroom mirror neatly outlining my lips, about to put on a dress-for-success suit and silk blouse. These were the people who dislike welfare recipients for fitting their stereotypes and who despise me because I do not. The users of "the blacks" make no distinction, unlike the liberals who in their weaker moments will say: "Well, I wouldn't mind having *you* next door. You're different, you know." Leanita McClain. "The black." Just another nigger.

The tears returned when Jane Byrne, soundly defeated in the primary, announced a write-in campaign to save the city from the brash black man and his opponent, the avuncular Jew. My editorial-writer colleagues were probably left in as much disbelief by the obscenity I spat at the television as by anything that little snow queen had just said. With my back to the

closed door of my office, seemingly focused on my word processor, I cried
in anger. My God, I implored. *What do these white people want of us?*

* * *

My transformation began the morning after Washington's primary
victory. Everyone in Chicago stayed up until 2 a.m. when Washington
claimed victory. Horrified white Chicago turned in for a fitful night. But
no one black slept either, though there were never so many bright black
eyes as there were the next morning. That morning black people had a step
and a beat that was more than the old joked-about "natural rhythm."
Smiles shown as brilliant as the blue Washington buttons that a white political editor astutely interpreted as "blue buttons of hope." Those buttons would become a badge of courage, of oneness. Even now many
blacks continue to wear them.

Black strangers exchanged sly smiles on the streets. A jubilant scream
went up, but it was a silent one, something like the high-pitched tones only
animals can discern. The black man won! We did it! It rose to the strato-
sphere, crystalized and sprinkled every one of us like sugared rain. We had
a feeling, and above all we had power.

No one in this town had talked about anything but the election for
weeks. But suddenly the morning after the primary, whites could not find
enough other things to talk about if they talked at all. Not just the most
bigoted of bigots, but all whites, even the more open-minded of my fellow
journalists. Even the standard niceties took on a different quality. Their
"good mornings" had the tenor of death rattles, not just the usual pre-
coffee hoarseness. There was that forced quality, an awkwardness, an end
to spontaneity, even fear in the eyes of people who had never thought
about me one way or the other before.

So many whites unconsciously had never considered that blacks
could do much of anything, least of all get a black candidate this close to
being mayor of Chicago. My colleagues looked up and realized, perhaps
for the first time, that I was one of "them." I was suddenly threatening.
The difference that everybody had tried to cover up was there in the open.
It leaked right out and stared at us and defied us to try and put it away.
Whites were out of their wits with plain wet-your-pants fear. Happy black
people can only mean unhappy white people in this town. (I never realized
how far I had strayed.)

I would begin that morning to build my defenses brick by brick, to
shut out people I had cried with, people I had never felt more akin to than
when we traveled to foreign lands, touting our shared Americanism. I
would begin to discern the full frontal view of the evil. It is the evil that
caused white coworkers to stop talking when blacks strolled by. It is the

evil that led blacks to caucus and revert to the old days of talking about "whitey." It is the evil of protesters, their faces red hot with hate, at a Catholic church where former Vice President Walter Mondale and Washington were jeered.

The theme of these ensuing months was set and hardening. So intense and oppressive was the atmosphere here that black and white *Tribune* colleagues sought refuge in my office from the foulness. A white colleague came in to explain away why he could not vote for Harold Washington, as if what I thought of him was really important, as if my office were a confessional. One black female on the staff was thrown into a fit of anxiety one day, troubled by suddenly not even wanting to go to lunch with one of the white women on the staff with whom she is close.

The lone black *Tribune* reporter on the campaign trail, Monroe Anderson, was so beaten down by what he was seeing in the streets that he came into my office-turned-retreat, enfolded himself in a chair and just stared at the floor. Anderson is indisputably one of the most devil-may-care persons on the staff—the one with the slightly bawdy joke, the one who keeps the party lively, the one with the quick line. His exceptional sense of humor keeps everyone going. But during this election it failed even him. As the hate campaign against Washington got meaner, I began to realize I had not been overreacting. I had been playing it safe, as each day up to the election would verify.

* * *

The *Chicago Tribune* endorsed Harold Washington in a long and eloquent Sunday editorial. It was intended to persuade the bigots. It would have caused any sensible person at least to think. It failed. The mail and calls besieged the staff. The middle range of letters had the words "LIES" and "NIGGER LOVERS" scratched across the editorial.

Hoping to shame these people, make them look at themselves, the newspaper printed a full page of these rantings. But when the mirror was presented to them, the bigots reveled before it. The page only gave them aid and comfort in knowing their numbers. That is what is wrong with this town; being a racist is as respectable and expected as going to church.

Filthy literature littered the city streets like the propaganda air blitzes of World War II. The subway would be renamed "Soul Train." The elevators in City Hall would be removed because blacks would prefer to change floors by swinging from the cables. (Anderson, temporarily regaining his jocularity, plastered the flyers like art posters all over his work cubicle. Most black staffers knew it was laughing to keep from crying. Whites grew more silent.) In the police stations, reports were whispered about fights between longtime black and white squad-car partners. Flyers proclaiming the new city of "Chicongo," with crossed drumsticks as the city seal, were tacked to police station bulletin boards. The schools actually formulated plans to deal with racial violence, just in case.

I brought the madness from the streets into work with me.

I dissected why some people had cultivated my friendship, why I was so quick to offer it unconditionally, straining as hard as they to prove a point—to say, see how easy it is if we all just smile and pretend?

I had put so much effort into belonging, and the whites in my professional and social circles had put so much effort into making me feel as if I belonged, that we all deceived ourselves. There is always joking about "it"—those matchings of suntans against black skin, or the exchange of dialect or finding common ground on the evils of racism. But none of us had ever dealt with the deeper inhibitions, myths and misperceptions that this society has force-fed us. The issue is there, no matter the social strata.

Now I know solving the racial problem will take more than living, marrying and going to school together and all of those other laudable but naive goals I defend. This episode made even these first steps so far from reach.

* * *

What is there, then, to believe in? Who was I to trust? How was I to know which whites were good and which were bad? How many of my co-workers wouldn't even want *me* next door? After all of these years of lunch dates and the familial togetherness that comes naturally from working next to someone 40 hours a week, how could I know who was on the level? If I was feeling this way, what were my brothers and sisters in the street feeling? Could this town be razed in a deranged moment?

What litmus test could I devise? I distanced myself from everyone white, watching, listening, for hints of latent prejudice. But there were no formulas to follow. Even an expression of support for Washington would not convince me, so certain was I of everyone's dissemblance. I drew up a mental list of those whites who could and could not be trusted. Revelation after revelation, doubt after doubt assaulted me.

First on the list was Kay—bouncy, smiley Kay. (No real names are used.) How she had used me all of these years, like a black pet, to prove her liberalism. I was safe; she could show me off without ever having to deal with the real issue. The next time she came skipping in to show me the "neat" pair of shoes she had found during her lunch hour or to talk about the "neat" movie she had seen or the "neat" restaurant we should try, I would throw my dictionary at her and advise her that having one black person—me—on her Christmas card list did not make her socially aware.

What about Clark? He always said the right things about race, viewed injustice with the proper alarm. But suddenly I questioned his sincerity. The next time he showed up at my office door, I would make him halt at the threshold. I would deny entry to my neighborhood on the ground that he was white. Then ask how it felt to be discriminated against to make the point that his talk was just that. What did he know? He had not lived in this skin.

What about Ken, kind-eyed, sensitive, cultured, thoughtful, cerebral Ken? No, he couldn't be a racist. Or could he?

What about Nan, with whom I had traveled? She headed the boards of church agencies in the poorest black neighborhoods. Now *there* was an exception. We had talked about race matters, about matters of the heart, about the differences that somehow did not alter those things that made us the same.

What about Lydia in Michigan, who had shared all my life's secrets? She too, passed.

It would be so easy just to dismiss everyone white. Why was it so easy for whites to classify me—"the blacks," or you exceptional blacks and the rest of "the blacks"—but not so easy for me to classify them?

When white friends begin to initiate conversation with, "Well, I'm no racist, but—," I no longer had to worry about my test. Everyone was suspect.

* * *

Bitter am I? That is mild. This affair has cemented my journalist's acquired cynicism, robbing me of most of my innate black hope for true integration. It has made me sparkle as I reveled in the comradeship of blackness. It has banished me to nightmarish bouts of sullenness. It has made me weld on a mask, censor every word, rethink every thought. It has put a face on the evil that no one wants to acknowledge is within them. It has made me mistrust people, white *and* black. This battle has made me hate. And that hate does not discriminate.

I've abhorred the gaggles of smug, giggly little white kids, out spending daddy's money, who start life a thousand yards ahead of black kids. I've detested my colleagues at the *Chicago Tribune*, whose antiseptic suburban worlds are just as narrow, who pretend to have immense racial concerns and knowledge but who don't know blacks other than me and who haven't even come in touch with ordinary whites in decades.

I've been repulsed by the scruffy black kids with their shoeshine kits on glitzy Michigan Avenue, all too real a reminder of the station to which some would like to remand blacks and the limits that I've tried to overcome. I've detested the pin-striped white junior executives who make their contribution to race relations in the quarters they flick to these kids. (Fortunately, I've noticed no rubs of the kids' heads for good luck.)

And of course, I've despised the bigots, the only group toward whom I do not continually have to re-examine my emotions.

The election has come and gone. Washington won, but to look at the battlefield, the rebuilding that must be done is defeating.

I have resumed lunching with some of the white colleagues I avoided for weeks, though the conversation will stay forever circumscribed. Some have fallen away, failures of my litmus test. New ones have been found. But no white will ever be trusted so readily again with the innermost me. It is difficult to have the same confidence in my judgment about whites that I used to have. It is difficult to say "friend."

Is that saying I have become a bigot? Let's just say I have returned to the fold, have become "integration shy." At least I tried once to extend my hand, which is more than most whites can say; they do not encounter enough blacks in their lifetime to try.

Why is Chicago this way? Why my beloved city, so vital, so prosperous, so exhilarating? I do not have an answer. I wish I did.

So here I am, blacker than I've ever been. But above all, human—a condition I share with everyone of every hue. I feel. I mistrust. I cry. And I now know that I can hate. ■

August 29, 1983

Tree shaker or jelly maker?

This is the land where every boy is supposed to be able to grow up to be president. The old saying made no mention of females or blacks, but it may yet be reworded, what with *Savvy* magazine profiling San Francisco Mayor Dianne Feinstein as White House material and the Rev. Jesse Jackson poised to join the race among the six announced Democrats. That a black or female has every right to run for the nation's highest office is at last accepted, and that bit of progress should not be ignored.

Now comes the hard part, whether there should be a black presidential candidate at all in 1984 and, if so, who.

Should there be a black candidate? The Democratic contenders are more in agreement on this than much of black officialdom. Former Vice

President Walter Mondale, considered the frontrunner, has the most to lose. Yet he and the others have said publicly they welcome the competition and that it would not hurt the party's chances of defeating President Reagan. Privately, though, they may be keeping fingers crossed that one never materializes.

Black elected officials are divided about whether anyone black should run, and they are in rancorous dispute about Rev. Jesse Jackson. Mayors Andrew Young of Atlanta and Coleman Young of Detroit, both backers of Mondale, assert that a black will drain energy from the effort to unseat Ronald Reagan, which is necessary at any costs. This view is endorsed by the NAACP's Benjamin Hooks.

But Mayors Harold Washington of Chicago, Richard Hatcher of Gary and John Ford of Tuskegee, Ala., counter that a black candidate is the best way to work up enough enthusiasm to get blacks to register and to vote. Would that the democratic process was enough of a reason.

They also argue that it will force the white presidential candidates to look at issues that concern blacks. This last is a dubious argument because in the political season every smart politician gives lip service to everybody's issues anyway, and none does so with any more sincerity than the next. Even Reagan has gotten religion of late about blacks, women, Hispanics, the hungry and everyone else he previously disregarded.

With a black or not, black issues will be addressed. The Democrats can be smug, knowing that blacks really have no other way to vote, but they can't be stupid. Chicago's recent election and the growing Hispanic voice automatically have impact. There doesn't need to be a candidate representative of any group. But why shouldn't there be? Politics is about getting the numbers, however they might add up.

But Jesse?

Jackson is acting more like an official candidate every day, racing between speeches with thrice his usual energy and planning European jaunts and audiences with royalty to show that a black candidate can have more than domestic social concerns on his agenda. He has asked Gary Mayor Hatcher to head a committee to look into the practicality of his running, though he has not yet officially declared. Until last week the biggest debate was whether he really was serious or just basking in the attention until such time as the demand for commitment became too pressing and he would, gracefully of course, bow out.

Don't look for an endorsement here. Captivating, stirring, brilliant he can be, but his zero experience in public office is a big question mark. And while Jackson has a significant place in the civil rights struggle, his aura is still of the streets, not the Oval Office. To put it in his own inimitable fashion, some people are tree shakers and some people are jelly makers. He has long maintained that he is a tree shaker, the agitator; others can make the jelly, take care of the follow-through, though they would be nowhere without his mighty hands shaking the tree. That, it appears, is just what he's doing in presidential politics, shaking things up. That's not all bad, but to survive in politics you have to make the jelly, too.

And finally, it is insultingly presumptuous to think that blacks will fall in line behind a black candidate on a national scale, particularly Jackson. The chants of "Run, Jesse, run" (from blacks and whites) that are greeting him throughout the country are not official polls.

One can go on forever about the subject, but the bottom line is no black is going to be president of the United States for so far in the future that it isn't worth pondering. And even though the Democratic contenders have said they would consider a black vice presidential running mate, don't hold your breath on that one either.

So what is there to lose in running a black candidate? The animosity black voters have for Reagan will not be turned on a white Democrat who appears to thwart a black candidate because of the simple logic above— blacks don't fool themselves that a black candidate will make it. The exercise, the reactions would be harmless and educational, a drill leading up to someday doing the real thing.

But Jesse? ■

August 27, 1983

Who will help black America?

Are black people hopeless?

No black person with any dignity could accept this thought for a millisecond without disintegrating into madness. And yet the question nags the thinking person, no matter what color, or how poor or well off.

Black unemployment, the inmate population, suicide, homicide, neighborhood crime, illegitimate births, single-parent homes are on the rise. Black life expectancy, test scores, income are generally lower than those of white America.

It is easy for some of other races to dismiss this. The most narrow-minded, of course, cling to theories of genetic inferiority as the reason for these ills. On the other hand, even the most thoughtful whites sometimes view as empty excuses the arguments that there are socioeconomic reasons for black failure to advance.

But anyone black must confront these questions daily: Is the lot of black America doomed eternally, some cruel hoax perpetrated by laughing gods? How long must a people yearn for betterment? And for those blacks who are fortunate, there is sometimes the added curse of guilt for having made it when so many others, from the same neighborhood, indeed the same homes, continue to suffer.

There is, of course, that thing called racism, as everyday as tying one's shoes. It is the way in which one approaches blacks with a ready set of assumptions about their intelligence, or job, or speaking abilities, or even more basic, whether they should be approached at all.

But even civil rights veteran Bayard Rustin writes in *Newsweek* this week "it would be convenient to ascribe all the problems confronting black Americans to the persistence of racism. But while racism continues to exert a baneful influence upon our society, the plight of black Americans today is more and more the consequence of a number of important nonracist, structural features of our economy."

The occasion for my reflections and Rustin's essay is the twentieth anniversary of the March on Washington, when 250,000 people let freedom ring on the Capitol mall and helped make history. A march in remembrance will take place today. What has changed since that tumultuous time when Martin Luther King Jr. was indeed a king to much of black America?

Much of the news from black America remains grave; a third of the 26.5 million population still lives in poverty. It is not, of course, as bad as it would have been without Dr. King's stirring words, marches in the face of attack dogs and hoses and days in jail. But the essence of his message—equality—still is a long way off. And that is the rub, that is why even the black middle class, which one would think content, complains as much as it does. In fact, media stories reflecting on the anniversary have found that many of those blacks who have "made it" are the most pessimistic.

A layer of black America called the "underclass" is in a frightful, directionless state. The recession, President's Reagan's policies, and a right face in politics have been detrimental, to be sure. But there is an underlying hopelessness now that goes beyond these factors, and it even distresses the middle class.

A generation of children has been lost to educational experimenting, the sexual revolution, the changing family, drugs. Whatever goes wrong for white America has a worse impact on black America, and what goes well always has a lesser impact. So that the breakdown in the family generally, with working wives and more divorces, has meant that 41 percent of black households are headed by single women and that 70 percent of these fall under the sociological catchphrase "the feminization of poverty."

Likewise, even if the economy gets better, it will affect blacks last and least. Even the black middle class that the media could not write enough about some years ago is largely dependent on government jobs, not sharing equally in climbing the corporate ladder.

The greatest commitment now in the civil rights struggle must come from the black middle class, which at the same time must guard its own sliver of the economic pie. That is not dishonest or selfish, simply American. And it will be triply hard without the very dollars-and-cents social programs that helped them, programs that have been stripped bare by the Reagan administration. They could not have achieved what they did alone, and they cannot now do for others without that assistance.

It will be black self-help that will have to save the underclass, to educate and call for an end to rampant teenage pregnancy, to offer reforms in welfare that will allow fathers to stay in the home, to decrease criminal recidivism, to demand better schools and community services. It will take, for example, the efforts of an Edward Gardner, the South Side black hair care manufacturer who has begun a "Black on Black Love" campaign to combat black on black crime. It will take electing responsive politicians, be they white or black.

White America may tire of what it views as grousing by black Americans about their condition, but blacks, who are touched by those conditions, tire of it and agonize over it a thousand times more—and are not simply looking for a handout.

Blacks will always have as their primary defense "racism," that generic, omnipresent miasma they alone can feel. And their frustration is compounded by the difficulty of persuading those who do not feel that it even exists. As impossible as it seemed to earn the right to sit anywhere on a bus, it will be far more difficult to prove that the person next to you has a sign blocking his mind.

Yet more despairing still is that 20 years hence the very questions posed here may remain unanswered. ∎

September 21, 1983

Beautiful is black in Miss America

This has been a watershed year for "first blacks." Harold Washington was elected the first black mayor of Chicago, Lt. Col. Guion S. Bluford was the first black astronaut in space and now the first black Miss America has been crowned, Vanessa Williams, 20, of Millwood, N.Y.

Why is the first black anything still significant? Because the progress of blacks since the 1960s has been nothing short of earthshaking. Because so much has been done in so little time to reverse centuries of inequity. All it took was for opportunities finally to open, though many are still flowering. Most important, blacks are grasping those opportunities, as they always knew they could.

That should not be lost on Miss America as she protests too much about the attention paid her race. Her crowning is historic because it has taken 62 years, and it is made all the more fascinating because the first runner-up, Miss New Jersey, Suzette Charles, also is black.

Miss America represents the nation's highest standards of beauty; it is surely a new day when a black woman is an ideal for little white girls to emulate.

But Williams is miffed. "At times I get annoyed because people and the press aren't focusing on me as a person and are focusing on my being black," she said.

That, unfortunately, comes with the "first black" territory. What Williams should keep in mind is that she, like other "firsts," achieve what they do for the most part by not being overly "black." That has nothing to do with skin coloration—the subject of a minor and stupid debate over Williams' light complexion that one hopes will quickly dissipate in the black community.

Rather, it has to do with meeting "colorless" standards and qualifications that any individual would have to meet. That was the message of civil rights: Give blacks a fair, equal chance and they will advance. Williams provided it stunningly. The traits that swayed the judges radiated from Williams the individual, not Williams the black curiosity. But however gorgeous, dramatic and delightful she may be, she also is black. Though her other gifts were acquired, that last is a natural—and a gift as well.

If she is a strong person, and her statements indicate she is, she will not be co-opted into becoming a spokesman for black causes. An individual's personality can ensure that the color of that person is not turned into a symbol, as even Williams recognizes: "I don't think I'm going to be torn. Just because I'm black doesn't mean I'm going to support every black position."

It is not every black's lot in life to be "upfront" about color, to be the protester or agitator. There will be those in the black community chiding Williams' "lack of identity," or some such. Williams' victory placed her in a leadership role, but that role does not require her to organize a march or speak out on South Africa. Its demands are different.

Civil rights leaders are right to make a fuss over her, but they may be making too much of the blow to racism; it's far from dead. Every "first black" chips away at it, but it will not be defeated until there are second, third and even twentieth blacks; in other words, until blacks are in all strata of business and social life as a normal, everyday occurrence. In American society today, that just isn't so. Would that the day would hurry when being black were coincidental to someone's achievement.

Williams is not the first black to be annoyed about being the first black. John Thompson, the spit-and-polish basketball coach at Georgetown University, shocked everyone with his seemingly ungracious statements in 1982 upon becoming the first black coach to get his team to the NCAA finals. He said it wasn't so great an honor because to admit as much would be to say there had been no qualified blacks before him, and that would be an insult to other blacks.

To use Thompson's analogy, did the naming of Justice Thurgood Marshall as the first black on the Supreme Court in 1967 mean that there had been no worthy black men of jurisprudence before Marshall? No, it meant only that blacks were deemed unworthy—wrongly—and doomed by historical circumstance.

There are times to be black, and there are times not to be black. That is an early and indelible lesson of childhood for most black people. During her reign, Miss America will find the beauty and the beast in that lesson. ■

September 25, 1983

Beauty brings out
the beast

No sooner did I label the debate over the light complexion of Miss America 1984 "minor and stupid" than it quickly turned major and stupid.

The office phone was jingling crazily.

"Of course, they'd pick her," said one caller, referring to the crowning of Vanessa Williams, 20, of Millwood, N.Y., the first black to win the title Miss America, "she's the least black-looking person they could find."

"Why did they pick someone so fair that they had to ask her if she was half white?" one upset caller asked.

The comments continued: "Picking her was an insult. Whites always set the standards for blacks. So to pick someone like that, who is near-white, subjects us to their standards."

Others were incensed that Williams herself did not want to dwell on the racial matter, some questioned whether she really considered herself black.

Even a *New York Times* television critic noted that with the victories of Williams and first runner-up Miss New Jersey, Suzette Charles, also black, the beauty pageant could "chalk up one for diversity, but put something down for homogenization. It is unlikely that many viewers knew for sure whether the two young women were black or white."

Back on the phone, someone else suggested that crowning Williams was "an effort to help the Republicans get black votes. It's not inconceivable that this thing was rigged." And, this same person suggested, they probably picked a black first runner-up to keep from insulting the black community just in case the alleged rigging to pick Williams is uncovered and she is disqualified.

Whoa! I'm as intrigued by juicy conspiracy theories as the next person. Two blacks at the top in the same contest is a mite suspicious. But this kind of response is too much.

I never expected I would have to write on this subject, certainly not in the forum of a newspaper with a predominantly white audience. But I plunge now with both feet into the silly little business of "color consciousness"—status and black skin tones.

Color variations are joked about uninhibitedly among black people, but any serious discussion of it is whispered; and it is an unmentionable in the company of whites. Even civil rights has not relieved this twisted, parasitic tendency.

Miss America is black—light skin, green eyes and all. And I may as well admit to being of the same persuasion before someone calls to make an issue of it, though you'll never catch me competing against Williams in a bathing suit.

Those people who choose to feel superior or inferior to others of their own race on the basis of skin color ought to spend more time looking over themselves.

Whatever happened to the message of "black is beautiful," to the thinking that blacks were a melting pot all to themselves, to the poetry that celebrated shades from honey to ebony?

White society for years set all kinds of literal measures for blackness—"one drop of blood"; and "octoroons," who were persons having one-eighth black ancestry, or by a different formula the children of a quadroon and a white. In a recent Louisiana court case a woman who looked white and had lived as a white tried unsuccessfully to be declared so legally when she discovered after all of these years that her birth certificate listed her as black. The state law that makes anyone with 1/32d "Negro blood" legally black was upheld; the woman was found to be 3/32ds black.

With all of these definitions, why do blacks waste time with nitpicking, self-effacing refinements?

Black people throughout history have taken in the fairest and the darkest of siblings. Of course there were people who "passed," disappeared into white society, but that made them no less black in actuality. And there were social clubs for the light-skinned only in those days when everyone was a "Negro" and proud of it and the word "black" was an insult (that debate isn't over yet either).

There will always be people—black and white—with acute cases of color consciousness, individuals concerned about how light or how dark someone's complexion is, how straight or how kinky someone's hair is. But the bottom line is black is black, off-white is black and so is every color in between.

There are too many other substantive issues confronting black people today. Isn't it about time to blend together and move on? ■

October 26, 1983

My defense of an offense

The Reader *is a free Chicago weekly that has achieved remarkable success as a "sea-level" successor to Chicago's underground press that was fading out in the early 1970s. Directed at students and young professionals along Chicago's lakefront, it became the nexus of local conflict over its tolerance for anonymous individuals who used its free ads as a forum for racial, ethnic and religious hatred. The ads became the subject of the following column, which touched off freelance "Point of View" Tribune columns on both sides of the issue. The* Reader *quietly ceased the practice a few months later.*

I could not have been more offended. Yet I cannot be more righteous about defending the laws that allow the offender to express his views.

In every issue of the *Reader,* Chicago's free alternative weekly newspaper, there are ads in the personals that put forth the most venomous racial and anti-Semitic and anti-Catholic epithets. They are so objectionable that most cannot be reprinted here. They are usually signed "White power."

"Where is Hitler when we need him," reads one. And there is the indiscriminate discrimination of another that begins, "I'm sick of Jews and Catholics. Aren't there any Protestant girls in Chicago? . . ."

No need for more. You get the idea. They are the kind of ideas you don't like to think people think, much less take the time to place in a newspaper, even one that is free.

A fuming friend, who is Jewish, pointed them out to me, obviously seeking a like mind to blast the perpetrators. "This to me is the equivalent of yelling 'Fire' in a crowded theater," he said, using the oft-cited measure of where First Amendment free speech rights end and the endangerment of the general welfare begins.

Of course, I agreed initially, and not simply on the basis of color. But then I had to re-evaluate my position. Shouldn't free expression be free? Isn't the expression of these opinions as protected as those in this column? Was this yelling "Fire"?

The "phone sex" and "escort" ads in the *Reader* as well as many of the idiotic messages between jokesters and lovers also can be offensive. But do the ads, or those in any number of other free-spirited publications, incite disorder? When you begin to try to draw an exact line between what is and isn't acceptable, the next step is to forbid all such dissent. That essentially is un-American.

The line drawn by the *Reader* goes beyond that drawn by the *Tribune,* for example. Yet within the First Amendment is protection for them both. It ensures freedom of speech, press, religion and the right to assembly and petition. Anyone who doesn't like the *Reader* ads can send in his own, or start a publication, or march in protest under the very same amendment that permitted the offending material. And the Constitution also allows some room to take a publication to court to try to make the judiciary redraw the line.

"We do get complaints every once in a while," said Robert A. Roth, publisher and editor of the *Reader.* "What it comes down to is a choice between running offensive opinions or censoring offensive opinions. I prefer not to be the censor. And it's not that I like the contents of our personals. In fact, I never read them, and it is my recommendation to anyone who finds them offensive that they never read them [again]. I don't know anybody who reads them but I know they are very popular. Should someone allow shameful or distasteful opinion to be expressed? I say yes because the alternative is so dangerous. We don't care if people picket us or whatever, we're not going to allow the 'thought police' to control what gets published."

Roth says the standard for advertising is that the item not be illegal. "You may find hate ads, but not ads that advocate murder. We have thou-

sands of classifieds in which these fine distinctions and judgments calls
have to be made." (Housing discrimination is a real thicket for his ad
staff, he said.)

"The official policy is that we want to allow the maximum possible
expression of opinion. So you won't find us denying the military the right
to run recruitment ads, or the anti-military point of view, or abortionists,
or the pro-life movement. You won't find us attempting to decide for our
readers what's healthy, wholesome and edifying. We're just going to let it
run. Even if it promotes lung cancer and we know that, we're not going to
step in to protect them from lung cancer. We're not going to step in to protect them from opinion.

"The danger in our society is not from someone having the opinion
that 'Martians are scum' but from those trying to keep another person
from saying who he thinks are scum. They are transparently in favor of
freedom of speech for themselves, but they want to deny the other guy's
freedom of speech because they say he's a cretin. Maybe they're right; the
person who puts in the offensive ad may be a cretin, I'm just not going to
leave the determination up to those accusing him."

I stand offended, but ready to defend. ■

November 6, 1983

Black votes and
Jesse Jackson

It will be nearly impossible to be black and publicly against Jesse Jackson
in the presidential race. And yet blacks must keep in mind that as he has
every right to run so too have they the right to vote for whomever they
please, for whatever reason they please.

Julian Bond, the Georgia state legislator, has put it in words that display the proper diplomacy: "If we insist that white candidates cease taking advantage of us, we must make the same demand of black candidates,
too."

Plenty of big-name black opponents of Jackson have not wished him
well. Among them are Coretta Scott King, Atlanta Mayor Andrew
Young, Detroit Mayor Coleman Young and the NAACP's Benjamin
Hooks. Mayor Harold Washington is so far noncommittal and definitely
distant.

There is, of course, a matter of egos underlying this rift: Jackson does not need the blessings of any of them, but some of them wish he had asked. Yet there is enough ego on his part, too, to have dragged out his official announcement, made several announcements that he would soon announce and finally, last Sunday, announced to CBS' Mike Wallace that he was going to announce. Jackson is adroit at doing what is good for the masses by doing what is good for himself.

Emotions are feverish among blacks; to express any doubt about which lever you might pull is heresy. Already he is the candidate to be for if you are black because he is black. Contrary to myth, that was not the best or only reason black Chicagoans had for voting for Harold Washington. Washington brought together the black poor and middle class, giving new courage to black businesses, politicians and clergy to free themselves of the old power structure's grip.

There are signs already that Jackson is doing just the opposite. Many of those whom Jackson is hoping to find at the end of his "rainbow coalition" cannot hope to contribute to the pot of gold that should also be there to run a campaign. There haven't been this many charges of "Uncle Tom" in the air since the sixties. If black people get hung up on using sentiment for or against Jackson as a measure of each other's blackness, solidarity to the cause or some other such sloganism, it will hurt not just Jackson but the real symbolism his candidacy represents.

And there is undeniable symbolism in his running. "If I have a chance just once in my life to vote for a black man for president, I'm going to do it," said one supporter testifying to the pride Jackson has sparked.

And white support should not be written off.

Let's look again at the oft-cited pros and cons. First, Jackson has little chance of becoming president. True, but who is to say he won't perform well? Even the likelihood that he will be vice president is slim, although his most ardent disciples prophesy a winning John Glenn-Jesse Jackson ticket.

Second, he has not paid political dues. Despite a run for mayor, this is a valid but minor complaint. Even without a list of political courtesy titles or appointments Jackson is attractive against the whole field.

Third, Jackson will ruin the chance to get Reagan off the stage. People who are going to vote for Reagan are going to do so regardless of Jackson's presence in the primaries.

Fourth, Jackson is going to bring up issues that no one else would. So too would a Hispanic female. Jackson will add interest and voters on the strength of his oratory alone, and he will lose equal numbers for it. But to think that dozens of black politicians at the local, state and national level will ride in on Jackson's coattails is to overestimate the length of those coattails. State comptroller Roland Burris, who has announced for the Senate race, could do quite nicely even without Jackson. Must there be a black candidate in order for blacks to vote? If you were the only black in a community, would you not vote just because there were no black candidate?

Jackson's candidacy is a fascination. Most black people, asked who among the frontrunners they would trust with their future, would pick him. But have they really thought about the reasons why? ■

December 7, 1983

The black "quarterback syndrome"

The defection of quarterback Vince Evans from the Chicago Bears provides an ideal introduction for the fable of the black everyman and his drive to life's greater goals.

Evans recently switched from the National Football League to the United States Football League's Chicago Blitz after seven years with the Bears. He is being touted by the Blitz for his "market value," his drawing ability, his name. He has negotiated a four-year, $5 million contract, which may seem reason aplenty to some for his move.

But while Evans' accountant has a stake in his move, there is more to it than money. There is more to it than Evans' pride versus that of Jim McMahon, whom Bears coach Mike Ditka has knighted as his starting quarterback. There is more to it than sports.

To a great many black Chicagoans, Evans is the literal embodiment of "the quarterback syndrome," this society's pathological unwillingness to accept blacks in leadership roles. His predicament is representative of black life in sports, in politics, in business, or whatever.

Before someone jumps to conclusions, there is no name-calling against anyone connected to the Bears. And Evans has neither implied nor engaged in such charges; the man just wants to play football. I offer no armchair psychology about Evans himself or his action, and I leave to my capable colleagues in sports the duty of reviewing Evans' career, his wins and losses, his passing yardage, whether he did or didn't make the grade.

But I do presume to offer some psychoanalysis about blacks and the "place" assigned to them by the larger society, which seems always to have to have a "great white hope" to reaffirm its domination.

Why am I trying to use an athlete's professional decision to switch teams to discuss prejudice? Because it is so subtly pervasive and subversive that, through black eyes, very little can be discussed exclusive of it.

Blacks follow the weekly ritual of awaiting the coach's pronouncement on who will be starting quarterback for more than its informational value. The significance of Evans' being the starting QB is difficult to express. What blacks want to see is one of their own at center stage. Running back Walter Payton is a whiz, and the ball would go nowhere without him as well. But to illustrate further this application of sports to the game of life, why must blacks always be receivers and runners?

It is uplifting to see Evans at work because a black man is in control of something in this world for just a few hours, win or lose. It is a snippet of success, and each is accumulated, just like string in anticipation of the day when it may add up to a substantial skein.

This may seem too heady a discussion of a simple sports story, but here is an example applied to politics: Many blacks maintain that it was "the quarterback syndrome" that defeated Los Angeles Mayor Tom Bradley in his bid to become California's first black governor. No matter what the voting patterns or statistical analyses show, many blacks feel that once white Californians were in the voting booth, a lot of them were hit by "the syndrome" and they were suddenly and unthinkingly gripped with dread at the prospect of a black person running their state. The effect "the syndrome" would have was much talked about during the election of Harold Washington, too. How many whites simply could not—cannot now—accept black leadership?

You don't have to hate anyone to be so afflicted; you simply have to live from day to day in a world in which there are too few black quarterbacks in industry, in sports management, in government, in corporate board rooms, in small business. In this world blacks are relegated to second string, or "tokens."

"The syndrome" can afflict anyone. In fact, blacks are victimized twice by it. First, they are left out. Then they must confront the horrible truth of their own stunted expectations when they are flabbergasted to find a black in authority "quarterbacking."

If in an imaginary land of blue and green people, the blue people were always shown in a good light and the green people were always shown in a bad light, isn't it conceivable that the blue people *and* the green people would come to see blue as better?

If, as is traditional in this society, you never see a particular group in control of something, this distorted view becomes the accepted and then the acceptable way of life. Think of the adjustments society is still trying to make to see women as more than mommies. If people can begin to understand how image can feed bias as it applies to gender, why do they close their eyes when blacks try to apply it to race?

The more black quarterbacks there are—trained adequately, competing equitably, trusted unquestionably—the fairer life will be. ■

January 15, 1984

Curious can't undo
King's heroism

Today is the birthday of the Rev. Dr. Martin Luther King Jr., in its way a holy day for blacks.

Dr. King's heroism and power to stir remain with me and millions of other people of all colors who seek and work for goodness and justice, though they may never find it. The nonviolent teachings, the valor, the love of Dr. King remain as surely as the remembrance of the sight of him, gesturing, enunciating and rising up physically at the lectern as if to soar along with the crescendo of his awesome message.

This is the first time this day has arrived with deserved national recognition, although the official federal holiday will not take effect until 1986 (on the third Monday of January). After 15 years of oversight, Congress last October finally passed the legislation making Dr. King's birthday the 10th legal federal public holiday. The legislation was originally introduced within days of his assassination in April 1968.

In death, as in life, the perseverance espoused by Dr. King ultimately frustrated his maligners. Yet one of their ringleaders, Sen. Jesse Helms (R., N.C.), could not let the matter come to a close without vilifying Dr. King as an "action-oriented Marxist." Worse, Helms tried to impart some honor to his true intent by decrying the cost of yet another paid holiday for federal workers. And most unforgivable, he sought to have the courts lift the seal on FBI bugs and wiretaps of Dr. King, shamelessly disregarding the family's desire and agreement with the government that they be sealed for 50 years.

There is an issue on those tapes. It is: How solid are one's heroes?

Curiosity would have you wonder what is in them that is so spurious, that would be so calamitous if revealed. What is suspected about the contents of the tapes already gives them "negative inference," a legal term essentially meaning that the absence of proof that they are not damaging becomes the proof that they are.

The tapes reportedly contain snippets revealing that the amazing marcher and preacher was also an amazing womanizer. I believe it was Jesse Jackson years ago who brushed aside the sexual innuendoes with a remark to the effect that if indeed "Martin could have done all that marching and all that preaching and still run around, he was surely a 'king'."

On this, his birthday, I respond with a similar "So what?" Curiosity has me itching to know what is in the tapes, yet I respectfully grant the King family's right to and wish for privacy, in perpetuity if necessary.

Sources with even the slightest notion of the tapes' contents warn that a revelation might undo Dr. King's image and perhaps some of his social good, that besides the embarrassment to his family, bigots would have cause to revel.

But a crack in one's idol is not cause to smash it, to denounce it and turn away.

Such is the price paid by public people in their private lives. Or sometimes in their public lives, since the most fascinating twist on the story is that then-Atty. Gen. Robert F. Kennedy, who is perceived as having been in step with civil rights, authorized the eavesdropping. Sen. Edward Kennedy, having to lower himself in acrimonious debate with Helms, defended his late brother: "If [he] were alive today, he would be the first person to say it was wrong to wiretap Martin Luther King."

And I think that, were Dr. King alive, he would be the first to forgive the authorization.

Such was the manner of the public man in life, and such will he be throughout time.

What Dr. King did publicly was to shame this nation into searching its conscience and giving to a people what should have been theirs anyway. He flung words so mighty they pierced the hardest hearts and brought about civil rights legislation. These are what will last. What he did in private will not, not even on tape. ∎

January 22, 1984

Rights commission looks backward

Racial quotas were fine in the days when they were unwritten, unquestioned and understood to be: whites 100 percent, blacks 0.

Those percentages were simple, easy to maintain. But then blacks started complicating everything, calculating that they were 10 percent of the total American population and 40 percent or even 60 percent of municipality or school or voting age populations in some places.

And so came the civil rights movement, which brought affirmative action and quotas. The former is a stated intent to take action to correct wrongs to some degree. Quotas are actual, verifiable numbers that are suggested—or often demanded at very high decibels—to get this nation to adjust the historical ledger that has listed blacks as liabilities rather than assets.

Last week the reconstituted U.S. Civil Rights Commission began looking at those figures and reverting to the old system of bookkeeping. By a vote of six to two, the commission declared that the use of racial quotas in affirmative action programs by public employers was not the way to correct job discrimination.

So what is? I can hardly wait for the commission's pronouncement that old-fashioned American freedom and sense of fair play will out over discrimination; that same old American freedom and sense of fair play that kept—keeps—blacks behind.

The nonsense on quotas capped a week of policy reversals, absurdities and outright heartlessness by the new but hardly improved commission. It took out after affirmative action, bilingual education, busing and other mandatory "racial preferences"; labeled as "radical" the theory of paying women equally with men for comparable work; suggested discarding two studies already underway, one on how cutbacks in student financial aid affect colleges with black and Hispanic majorities and the other on admissions, hiring and promotion of minorities at universities generally; and decided to study instead how affirmative action had hurt Americans of eastern and southern European descent. (While the commission is feeling so energetic, it might want to review history on the different means of transport used by blacks and Europeans to get to these shores. But I'd be afraid to read the report.)

The commission surely has taken up as its banner "Our President, right or wrong." It turns out the old six-member commission the president tried to undo has been undone in the new eight-member body whose appointees are divided equally between the president and the Congress.

Uneasy as I was with the president's effort to replace some members of the old commission, the authority was his to exercise as long as the commission was under the executive branch. But some finagling, and not a little arm-twisting of congressional leaders, I'm sure, has resulted in a commission under the legislative branch that still seems bent on following Reagan down the yellow brick road. That road leads to the days of old when, as only the president could have put it, "America didn't have a race problem." No one yet has been able to convince the president that America didn't have a race problem when he was a boy because blacks were invisible people, if they were recognized as people at all.

This commission could be a clever plot by the Democrats to foil the president's re-election, but that would be giving the Democrats too much credit. No, the president can take all the credit for this. And minorities and women can return the favor by taking their votes elsewhere.

On the central question of quotas, they can be made to work and turned to good, so long as they are reasonable and flexible. But many think any special effort to aid minorities is unreasonable, and they don't want to be flexible on taking in even one token; thus the fashionable cries of reverse discrimination.

Yet those who support quotas must be reasonable and flexible, too. The demand may be for ten black or female positions, but even three or five or seven would beat the old zero.

Quotas can be set in certain cases, with certain deadlines and with an understanding that, once attained, maintenance will be based on performance. Minorities and women deserve special help in many cases, but they should not be excused from accountability for their performance. In the meantime, their chances for success should be helped through education, with the goal of ending quotas one fine day when that American sense of fair play really is fair.

Someone should tell the president and the Civil Rights Commission that that day is not yet in sight. ■

February 8, 1984

How blacks can influence media

The black community and the media have discovered each other in the past year, but it has hardly been a "pleased to meet you" exchange.

Around this time last year, when things were gearing up and growing ugly before the mayoral primary, there was a rude and sudden awakening by the black community to the caliber of reportage and to the color of those presenting it. There was indeed a hypersensitivity all around, among blacks and whites, to every word written or broadcast, every photo angle, every facial expression of a television commentator.

The media, long accustomed to being lambasted by the public for being the bearer of bad news, was stung as never before. That, however, is the nature of this profession; it is not a job in which one expects to be liked.

But the black community, understandably and deservedly heady in this last year, remains at boiling. Every unkind word about the mayor, anyone on his side, or anyone black—period—is cause for protest. The reactions are too often automatic and emotional, without considering that unfavorable reporting can be valid and appropriate; or that opinions, such as these presented here, are one person's only. It is incumbent upon the black community to learn this and to learn to disagree with such comments without being disagreeable.

Over the weekend, on a black radio talk show, the idea of boycotting the downtown media came up again, as it has too often. Attorney Thomas Todd, who is heading Operation PUSH while Jesse Jackson seeks the presidency, explained to a caller that action against the media is warranted but that opposition to the boycott is coming from those black vendors who brave walk-ups and the weather to deliver and sell the newspapers.

Let me add my voice to that of the vendors, and for the self-same, and candidly self-serving reason: my livelihood.

There is a course of action for the black community other than a boycott. Rather than removing itself from the media after a year of heightened and productive involvement with them, the black community should do just the opposite. It should immerse itself in the media.

Those of us who are blacks inside the media are quoted all the time as saying our employers are not pristine on racial matters, in coverage or in hiring and promotions. There are biases to be overcome within the institution and among individuals. There is a need for more minorities and women in positions determining what will be covered and how it will be presented.

Yet it is the ideal of balance I hold as a professional that allows me, as a black, to speak my mind in this space. And I defend that balance even as I see how futile efforts sometimes are to attain it.

If the black community wants to do something about the media, here are some suggestions:

For a start it should study them, buy them, read them, watch them, contact them, know them, use them to advantage. It should congratulate as well as denounce the "white racist media"—as we (yes, we) have come to be called these days, all in one breath.

If you feel the media don't know your community, consider that the "conspiracy" is borne more of unfamiliarity than contempt and help the unenlightened white reporters. When was the last time you submitted a good or bad letter to the editor, opinion piece, or idea for a feature story on a black subject, or took up your cause with an editorial board or sought to rebut a broadcast commentary? And if in such instances you were rebuked, did you consider first that the reason may have been a staffing or deadline problem, or that the idea or the writing were unacceptable or untimely, before concluding that maybe, just maybe, it was racism?

And if you really want to do something about the media, encourage creative young black writers to start freelancing now, and contribute to scholarship funds to send them to college and out into the working world. And get those reinforcements in here in a hurry, because my fingers won't hold out on these keys forever.

Now that the black community and media have discovered each other, it's time they discovered what each other is about. ■

February 12, 1984

An ugly sign then, a talisman now

In my living room hangs a sign:

COLORED
WAITING ROOM
N. C. & St. L.

It is an authentic glass sign from the 1920s from an authentic colored waiting room of the defunct Nashville, Chattanooga and St. Louis Railway.

It hangs strategically above the fireplace, so that it is the last sight upon leaving the house and the first sight upon returning. How many other black eyes beheld it, accepted its directive and then averted their eyes from it, perhaps wishing it away or heading somewhere they hoped never to see the likes of it again?

The sign was a rare find at an antique store. The dealer so understood my yearning to have it that he broke a promise to someone else, someone white, so that I could have it.

But not everyone understands that yearning.

"Why," many wonder, and not always aloud, "would anyone want such a thing around?"

A few have taken offense at it. But what it symbolizes was so inordinately offensive that any momentary, modern-day discomfort seems trivial.

A few laugh, but it is not there for laughs. What it symbolizes is sacred and solemn. It is as precious as a collection of Ming dynasty vases. It is, in its way, a religious symbol, a talisman. It is sustenance and strength.

And during February, Black History Month, I would like to use it to explain the beauty and ugliness of being black in America and why this month is not for blacks only.

It was only 20 years ago that such signs slowly began to come down over water fountains, doorways, bus seats, train coaches and entrances to hospitals and stores. It will be many years more before some people remove them from their minds, for there are psychological barriers of paranoia and superiority far uglier than any words on a sign: These jobs are for blacks only, this real estate is for whites only, only this much of the economic pie should be for blacks.

There are many blacks who want to put the thought of the sign behind them; the depth of their hurt is understandable. But history is undeniable, and the good and the bad of it must be acknowledged.

A local media analyst, Brenda Verner, makes this point in her presentation on images of blacks throughout history. She has some 4,000 articles of memorabilia, books, photos, cards and advertisements in her private collection dating from 1760. They depict the most callous dehumanization of a people, woolly-headed caricatures, bare-bottomed pickaninnies and rotund mammies. Her slide show presentation elicits distressed gasps, and she brings the awful stereotypes up to date with criticism of television shows. What she holds up is not pretty by any means, but as blacks must face it, learn from it, so should whites.

It is because of the stereotypes, the centuries of degradation, that Black History Month is celebrated. It is something that whites should feel free to share. Nothing can reverse history, but Black History Month at least tries to correct the imbalance.

The celebration was begun by black historian Dr. Carter G. Woodson in 1926 as Negro History Week during the week of the birthdays of President Abraham Lincoln and Frederick Douglass, the freed slave and abolitionist newspaper publisher (Feb. 12 and 14, respectively).

As it has grown into a month-long tradition, however, so has opposition to it from those who wonder why there is not a month of homage to their culture.

The answer is that other cultures' contributions are acknowledged; their history was not misplaced. Their goal when they came to America was to meld, to melt into the pot, and they did so by choice.

Blacks did not come here by choice, had no choice as to blending in, or still lack complete choice over their destinies. And their contributions, made under duress and without compensation, have yet to be adequately chronicled and appreciated. Black children were taught others' history when they knew not their own.

In truth, even during Black History Month, there is not enough immersion in black culture by other ethnic groups. And, sadly, it is the only time many black youngsters are in touch with it.

But every day of every month, that sign in my living room reminds me whence I came: from a history fertile and exuberant despite adversity, about which I continue to learn and am not ashamed.

My people could be sitting still in colored waiting rooms. And so, that sign reminds, could I. But more important, it reminds that, with a sense of self, we never will again. ■

February 19, 1984

Marcus Garvey
deserves a pardon

There would be no better time than during Black History Month to grant a pardon to Marcus Mosiah Garvey.

The Jamaican-born Garvey became one of America's earliest advocates of black self-help and self-pride during that period of black literary blossoming in the 1920s called the Harlem Renaissance. His movement, though unsuccessful, helped to germinate the philosophy that "black is beautiful."

Garvey's campaign borrowed from the Russian revolution, the embryonic movement for a Jewish state and Irish independence. "Africa for Africans" was his call for the continent's freedom from colonial rule. His oratory attracted thousands of blacks to his Universal Negro Improvement Association, and he had these multitudes signed up and ready to board his Black Star Line ship to return to their motherland.

Although his idea was not original (freed slaves had founded Liberia in 1822), he perhaps came closest to making it seem workable on a large scale. It is ironic that bigots say offhandedly that blacks should return to Africa, when Garvey's efforts to do just that were thwarted as a national security risk.

Garvey's solicitations, which reportedly reached $10 million, were the basis for federal mail fraud charges against him and led to his deportation to Jamaica in 1927. He resettled in London in 1935 and died there, at 52, in 1940.

Now, some 60 years after his ill-fated adventure, the Jamaican government has requested that the U.S. government grant a pardon to Garvey. Prime Minister Edward Seaga asked this gesture of Vice President George Bush when Bush visited the island last October. Seaga said, "If the President of the United States . . . found it possible to grant a full pardon to Marcus Garvey, wiping the slate clean and clear for posterity [it would] enhance the consciousness, pride and dignity of black people throughout the world."

And a new book reveals the campaign to depose Garvey, a campaign of surveillance and infiltration led by none other than a young J. Edgar Hoover; history does indeed repeat itself, since Hoover conducted a similar campaign against Dr. Martin Luther King Jr. in the 1960s.

The first two volumes of a planned 10-volume set, *The Marcus Garvey and Universal Negro Improvement Association Papers,* have just been completed by Robert A. Hill, a professor of history at the University of California (Los Angeles) who has been active in the pardon campaign. The volumes make for an unusual, if soporific, biography that is told chronologically in an avalanche of papers. Hill culled more than 30,000 documents worldwide, including newspaper stories and Garvey's and others' articles and letters and news stories. One includes an invitation to Theodore Roosevelt to attend the Garvey organization's musicale. But most fascinating, through the use of the Freedom of Information Act, Hill has uncovered documents proving the conspiracy against Garvey by Hoover.

One Hoover memorandum reads: "He [Garvey] is an exceptionally fine orator, creating much excitement among the negroes through his steamship proposition; in his paper the 'Negro World' the Soviet Russian Rule is upheld and there is open advocation of Bolshevism."

An aging Hoover used this preoccupation with communist influences as justification for spying on King, too.

Yet Garvey was not opposed only by those of like mind to Hoover. Many prominent blacks of the day opposed him philosophically, including W. E. B. Du Bois, perhaps the greatest black mind of this century. Letters from Du Bois in the volume denounce Garvey as a charlatan and advise against investing in the Black Star Line.

And in Chicago, Garvey and Robert Abbott, founder of the *Chicago Defender,* were forever feuding, countersuing each other for libel. In its Weekly Comment, the *Defender* advised on Sept. 6, 1919: "Such meetings as that of Marcus Garvey . . . are more harmful than helpful to the Race. . . . Our Race, it is true, is struggling hard here for justice, but the fiery little man who wants to start a black star line to Africa will find conditions almost as bad in his own country, where he might better center his activities."

Still, Garvey's surprising vision easily preserves his place in American and Jamaican history. Now, through a posthumous and harmless pardon, it deserves respect. ■

February 29, 1984

Jesse Jackson and the Jews

So Jessie Jackson actually did call Jews "Hymies."

Now, will everyone who ever called a black, a Jew, or a member of any other ethnic group something despicable please stand up.

I do not mean to lessen the blow of what will go down in campaign history as "Jesse's Jewish incident," but I certainly mean to point out that there is less to it than many insist.

My reaction upon first hearing the reports of the slur was disbelief; not that I didn't think Jackson capable of anti-Semitic remarks, but that the remark itself was such an "un-black" usage. I've heard plenty of black people insult Jews (and others), but never with the word "hymie." It just sounds like such a "white" insult. But Jackson had an explanation for that, too, saying it was used in his native South Carolina. I guess it's an Eastern, not a Chicago, usage because even a Jewish friend found it obscure in his own informal poll.

But be that as it may, Jackson has repented, and better a week after the fact than not at all. Like any politician, he had to delay and choose the right moment. And Jackson did it as only he could—with chutzpah, from the podium of a synagogue. And he has again managed to get more news coverage than the other candidates combined, with the help of media that are both enticed by this peacock and the great copy he makes and bent on finding ways to pluck his feathers.

But the manner in which he apologized does not take away from the regrettable insult, nor does his reprimand of the black Washington *Post* reporter who revealed the slur, supposedly spoken in private conversation. Jackson has been a public figure long enough to know that anything he utters can end up on page one, no matter the color of or rapport with a journalist.

And the slur was not justified because of what Jackson called an organized "attempt to discredit, disrupt and destroy my campaign" by the Jewish community. A late-January incident that built up just before the New Hampshire primary is suspect, but surely the reverend knows about turning the other cheek. The Jewish community's complaint has been about his coziness with the Arabs. It is a substantial and fair issue on which to attack him—and they have, often stopping short of their own slurs.

Jackson is right in that this one remark does not make him anti-Semitic, just as an unkind word about blacks in general can be spoken by someone who claims "some of my best friends are." Despite the uncharitable remarks on both sides, the recent disagreements over quotas, the old Jewish-black alliance is not dead.

Certainly, Jackson should not have used the term, even if "innocent and unintended."

Yet if every politician owned up to every racial or ethnic slur he had ever uttered, voters would have a truer picture of his personality and probably would have a lot more to vote on than a smile, party loyalty or a position on some critical issue that they should care about but don't.

What makes Jackson's case so peculiar and so uncomfortable is that blacks have been on the receiving end of so many insults for so long, and Jackson has been fighting the very thing he now stands convicted of.

Such fallibility has been the undoing of politicians before. This alone will not "undo" Jackson. James Watt's list of sins was already long before his exit following a similar incident.

But underlying all this attention is a campaign to make Jackson the black candidate, and nothing more. I am one of those who has been hesitant about his candidacy, looking for a selfish motivation where perhaps there is none. But whatever doubts I may harbor, I have been appalled at the spectacle of my fellows in the media making Jackson *the* black candidate for blacks only. Black he is, but he has reached out to other constituencies, taken risks that his fellow presidential aspirants will not, including his Arab views.

His rainbow coalition is being treated as if "all of the colors are black," to borrow a line from songwriter Paul Simon. It's not that the colors aren't there, it's just imagination that many of the media and the electorate lack.

I can waffle about and look askance at Jackson. But it would not be fair of me—and is not fair of others—to dismiss his ability to attract women, Hispanics, the elderly and everyone else to whom he has extended his invitation, to dismiss the legitimacy of his candidacy. Jackson is a great draw.

If his detractors didn't want to accredit him as more than a black candidate before, the "Jewish incident" is payment in full for his membership in the fishbowl. ■

March 7, 1984

Fisk University rises to challenge

Fisk University in Nashville, one of the nation's earliest and finest black colleges, has fallen on hard times. But it remains dignified and undaunted.

Late last year the university was in arrears on a $170,000 natural gas bill. Service was cut off, leaving students to study while swathed in blankets in midwinter.

Through the efforts of alumni, black fraternities and churches and even rival black colleges such as Howard University in Washington, D.C., a fund drive was begun. The university and the gas company reached agreement on time payments, and service was restored. But more than $2 million in bills remains past due.

So Fisk is, as always, struggling, just like most of black America. It is nothing unusual, nothing of which to despair. Indeed the only certainty of black life is that it will always be tough.

But the intent here is not to maintain a "woe are we" lament. Many who are not black may find it hard to believe, but blacks tire of the state of permanent tribulation and the accompanying bewailing of it.

The national effort to save Fisk University offers black America a chance to show that it can do more than bemoan its status, that it can do for itself—not that help from friends wouldn't be appreciated.

Ironically, Fisk University has a history—again reflecting black America generally—that is noted for adversity and for stubbornness in conquering it.

The school, with an enrollment of about 800, was founded in 1866 in an empty Union Army barracks in Nashville. Four years later, it was already bankrupt.

That first fundraising effort in the early 1870s is a captivating chapter from black history.

A Fisk music teacher started the Fisk Jubilee singers. The group, in addition to helping save the school, helped to make the Negro spiritual an "acceptable" musical form.

The group went on tour to sing about the plight of the school and the need for higher education for newly freed blacks. They often were denied lodging and meal accommodations or even a chance to perform. Then, at a program at Oberlin College in Oberlin, Ohio, fortune turned in their favor. They were being kept backstage, and it appeared that once again they were to be ignored. They began singing offstage during a lull in the regular program and so moved the audience that they soon were in demand, even performing for Queen Victoria in England.

Today's crisis will take more than song, but music is part of the effort; a special benefit concert will be held in the spring at the John F. Kennedy Center for the Performing Arts in the nation's capital.

Among other efforts, some 70 black leaders were called together under Howard University's auspices and formed the National Committee for the Preservation of Fisk University. They pledged to raise $5 million this year.

And the hat-passing in the black community included one Sunday's church collections in February for Black History Month, especially significant given Fisk's role in that history.

The role of black colleges has been to ensure a flow of black leaders whose considerable talents were not appreciated by other institutions. They were born to be separate and remain so, even though they have white enrollment. In a turnabout in recent years many have had their autonomy threatened. Why do black colleges fight so hard to maintain that separatism, when blacks have indicted separatism, whether it has been unequal or equal? The answer can be found in an institution such as Fisk, in the laurels it has won and in the pride it engenders in a race once thought incapable of and barred from the most rudimentary academic training. It has come too far to fail now. ∎

April 1, 1984

There are no white people

There are no white people.

This bit of profundity is put forth by no less a thinker and agitator than author James Baldwin. The black writer is best known for efforts in the 1960s to censor his book *Another Country,* which dealt with homosexuality and interracial love affairs.

In the April issue of *Essence,* a magazine for black women, he once again aims his pen at the core of racism in America. [His latest book, *Evidence of Things Not Seen,* about the murders of 29 children in Atlanta, is forthcoming later this year.]

In the magazine article, "On Being 'White' and Other Lies," Baldwin is, as always, explosive, defiant. He lets loose with his theory of whiteness: that it is a fraud ethnics who arrived on these shores perpetrated against themselves out of the necessity to deny the humanity of blacks; and they have built upon and fortified this lie until it has become their most abiding truth. And "blacks" were "branded" as such, and had no say in choosing their identity.

He says no one was "white" before they came here, were, in fact, proud to be hyphenated Americans, with strong ties to their mother country. But then their fear of people of color led them to fade into a generic whiteness to better ensure and exert their collective power.

But Baldwin speaks quite ably for himself:

"There is, for example—at least, in principle—an Irish community: here, there, anywhere, or, more precisely, Belfast, Dublin and Boston. . . . And there is a Jewish community, stretching from Jerusalem to California to New York. There are English communities. There are French communities. . . . There are Poles: in Warsaw (where they would like us to be friends) and in Chicago (where because they are white we are enemies). . . .

"No one was white before he/she came to America. It took generations, and a vast amount of coercion, before this became a white country."

"White men—from Norway, for example, where they were *Norwegians*—became white: by slaughtering the cattle, poisoning the wells, torching the houses, massacring Native Americans, raping black women."

And Jews, he says, have paid the highest price:

"For the Jews came here from countries where they were not white, and they came here, in part *because* they were not white; and incontestably—in the eyes of the black American (and not only in those eyes) American Jews have opted to become white. . . ."

Is this theory, you may wonder, what many or most blacks believe? It is not far from the thinking of most blacks, whatever their political or philosophical bent. And while neither Baldwin nor anyone can speak for an entire race, there is continual thought among blacks as to the why of being white: why it must be maintained so stalwartly, why it is deemed better, why it so shamelessly relegates others to a lesser stature without a fair trial and, above all, how it justifies itself morally.

Baldwin's response, and he does paint a wide swath, is that it is immoral. "This necessity of justifying a totally false identity and of justifying what must be called a genocidal history has placed everyone now living into the hands of the most ignorant and powerful people the world has ever seen . . . and has brought humanity to the edge of oblivion: because they think they are white. Because they think they are white, they do not dare confront the ravage and the lie of their history. Because they think they are white, they cannot allow themselves to be tormented by the suspicion that all men are brothers."

What does Baldwin want? He wants what black people in general want, that white people look upon them as people. And like Baldwin, many blacks wonder whether the distance between races is so great now that members of one will never be able to see the members of the other with clarity, or whether anyone cares to try.

As incendiary as the words seem, he does not want, nor do blacks generally want, revenge. They only want an acceptance that their condition was not of their making; that whites acknowledge and start tearing down their own psychological barriers.

Despite its potency, Baldwin's essay is not a diatribe. To those who believe it is, take up his challenge and look within to see if the seed of hate has not been embedded there, unnoticed and perhaps unwanted.

Maybe then there will be no white people, or black people, either. ■

May 9, 1984

Jews and blacks
still shipmates

The old alliance between blacks and Jews is strained, but hardly about to collapse.

The split in this traditional twosome was apparent long before Jesse Jackson's "Hymie" incident. Two weeks ago, 10 blacks and Jews in the New York congressional delegation issued a letter of unity: "Today on the eve of Passover we join together in an effort to reaffirm [our] longstanding bond and community of interests. . . ."

The *Chicago Reporter,* a newsletter on race relations, talked with leaders from each community in this month's issue. It concludes that the alliance cracked because blacks felt Jews had betrayed them by abandoning the civil rights movement, and because Jews felt blacks had been ungrateful for their aid, especially after the riots of the 1960s.

Certainly, some blacks dislike Jews and vice versa. Yet the link forged by their shared history of oppression has been so strong that many blacks make the distinction that there are Jews, and then there are whites. Jewish merchants stayed behind after neighborhoods changed. As the *Reporter* cites, many blacks always thought those merchants were cheating them, but the fact remains that the merchants were there.

Jews helped found the NAACP in 1909 and bankrolled the Harlem Renaissance of black art and music in the 1920s. No black social agency seems to lack Jewish members on its board.

But what bound blacks and Jews also has entangled them.

The "oppressed" link has turned into a game of one-upmanship, with blacks saying they have suffered more. Blacks feel their calamitous history is not accorded the same importance as the Holocaust, even though recognizing that many people don't want to hear about the Holocaust either. And blacks know that Jews have one route to acceptability that they will never have—all the name changing in the world won't change skin color.

The philanthropic link also has been twisted. As the civil rights movement grew into a black power movement, Jewish supporters came to be seen as patronizing and patriarchal. Many blacks turned on the Jews marching and praying beside them, accusing Jews of wanting to be part of the movement only so long as blacks did not control it. This was a wrenching parting, but probably a natural progression. As Jews arose from European ghettos through education, self-pride, self-help and inspiration drawn from a cruel yet cherished history, so must blacks.

Adding to the tensions have been differences about the use of quotas to help end discrimination; Zionism and unquestioned U.S. support of Israel; and of late, Israel's trade agreements with South Africa.

Jews view quotas as a tool of discrimination because they were used in the past to limit Jewish participation. In the Jewish view, every quota is restrictive: If the numerical goal is seven entrants, then the eighth entrant will be shut out. Blacks may come to share that view eventually, but now seven looks better than zero.

On Israel, some of the bitterness was fostered by the rise of the black Muslim movement and its identification with Islam and Middle Eastern Arabs. But for most blacks there is no such religious consideration; they simply do not understand why a people who so wanted their own homeland are insensitive to the Palestinian longing for the same right. And the two groups' shared contempt for prejudice should dictate that Israel not trade with the perpetrators of apartheid in South Africa.

But these differences are not enough to destroy one of the most well-maintained alliances in history.

How will it hold together? One way was put plainly, if crassly, by Republican mayoral candidate Bernard Epton last year after blacks did not vote for him: "I certainly will save a lot of money in the future on charitable causes." To be plainer still, black groups still need the support, monetary or otherwise. (Epton, who is Jewish, lost 43 percent of Jewish votes to Harold Washington.)

There is another reason the alliance will hold together. Jews, no matter how they have assimilated, recognize that they are not so far removed or safe from discrimination. They have an interest in seeing that blacks win respect. For if you scratch a person who hates blacks, you are likely to find an anti-Semite, too. ■

May 13, 1984

Opting for life in the gray area

Life isn't always black or white.

City Councilman Mark Stebbins of Stockton, Calif., retained his seat in a special election Tuesday that had less to do with his qualifications than his true identity. Stebbins, curly-haired, blue-eyed and white-skinned, claims to be black. The man who lost to Stebbins originally, Ralph Lee White, who is undoubtedly black, claims that Stebbins is a white man with an identity crisis.

White pushed for the recall in the predominantly black district, saying that the constituents had been hoodwinked and were not being represented because, contrary to Stebbins' claims, he was not, like White, black. White, who represented the area for 12 years, offered Stebbins' birth certificate as proof.

Stebbins, 41, comes from a family of six children whose other members all look and identify themselves as white. His parents, who live in Washington state, said they think of their son as white, but his "outlook" is black. His wife can obviously be categorized as black, but he has two former wives, one black, the other white with two white children.

But Stebbins has his disclaimer: "In America, if you have a drop of black blood in you, then you are black. That's where I have established myself. As a child I didn't have a racial identification, but I had feelings of being different at 14, when we moved to a more racially mixed area, and I began to get 'nigger hair' comments from white kids."

Stebbins is just one case in the renewed debate over that gray area which defines a person's race.

A Louisiana woman who had lived as a white discovered when she went for a passport that her birth certificate labeled her as black. She lost a court fight to be white based on a state law that anyone 1/32d black was black. The court ruled against her 29/32ds whiteness.

When Vanessa Williams became the first black woman to be crowned Miss America, black tongues clucked about just how black anyone that white-looking could be. They called her election a fraud and an affront because she was as close to white as black could get.

This debate will never be settled, but labels can be as helpful as they are harmful. Most people find it disconcerting when they can't slot someone: white or black, liberal or conservative, Democrat or Republican, middle class or upper class, etc.

How nice if the racial label could be chosen.

Maybe Councilman Stebbins has something here. From all indications, Stebbins is what 99 percent of most anyone who was asked would call white. If it behooves Stebbins to be black to get elected in a black district, if he wants to try "reverse passing," more power to him.

Light-skinned, straight-haired blacks have "passed" for white for centuries. There aren't nearly as many of the opposite case. So maybe it's a sign of progress that we now have some equal-opportunity passing.

Let's open membership now to anyone of any race who has ever wondered what it's like on the opposite side. It might be just the way to foster understanding; it could be the first step to reaching that idealistic (and elusive) colorless society.

All those white people who have preconceived ideas about the people in Robert Taylor Homes could move in, become unemployed and file for welfare. Since they think that blacks have this cushy life on their tax money anyway, they could try to get some of it back.

If all those white ethnics who are plotting to protect the sanctity of their neighborhoods were to become black, they could find an honorable pursuit in trying to keep each other from living next door.

All those black folks who think it's easy being a corporate executive could get firsthand experience at those long hauls back and forth from the suburbs. They also could suffer anxieties over their kids having the latest computer, braces, designer togs and acceptance at the right Ivy League school.

Just sign here, put it in black and white, and be the race of your choice. Oh, forget about the fine print. It just says that if you decide you don't like being the opposite of what you were, you can't go back. A mere technicality.

Any takers?

The line forms behind Mr. Stebbins. ∎

May 16, 1984

School decision
thirty years later

Brown vs. Board of Education, the U.S. Supreme Court decision that declared an end to racially separated education, marks its 30th anniversary Thursday.

Yet the mission of Brown is hardly begun. As efforts were made to live up to the decision, its intent became obscured. The means sidetracked the Brown decision from attaining its end. There was a furor over busing, angering black and white parents, and subsequent court orders that had judges ruling on everything from desegregation plans to allocation of sports equipment. The demoralization and deterioration within education generally also deflected the focus from integration.

Ill-spent time and white flight worked against Brown; most big-city school systems lost too many white pupils before Brown's hypothesis could be tested. There has been an increase in private schools nationwide to circumvent the order. And many black parents now believe Brown is unworkable; instead, they're demanding quality in an all-black setting and dismissing that their children need to rub white elbows.

Chicago's own desegregation battle took 20 years. It began with a suit by parents in 1961, when the schools were still 50 percent white. With that ratio, desegregation might have been achieved—and so might neighborhood stabilization.

But it was two years later before the Chicago Board of Education agreed to appoint a group of experts to develop a plan. In 1977, a citizens committee joined in the effort, but in 1979 the U.S. Department of Health, Education and Welfare rejected the plan and referred the case to the Justice Department. In 1980, the board and the Justice Department signed a consent decree in which both sides agreed to desegregation guidelines. U.S. District Court Judge Milton Shadur accepted it just last year and continues to pass judgment on every student transfer, every cent.

But beginning math proves what a farce much of the agreement is: 16 percent white students just won't go into 62 percent black and 22 percent Hispanic by anyone's figuring.

So the Chicago system touts that it is desegregated, but only 29 percent, or 112,000 of 435,000 students systemwide, are in such schools, and those schools are defined as having between 30 and 70 percent white enrollment.

And there remain 379 schools where there is no pretense at integration. They are euphemistically called "racially isolated," which means that there is no way, no how, given the geography, that they can get anyone white into them. What they are is still separate, and all too often still unequal, despite special programs.

So in this city alone, much of what the Brown decision tried to stymie is actually thriving.

That does not mean Brown is worthless. There are schools in which sitting next to a child of a different race is commonplace, and there isn't the remotest notion among the youngsters of how unusual such a scene appears to their parents.

Where Brown falters, the whole society is to blame. There will never be mutual respect or understanding until people share all aspects of their lives—housing, work, education, recreation. And even then there will be prejudice.

Brown's objectives are still worthy; perhaps because they have been so difficult to institute, that is all the more reason to continue trying. The decision may reach its centenary and receive the same evaluation.

Brown stands as a monument to good intentions and to the fallacy that the force of law can really change human nature. But Brown stands, nonetheless, and stately.

If the changes demanded by Brown never materialize, the decision will have done its work just by putting on record America's disdain for and regret about what had gone before. The idea of a just, tolerant and equitable society may be fanciful, but there is good in the expression of such an objective; intent requires a different judgment than methodology.

And what Brown said was that something was frightfully wrong in this country. On that, its vision was keen. It could not have been expected to see into people's consciences. ■

POLITICS

Leanita McClain's columns presented not only the perspective of a black woman but also the viewpoint of a lifelong urban dweller who was married spiritually to a love for all that the nation's cities have to offer. As such, she held nothing but disdain for the politicians who would sell out the city's best long-term interests for the sake of their own short-term political gain. As a result, she tended to approach politics in much the same way that her father would wait up for his daughters during their teen years: with a Bible in one hand and a baseball bat in the other. Her political analysis was tempered with an uncompromising sense of moral rectitude yet delivered in an often confrontational style well in keeping with Chicago's tradition of feisty journalism.

She concerned herself more with urban politics than any other kind and constantly searched for developments in Chicago and other cities that had national repercussions. As it turned out, her career as a columnist coincided with the stormy transition of power from Mayor Jane Byrne to Mayor Harold Washington, a political conflict that typified the way Northern industrial cities have moved from mostly white mayors to mostly black mayors and how traditionally liberal urban ethnic Democrats have been wooed and seduced by conservative Republicans who use racial fears to undermine old Democratic party power.

McClain's political sense came from her experience as part of a generation of Chicago youth who had known no other mayor but Richard J. Daley, the very prototype of the big-city "boss." Though many who mistakenly perceived McClain as antiwhite or subversively anti-Establishment might find it hard to believe, she often expressed an undying respect and admiration for Mayor Daley during his life and afterward. If there was anything she admired about Daley more than anything else, she said, it was that he cared about Chicago and that was a lot more than she could say for the movers and shakers who worked downtown every day, earning their keep from the city's resources, only to scamper to the suburbs before nightfall. It was a scenario that disturbed her deeply. She would often say that her value as a columnist was to provide a voice not just for black people's interests but also for those who loved big cities and wanted to help them to prosper as homes for the broadest possible variety of people and ideas.

January 12, 1983

Gender's impact on elections

What with the stifled mumblings about race and ethnicity in the city's mayoral campaign, the issue of gender has become even more muffled. Yes, there are a black and two Irish-Americans running, but one of them is also a woman. Discussions of the "gender gap" were all the rage in the November elections, particularly in Illinois with the tarnish of the failure of ERA still upon Gov. James Thompson. In the upcoming election, with a powerful woman incumbent, the subject of gender is curiously absent.

For a woman, Mayor Jane Byrne did a remarkable job of keeping that component out of her first campaign. But for a woman who was elected with the help of female voters, she has not done very much to further the rights of women. She donned a white dress in the summer heat and marched for the ERA, but all of her closest advisers are men.

She does have one high-ranking woman in her cabinet, but that woman runs the most women's issue-type department, Commissioner Lenora Cartright in Human Services. Other of her appointments of women also have been to "sex-role stereotyped" positions, Marie Cummings of the Fine Arts Council and businesswoman Sally Berger of the Library Board.

The naming of Ruth Love to run the schools was more a function of race than gender, a case of the lucky "twofer," in the parlance of corporate affirmative action headhunters.

To take nothing from these women, having a woman as mayor did not necessarily raise anyone's consciousness. So it was surprising when Pat Horne of the Midwest Women's Center here mentioned that Mayor Byrne had the vote of professional women sewn up (no sexist pun intended). If this is indeed the case, is it more honorable to vote gender than race? Both conditions are matters of birth.

The type of well-educated, business-suited, attaché case-swinging woman Horne is alluding to is the kind you'd think would not follow Byrne blindly just because Byrne is a woman. Is her holding office that symbolic? Horne believes that many of these Byrne supporters, some of whom are high-powered in their own fields, are one issue—ERA forever—and feel obligated to return the favor to the mayor.

If one wants to deal with women's issues, the two male candidates have credible records. Predictably—though last November's elections proved once again no election is predictable—Daley's female supporters are of the pro-life and/or pink-collar variety. The defection of State Sen. Dawn Clark Netsch from the lakefront "liberal-ati" to the Bridgeport home team surely has helped him.

As a state senator, Daley fought long and hard—and unsuccessfully—to kill the sales tax on food and medicine, which are still a woman's bailiwick. A woman heads the juvenile division in the state's attorney's office, which is an area dealing with youngsters but her "charges" are hardly children by anyone's definition. Daley's office also has done tremendous work on prosecuting domestic violence cases. Still, some women in the myopic ERA faction won't forgive him for not pulling more of his considerably long strings in Springfield.

If one were voting on feminist issues alone, Harold Washington's longtime liberalism and record on social programs should do him a world of good. Among working-class and poor women concerned about the feminization of poverty, Washington is the obvious choice. Apparently, black women know which accident of their birth carries the greater liability.

No doubt cognizant that the two men in the race are running circles around her, the mayor has just named a women's panel to look into allegations of discrimination in city government pay and promotions. The complaints are based on a study of the city payroll that found that four of five male city workers are paid more than $20,000 a year, but only one of five women makes as much.

The panel of seven women, headed by Day Piercy of Women Employed, will review pay and career opportunities. The group also will establish a career development program for women seeking managerial positions—perhaps like running a city.

In announcing the panel, the mayor recalled her days as the party's token female. During those years, in her "proper place" as consumer sales commissioner aiding homemakers, she zipped from supermarket to supermarket to ferret out short-sheeted rolls of toilet paper. She said men in the office were called "inspectors" and women "female shoppers" at lesser pay. Having had such firsthand experience with sex bias, it is especially peculiar that she has just come upon the idea of helping women a few weeks before the election. ■

January 16, 1983

New sparks in forensic fire

Marquette Park is an all-white Southwest Side neighborhood whose level of racial tolerance was indicated by its being the home of Chicago's neo-Nazi party until the organization's leader was convicted of child molestation.

"Pucinski country" refers to the all-white areas of the Northwest Side where Ald. Roman Pucinski, a former United States congressman, was a leading political figure.

The spectacle of organizations racing to cash in on the mayoral debates last week as the *Sun-Times* canceled and then reinstated its forum was as unseemly as the conduct of the candidates. The on-again, off-again debates supposedly are on again, but don't believe it until you see the post-debate media analyses. Everyone now has been dealt a piece of the action in four debates, including black radio station WBMX, the League of Women Voters and the City Club, cosponsoring with the Urban League.

However, there is yet another proposal in case everything falls through again. Mine.

The details are still being worked out, but who cares about details. I propose the following:

No. 1—The treasure hunt and road rally debate. Clues to the debate site will be hidden around the city, much like that contest to find a case of booze. The first candidate to reach the site will be declared the winner and guaranteed upfront 10,000 fraudulent votes. This way everyone will be spared a debate, which no one seems to want anyway. This also will make for the best media event.

No. 2—The sing-along debate. Again, no one will have to talk issues. All the candidates will have to do is come up with a new Chicago anthem, since the official contest to find one has gone through 1,500 entries since September with no luck and has been extended until June. Candidates must sing a cappella, and only music critics will be allowed to cover it.

No. 3—The clean-plate debate. Everyone over to my mom's for a soul food dinner of greens, cornbread and chitlins (translation: chitterlings). Again, no candidate will be required to talk, since it's impolite to do so with your mouth full. Besides, mom, having fattened up everyone and bored them with the family albums, will give a good piece of her mind on every issue from garbage collection, which she is for, to the CTA, which she is against.

To those who think this format gives Harold Washington an unfair advantage, I also propose two other neighborhood debates and ethnic food bakeoffs. One will be in Marquette Park, if Washington is allowed to speak and eat first and race out 10 minutes ahead of the picketers. The other will be in Pucinski country on the Northwest Side, granted the *czarnina* is served hot. In all fairness, the next debate will be in an Irish neighborhood—City Hall.

No. 4—The musical chair debate. Each candidate will sit and pose for the cameras at the desk in the mayor's office on the fifth floor. This will allow the public not only to decide which candidate is more mayoral-sounding but which is more mayoral-looking. All media will be allowed, since they normally prefer to hang out there rather than travel to a neighborhood.

Wait a minute. Scratch this debate. Mayor Byrne says she will not allow anyone into her office under any circumstances, even if she loses the primary. They'll just have to carry her out with the furniture, if they dare.

I have plans for 57 more debates, give or take a few, but will not disclose any details until I get agreement on the above, in blood, with a check for $1,000 from each campaign to cover my mom's grocery bill. Anyone interested in cosponsoring these debates can write me at the *Tribune* or meet me at my mom's for Sunday dinner. ■

February 18, 1983

Fear of post-election theft . . .

Forget for a moment the political ads and bravado and the voter registration numbers game. Since the Democratic mayoral primary is nothing but speculation and guesswork now anyway, assume it's the morning of Feb. 23 and Harold Washington has won.

Now what?

He becomes mayor, right?

"Yes, it's tradition," said one longtime political watcher, who is white. "The winner of the Democratic primary is mayor. Whatever else people in this town may be, they're Democrats."

A lot of people in the black community think the answer is not so clear.

"No way!" said a Washington backer. "Harold is going to win the primary. But they'll find some way to steal the mayor's office. Look, they wouldn't let Wilson [Frost] have it for five minutes. You think they're going to let Harold have it for four years? They'll think of something."

This sentiment is more widespread than anyone, especially blacks, would like to admit. If this is the case, though, why is there a Washington campaign at all? Why would supporters think Washington could win the primary yet maintain that he won't become mayor? How could blacks be so skeptical even as they stand at the threshold of what could be their greatest political coup?

The logic is simple. Blacks have learned from history to be eternal optimists and eternal pessimists simultaneously. It was a way to survive. The first quality has helped a race of people confront adversity. It is the fuel of the Washington crusade—and it is as much crusade as campaign. The second quality has helped a race of people endure adversity. It is the safety valve blacks can turn when all their hopes are dashed—and it has been much used. Optimism says integration can and should work; pessimism says whites just don't want you next door. Optimism says the progress of the sixties is astounding and will continue; pessimism says it was so astounding that whites want it cut off.

The psychology draws from the old proverb, "Look for the best; expect the worst." What it says about the despair black Chicagoans feel regarding race relations is revealing. Blacks, in their eternal optimism, had hoped they were finally fully accepted. Now, in their eternal pessimism, they can admit they are not. And the campaign has opened white eyes to this, too.

With even oldtime liberal friends deserting them for other candidates, many blacks have a circle-the-wagons mentality that makes speculation run wild that anything could happen, including the theft of a primary victory. The suspicions cannot be discounted. Blacks have always had good reason to look over their shoulders.

So if Washington wins, many are forced to ask, would Republican candidate Bernard Epton become the great white hope? Even a Southwest Side machine alderman thinks so: "[If Washington wins] Then Bernie Epton becomes mayor. White ethnics just aren't ready for a black mayor. It will be interesting, won't it—a black and a Jew?"

What would be more interesting is that Epton might be persuaded to step aside for a Democrat in Republican clothing, like Richard Ogilvie, whom the machine and white ethnics could better abide. Without doubting Epton's sticktoitiveness, by the logic of black pessimism this scheme is not illogical or implausible. And it is legally possible; if Epton withdrew, the Republican committeemen only need vote a replacement.

But suppose the political watcher is right, that Chicagoans are Democrats first. Will the machine embrace Washington, or co-opt him—from a goodly distance, of course? It did Mayor Byrne. Four years ago she was as much an outsider as Washington is and was given the same odds. But she's not black.

This is the likeliest scenario, knowing that the name of the game in this town is staying in power. Good Democrats all, they will fall into line with Washington whether they were in the Daley or Byrne camps, but the city council will suddenly acquire a mind of its own for the first time to make Washington's term difficult.

"If the party doesn't rally around Washington, then you may as well throw the party away," said a black machine alderman.

Milton Rakove, University of Illinois at Chicago political scientist and a historian who has written two books on the machine, agrees. "I know that race is a battle line in this town, but this is a very practical city. The machine learned to live with blacks and it will learn to live with Washington—and he'll learn to live with them."

Yet the logic of pessimism forces many blacks to ponder the most far-fetched alternatives, including that whites in this town would indeed throw the party and fairness away to keep a black man from gaining power.

There are mumblings that, just before the April election, Washington could be disqualified on a technicality, or tainted in a miraculously invented scandal—anything to force another election. Even though the filing date is past for a third party candidate, the logic of black pessimism says there's a machine hack lurking somewhere ready to pose as one, if the rules can be bent.

Just how severe is the distrust? Even the idea of metropolitan government is being whispered, that whites will seriously seek mergers with close-in suburbs to buoy white voter strength and make sure Washington will be the first and last black mayor. The presupposed schemes do not have to be practical. How many suburbs, for example, would want to annex themselves to the city? That these imagined fears are outstripping reason is proof of the depth of pessimism in the black community and of the gulf that remains between the races.

To think such thoughts is not to underestimate the political savvy of Washington. It is only to beware of the political treachery of others—and not to get caught optimistically off-guard.

Would those true white liberal friends, those who are expected to vote for Washington, be willing to storm City Hall if it appeared a fix were in to foil him? Blacks would like to think so, if for no other reason than those high-minded soundings about protecting the democratic right to vote. (That is optimism speaking.) Yet blacks can be certain of nothing in life except uncertainty and that, particularly in Chicago, real friends are outnumbered by real enemies. (That is the voice of pessimism.)

If anything, Washington's campaign has been a great liberating force. It has brought many blacks and whites to reality about the frailty of racial progress. And it has emancipated some whites from the bondage of fashionable pretense and allowed them to be public bigots again. ■

March 30, 1983

The wart on Chicago's face

In extended observation of the ways and
*   works of man*
From the Four-mile Radius roughly to the
*   plains of Hindustan*
I have drunk with mixed assemblies, seen the
*   racial ruction rise*
And the men of half creation damning half
*   creation's eyes*

I have watched them in their tantrums, all
*   that pentecostal crew*
French, Italian, Arab, Spaniard, Dutch and
*   Greek, and Russ and Jew,*
Celt and savage, buff and ochre, cream and
*   yellow, mauve and white,*
But it never really mattered till the English
*   grew polite;*
*   "Et Dona Ferentes"—Rudyard Kipling*

I hate to tell you so. But I told you so.

Right here in this space before the primary election was detailed the injury to race relations and the capacity for dirty tricks that black Chicagoans feared if Harold Washington won the primary.

Among them were: (a) Bernard Epton would become the great white hope; (b) the Democratic party would embrace Washington from a distance of 50 yards (it's more like 100); (c) Washington would be smeared; (d) Epton might be persuaded to withdraw and let someone else on the ballot (score 10 extra points for the plot, only five for thinking it might be Richard Ogilvie rather than Jane Byrne); and (e) whites would go so far as to promote a metropolitan government to ensure they would outweigh the growing black population—and votes—in perpetuity. Check all but the last, which took some stretching of the imagination and might take some more time. But the conduct of the principal players in this campaign begs the question of what is unthinkable.

The brief interlude provided by Mayor Jane Byrne's write-in campaign would have been unthinkable were it not for the source. There was more to her move than obstinacy, egomaniacal self-delusion and greed, although those were quite enough. Perhaps now she will salvage what grace and money she has left and go weigh veggies at the Randolph Street market, or teach urban studies at Barat College, her alma mater, or open a boutique with her daughter.

But in deadly seriousness, the happenings since the primary and Byrne's announcement and renouncement validate the worst suspicions of blacks. To dwell on whether Byrne would have hurt Epton, or whether she could have won missed the point. Her selfish intent was plain, and so was the public sentiment that fed it: to ensure, at any cost, that Chicago would not have a black mayor. Blacks told you so.

Like the English in Kipling's poem, blacks grew polite. They became, as the poem continues, "the men who fight with votes." Then did trouble arise. It matters not that after years of being labeled apathetic blacks turned out not just to register to vote but actually to vote when the numbers really counted. It matters not that Washington won the numbers. It matters not that there is a genuine chance for this town to erase its ugliest wart. It matters not how well-spoken or well-educated the candidate is, how moderate, how open.

All that matters in this town is what color one is. It is positively antebellum.

Who is doing the polarizing? Whites, who are all but packed up to leave town after years of running everything? Or blacks, who after years of voting for white politicians could get neither thanks nor dividends for their investment in others' stock—and the stock lies—except by putting forth their own candidate? Now, having won, and with only themselves to thank for it, blacks don't even merit a moment to savor their prize because of the plots to foil it.

What is it that makes Chicago so shamelessly bigoted? There are bigots everywhere, but what makes being a bigot more respectable here? With more than 200 black mayors nationwide, what makes the thought of the same here so distasteful? Could it be that whites think blacks now will give them equal opportunity at unfairness?

Mindless hatred requires an evaluation more penetrating than merely looking at quaint neighborhood ethnicity—though it cannot be coincidence that the runner-up for lousy race relations is Boston.

While greed is the deciding factor in the Three Stooges antics of the ward bosses, what is it that motivates people with no vested interest, no city job, to curl their lips and spit epithets at black children? Is it crime? Then blacks have the stronger case for anger, being victimized twice—first by the criminal and then by the criminal lack of police concern. Is it primordial xenophobia?

It is unforgivable simply to write all of this off as just the way things are. Lively politics make for great news stories, but there is no humor beneath it all. This town is beset by a wretched plague.

Chicagoans with any soul left to search should be asking themselves why. ■

April 9, 1983

Media ignorance is showing

With admitted immodesty, I feel uniquely qualified to take on one furor swirling about the mayoral campaign—racism and media coverage.

Some segments of the black community have labeled the media racists. (Interestingly, the white community is decrying the "negative" coverage of Bernard Epton. You can't please any of the people any of the time in this race.) Do I, as a black and a member of the press, deem the media racist? They are no more so and no less than any other institution that is held by and caters to the majority culture, much to the neglect—intentional or not—of minority cultures.

The other question from the black community is: Are certain columnists and commentators racists? This one is more disconcerting and not easily answered. I cannot read people's souls, not even after sitting next to them 5 days a week for 10 years.

I have suspected a few coworkers of storing white sheets in their lockers, suspected a few more on the morning after Harold Washington's Democratic mayoral primary victory. There were a lot of taciturn people in Tribune Tower that morning who suddenly could not look black colleagues in the eye. Their jokes about declining property values were unforgivably insensitive, betraying a grave, deeper fear.

But what makes a journalist's handiwork "racist?" Is it racist if a white reporter writes something unfavorable about Washington? If a black writes something favorable? Is it anti-Semitic if a black reporter writes something unfavorable about Republican candidate Bernard Epton?

The hostility of the black community has come to this kind of hairsplitting—complaining about the mention of Rev. Jesse Jackson's name three times in an editorial that both congratulated and cautioned Washington.

Editorials are by their nature opinionated. Reporting is different. For reporting to be fair requires facts that are indisputable, contacting the subject to allow a defense and care by reporters and editors of the use of judgmental adjectives.

Journalists are just like everyone else. They can despise and ridicule and admire. Their special mission, however, is to put this part of their humanity aside temporarily for the higher good of an informed citizenry. Everyone is the sum of personal experiences. Journalists are supposed to be able to sever the personal from the professional. Columnists and commentators simply have the luxury of not making so deep a cut.

Blacks in the media confront this duality naturally: Are we black journalists or journalists who just happen to be black? We begin a step ahead in understanding because the culture from which we come is invaded by the other; it is not a two-way exchange. White journalists have not had to struggle in this philosophical quagmire as often because of a natural kinship with their primary audience. With Washington's victory, the media encountered the black journalists' audience for the first time on the same level as the main audience.

The media's racial ignorance is not dismissible per se as bigoted and malicious; it is a byproduct of unfamiliarity. The media, if they are any good at all, will find ways to be perceptive interpreters of the black community, and they have shown evidence of this since the primary. That professional benefit of the doubt should be extended to black reporters covering a Seder in Rogers Park, or a Polish politician's rally, or a Puerto Rican Day Parade, or, more to the point, the black *Tribune* reporter who covered Epton at the South Side Irish Parade where T-shirts emblazoned "Vote Right-Vote White" and cries of "Go get 'im, Jew boy!" were the order of the day.

The black community—and I no more pretend to speak for all of it than William Safire speaks for all pedants—has a good case in knocking the media for its racial insensitivity. Yet to cry racist on the basis of nothing more than a difference of opinion is counterproductive.

In the wake of the primary, a black media coalition headed by Rev. Henry Hardy of the South Side Cosmopolitan Community Church has been formed to monitor coverage of the black community. It has the potential for doing good, but some of its missiles are misdirected at journalists who have a greater problem of ego than of race.

Part of its focus is on employment of minorities in the media, which I would not be foolish or presumptuous enough to get into here. There surely is a need for more blacks and Hispanics in every business and for more reliance on those minority-group members who are positioned in companies. But let's be candid, this is my livelihood and some business matters are best dealt with internally, even when there is a correlation to community dissatisfaction.

Better coverage of the black community is imperative. As a black, I feel as left out as does the black community at large, and I am just as appalled by some of the media's off-the-cuff remarks, poll interpretations and commentaries. I felt insulted by the sea of white panelists on TV primary night trying to explain a black phenomenon to viewers when they scarcely had a point of reference themselves. Yet as a journalist, I sought reasons to support my anger. Where there are inaccuracies, inequities and inconsistencies in coverage, those of us within the palace walls who have the ear of the king must—and do—protest.

Outside, the media coalition can best turn its attention to mobilizing the black community in letter-writing campaigns and in seeking rebuttals on broadcast stations, within reason. It is not enough just to get mad, but to become attuned to, to get involved with and to seek accountability from the media. This is the black community's obligation in promoting the two-way cultural exchange.

As for the media, they are not immovable. They are perhaps more easily altered than most institutions because of the flow, indeed the bombardment, of ideas. They will adapt. Individually, journalists with any integrity will find a way to keep their noses for news clean. ■

April 30, 1983

The storm has passed

This columnn was written shortly after Harold Washington became the first black mayor of Chicago. The "fistfight" that McClain mentions refers to a white voter who was charged with attacking Richard M. Daley, an unsuccessful mayoral can-

didate and son of the late Mayor Richard J. Daley. The attacker reportedly was one of many whites who were angry that Daley had siphoned off white votes that would have enabled incumbent Mayor Jane Byrne to stop Washington's victory.

This town was not a jolly place to live a few weeks ago. Remember?

All appears to be well now, after the charged words, the debate about why it was or wasn't acceptable to say or do or vote this way or that. Everyone's going on about life peaceably. Or are they? The fistfight between State's Atty. Richard M. Daley and an angry voter says otherwise.

Harold Washington's victory in and of itself doesn't buff the tarnish from Chicago, no matter how many votes he got on the Southwest Side. It is hypocrisy to talk about the divisions and say in the same breath that the city did not deserve the label of racist, or whatever watered down word approximates it without offending.

Just when the racial barriers had become worn, shown a crack or two, they were quickly tuckpointed, and the age-old misunderstandings that had never been dealt with, inwardly or outwardly, were sealed even tighter. Interracial friendships have been tested; some have fallen victim. Many people have taken refuge in cleaving to "my kind," and it will be a long time before they venture forth trustingly again. In desperation, the people and the candidates exhibited not their best, but their worst. People really showed their true colors in more ways than one.

Everyone's emotions have been wrung. Everyone has had enough of everything and yet nothing has been done to change people's hearts. There was a lot of talk, but no dialogue, no exchange. Everyone talked at each other from intransigent, distant positions, never hearing what the other had to say.

Whites don't understand black aspirations any better, and blacks don't understand white fears. And all the unity luncheons in the world won't change that, not until people pray and live and marry and go to school together. Working together eight hours a day isn't enough. But we have to try. We are supposed to be trying in the spirit of healing, though my lifetime will end before it's through.

Everyone's talking about unity. It's going to take nothing short of a miracle to achieve, and a mayor can't do it alone. Where is the reinforcement to come from? The proud warriors of the Democratic party? The businesspeople who venture out now that the storm has passed?

There is a task for everyone if the healing is to be in earnest. Before Washington's term is over blacks are going to have to learn to disagree with each other publicly, to vote against each other if need be. Sometimes the best support will be contrariness. And whites are going to have to make leeway for Washington to counterbalance their biases. This is not a charge of racism, it is a statement of the facts of life; people of different races do indeed approach each other differently, with different expectations, different outlooks.

This was apparent in the campaign. Blacks looked at this election as the natural continuum of the civil rights movement; whites saw it as just politics.

Now it really is politics.

It must not be easy today to be Harold Washington. On the one hand, the newfound messiah of many blacks; on the other the grim reaper come to pillage a vibrant city, and don't think the latter view does not persist. If he fails, he not only takes the city along, but the hopes of 26 million black Americans, not just the 1.4 million here.

Washington has a struggle ahead and very little help. After the prayers and thank yous, he'd better head for City Hall to try to persuade city workers that he will be fair. A great many won't believe him, will never like him, but at the very least they should work for him diligently and earnestly. He is the head of this city now and the hacks who didn't want to defer to him are going to have to swallow hard and try it. And so must he indulge them. A victor can afford to be forgiving, should be magnanimous. Smoothing a few ruffled feathers does not detract from his victory.

Then Washington had better hit the streets again with 10 times the vigor he showed in the campaign, going into every neighborhood, whether he anticipates a throng shouting grateful adulation or the echo of an empty hall. The police stations will have to be a special stop. He may even have to go behind closed doors with police, the partisans who compromised themselves most in this election, and have a shouting match before there is calm.

And after all of the symbolic gestures, he had better run this city the way he said he would, fairly, honestly, openly. He did not promise a black in every power-wielding slot, contrary to the most overblown hopes, the most irrational fears. And few blacks ask or expect that of him.

Washington's most important promise was to make the city solvent. That has nothing to do with color and everything to do with good administration and political pull, here, in Springfield and in Washington. He needs a thorough, respected No. 2, a known quantity who knows every piece of legislation, every alderman and committeeman, every bond issue and contractor, every community organization's complaint and every weak link. His top-level management team had better be better than his disheveled campaign organization. There will be friends and contributors to repay, as in any campaign, but appointments that turn to embarrassments may be irreparably damaging. No one will give him the benefit of the doubt of being "changeable" like Jane Byrne.

The crusade is over. This is the real world. Words now must turn to deeds.

It's your city, Harold Washington, splintered and troubled though it may be. ∎

May 28, 1983

Pinpointing political motives

City council drew new battle lines after Washington's election. Washington and his allied 21 aldermen faced off Ald. Edward "Fast Eddie" Vrdolyak's 29, which included Roman Pucinski and Edward Burke, the "aldermanic errand boys" to whom McClain refers at the beginning of this column.

City council meetings, which had been rubber stamp affairs under earlier administrations, now became argumentative and even vituperative. As a result, when the Cook County regular Democratic organization, chaired by Vrdolyak, held a party fundraiser, most prominent blacks boycotted the affair and held the alternative fete mentioned here.

It's politics.
It's race.
It's politics.
It's race.
Truth is, the fractiousness in City Hall is both. It is naive to think it is all one or all the other.

How much of the fight is political and how much is racial is where the true difference in opinion arises. The percentages are in the eye of the beholder. My own percentages are generally 50-50, but this varies with every council meeting, court decision or pronouncement from aldermanic errand boys Edward Burke and Roman Pucinski.

Each faction in the struggle surely realizes this. And each has been showing the political card but banking on the emotional racial card to win.

Mayor Harold Washington, of course, doesn't have to show his hand; his constituency plays it for him. At Wednesday's black Democrats' boycott dinner on the South Side, he said: "They're trying to make this a racial conflict . . . a racial division. It's not that at all. It's good versus evil." He can afford to say that it's politics, almost in code, knowing the bulk of his supporters will maintain the "it's race" side nonetheless.

The opposition 29 try to keep the race card hidden, but their bluff is transparent. Their public stance is "politics as usual." The dishonesty of it is that their private stance plays to their constituencies as much as Washington's just being mayor plays to blacks.

It was that seer Edward Vrdolyak himself who sorted out the psychology of this town as long ago as the February primary. He reminded his workers then, "This [election] is a racial thing." Now Vrdolyak, 10th Ward alderman, sees only politics. He speaks in code, too. It gives his constituency a chance to nod slyly in agreement with this publicly acceptable stance, knowing all the while the unspeakable factor of race is lurking somewhere.

With all of this doublespeak, no wonder so many people want to oversimplify the squabble as just race or just politics.

Those on the "it's politics" side are certain that the split among the aldermen is a good, old-fashioned fistfight, with bloody noses but no lasting damage, a prediction that could prove doubly naive. Don't worry until city business comes to a halt, they say assuredly. Meanwhile, let's just watch. This side also maintains that the power struggle would have occurred had all of the parties involved been white, had Washington been white and Vrdolyak black, or had everyone been purple.

And last, in this view Mayor Washington just did not get his act together and was defeated by his own delay, his own ego. He was bamboozled by those around him, whose sudden promotion from outsiders to insiders pumped up their pride but didn't necessarily make them skilled political wheeler dealers.

The "it's race" argument reverses some of the other side's examples. First, if you're black, there is no such thing as a good, clean fight, because the rules will be dirtied up every time. Blacks will never be convinced that a white version of Harold Washington, had he come charging in in the same way with the same battle cry of "End patronage," would have been treated to such public insult.

Second, perhaps Washington was given to a bit of self-delusion. Anyone else who had come so far so fast, swept by a vast and unparalleled social movement, probably would have been seduced, too. A victor ought to be able to enjoy his victory. The black community never said Washington was superhuman. Far from it, each of his personal and professional shortcomings was listed so often during the campaign they could not be forgotten.

Perhaps he did weaken his strategy by not being more conciliatory. Here is a man who, after breaking with the machine, made it by jousting, by being contrary. And he does not often lose. He would not have become mayor without that stubbornness, without taking risks. These are not excuses for Washington. One can acknowledge these faults without excusing them as long as one notes the opposition's faults as well. He should appear more deft. But the other side looks all too deft—in wielding a stiletto.

Why do some people want to deny there is any racial angle? The question is best answered with questions: In a city where even park benches are subject to discrimination, how can race be disregarded? Why is it so imponderable that those white voters who opposed Washington are reveling in this act of revenge? Why wouldn't they cheer on the Vrdolyak side to whip Washington into shape, to put him "in his place"?

Why can't the angriest of blacks see the political angle? Because for most of history, politics and racism have been synonymous to black people. Even with new political confidence, it is not possible to sever that tie overnight.

The next four years are going to be rollicking—and wracking. As long as there is a black mayor, just about everything is going to be simultaneously racial and political. Among the things that will separate us will be this fundamental disagreement about motive. ■

June 25, 1983

City's puzzling
prudent pol

Thomas Keane is a former alderman who was sent to prison when Richard Daley was mayor. Keane, who even his detractors admit is highly intelligent, was Daley's parliamentarian. He succeeded in having his wife elected to his post while he was imprisoned, and ran the ward from jail. The Shakman decree was an antipatronage court decision that sharply reduced the amount of city workers who could be hired or fired for political reasons. It went into effect shortly after Mayor Washington took office. Its restrictions were so severe it compelled Washington to appeal to the court for more political jobs, an embarrassing position for him as an antipatronage mayor.

Reports that the mayor's transition team chief, Edwin C. "Bill" Berry, threatened to resign because he could not get in to see the mayor made a splash and quickly evaporated. Berry himself begged off from reporters' questions, but enough sources have confirmed the story.

It is an unfortunate occurrence, but it provides a chance to examine the administration more closely. The study is revealing.

First, it is unfortunate because Berry, former head of the Chicago Urban League, is a first-rate organizer. Everybody knows Bill Berry, and it was his familiarity with people from struggling social agencies to academia to corporate board rooms that helped to shape a distinguished interracial transition team. His disenchantment so early in the administration's short but rocky life is badly timed, yet another stumble from which to recover.

Second is that the incident collided with the psychology of unity that has marked black Chicago for months. The scurrying to mend any crack in the works is an astounding sight. There is an incredible oversensitivity to any criticism of Harold Washington, particularly with the city council battle in midair. But the one should not be dependent on the other. To question Washington on one matter is not to desert him on any other. Yet even people close to him will not speak on the record about the directions he is going, or more correctly, their thoughts about where he is not going.

And third, the Berry incident leaves you wondering whose counsel Washington seeks if not the man he entrusted to construct the framework for his new government.

Who does Washington listen to? Many people say, so long as they are not quoted, that he listens to "Harold" and to no one else. He himself said it in an interview with the *Tribune* after the February primary. Asked who helps him make policy, the answer was, "Me." It apparently was not a joke.

"Harold does things in his own way and in his own time," says an ally.

The staunchest of Washington's defenders are baffled by his inaccessibility. They point to his inaction on appointments to commissions, the police department and city departments. (Why is he leaving the enemies entrenched?) Yet everyone is quick to add that those he has named thus far are sterling. (In fairness, the other side of this is that these very people would give him the business about "the Jane Byrne revolving door policy" if he named someone today and got rid of him or her tomorrow.)

Some supporters fret that the campaign's weaknesses and weaker personalities have been carried over into government. These people argue that because they care as much as they do about Washington, it pains them to see his image sullied, but they do not deny their impatience with him.

Washington's famous no-shows and reluctance to politick by phone are far overplayed, but they make for a tangible measuring stick, especially when some of those left indefinitely on hold are among the powerful whose support should not be taken for granted. Why would he shun the national forum of the U.S. Conference of Mayors in Denver, a quick flight in and out, to stay home and lobby for the state income tax? How many potential allies have been lost, or remained neutral, because the phone did not ring? Power brokers are power brokers because they know how to deal with people.

Even among the "21," there is uneasiness, which, black Chicago should be reassured, is not the same as dissent or betrayal.

"Harold has a legislative mind," says one. The implication is that, with Thomas Keane doing the choreographing for the "29," the mayor simply cannot afford to miss a step.

This all points to the fact that Harold Washington, the man, is still somewhat of a mystery to black as well as white Chicago. What kind of person is Washington?

"He's irrepressible, intense, single-minded and has a strong sense of purpose," says Grayson Mitchell, his press secretaary.

"He takes a long-range, strategic view of political problems," says Ald. Lawrence Bloom (5th), a Washington backer. "This is something different for people used to dealing with Chicago mayors. He's understandably and justifiably slow to make commitments until he knows the actors better. He's not interested in the immediate resolution just to avoid bad press."

"In a word, deliberate," says Dr. Quentin Young, who is helping to revive the city's health policies.

But that deliberateness is a blessing and a curse, for it is being perceived as indecisiveness and, worse, insularity. Still, Washington's caution might succeed.

"I was on the other side of the campaign," says David Schulz, who was retained in the Washington administration as acting budget director. "I saw her [Jane Byrne] characterized as precipitous, changeable. It's really interesting. I don't think the criticism of him is valid. He had some major hurdles in Shakman and the city council, but I think we're going to see an acceleration now."

"He doesn't rush to make decisions," continues Mitchell's defense. "Sometimes prudence dictates patience because some problems solve themselves. Harold can't turn around on a dime. He puts sound judgment over speed, and he advises us to do that, too. He's very grown up, and he is not easily rattled."

Deliberateness works in a deliberative body; it doesn't always work when you run a business of 42,000 employees serving 4 million consumers. And it may not seem a realistic strategy to use against someone whose nickname, for good reason, begins with "Fast."

Chicagoans may have to learn to be as patient as their mayor. ■

July 16, 1983

This is the
black monolith?

It's the biggest political free-for-all in a long time. It's democracy in action. It's the black monolith cracked. It's the lst Congressional District primary race to fill the seat Harold Washington vacated when he became the city's top official.

There are 18 (count 'em 18) candidates: 14 Democrats and 4 Republicans. And yet with all of those people clamoring for forums or pasting over each other's posters on the limited circumference of South Side street posts, it's been fairly ordered chaos. The issues have ranged from getting much-needed jobs and social programs for the district to cutting the defense budget to blowing up the Robert Taylor Homes, with little variance in candidates' opinions. The biggest issue is Mayor Washington's endorsement of labor leader Charles Hayes.

Washington's endorsement has met all manner of criticism, including that he twisted the arms of committeemen to line up behind him, that he doesn't want a representative as independent-minded as he himself was and may even be plotting to retake the seat after four years of headaches running the city. Some people thought he should not have made an endorsement, but let the people decide. Some thought he should have made one sooner, sending a signal to contenders to stay out and saving the people from having to choose among so many candidates.

Fact is, he has every right to endorse, and the people have every right to vote their minds.

The two top contenders early on supposedly were Hayes, the meat-cutters' union leader who won the endorsement of his old friend Washington, and Lu Palmer, the journalist and community activist who did not win the endorsement of his old friend Washington. Palmer's strength is in his grass-roots contacts. Some call him a rabble rouser, he says he's "doing for his people." He has been pressing for black political empowerment for years, and the success of Washington is seen as a byproduct of that effort.

Just when everyone was settled in for a race between these two, some other heavyweights decided to lengthen the ballot. Ald. Marian Humes (8th), State Sen. Charles Chew, State Rep. Larry Bullock, Washington campaign manager Al Raby, attorney Lemuel Bentley and Ralph Metcalfe Jr., son of the late 1st District congressman, all joined the race.

And then there are the "unknowns." Among them are Republican Betty Meyer, a white, Hyde Park homemaker who frankly admits she doesn't have a chance but is enough of a patriot to want to bolster the two-party system; Democrat Hiram Crawford, an abortion foe whose platform is prayer and fasting and II Chronicles 7:14; Democrat James Sterdivant, who makes bicycles in his home workshop and who intends to take over the country with his fraternity, Delta Nu Alpha; Republican Diance Preacely, a community newspaper journalist and former pin-up girl; and perennial U.S. Labor party candidate Sheila Jones, fresh from the mayoral campaign where she honed her skills disrupting debates. (Socialist Workers party candidate Ed Warren, who also ran for mayor, is actually the 19th candidate. He did not file for the July 26 primary but rather as an independent in the Aug. 23 special general election.)

Whoever wins, the victory will be anticlimactic to the exercise of individual thinking that is making some in the black community dyspeptic. This race has punctured black unity, but not all for the bad, and certainly not irreparably.

If there was overcriticism of blacks during the mayoral campaign for sticking together, there will be none of that in this instance. This race shows that blacks can and will disagree, that they have reached a level of political sophistication that defies analysts and pollsters.

Yet many blacks are supporting Hayes because Washington is and take the attitude that "we have to stick with Harold." This is a congressional campaign, not the City Hall brawl, as even the mayor should know. At a rally for Hayes last weekend Washington accused some members of his city council opponents, the "Vrdolyak 29," of contributing to Hayes' opponents' campaigns to undercut not Hayes but him. He did not name names. Even if contributions are being made, there should be no quarrel with anyone's right to give them; the black community can deduce for itself the motivations.

State Rep. Bullock, endorsed by the Fraternal Order of Police, was quick to chide Washington, saying the remark was "beneath the mayor." Ald. Humes, on Washington's side in the city council, called the charges a "smoke screen" to cover up for Hayes' lack of qualification. And State Sen. Chew said the mayor fabricated the charges. Chew further fumed that the mayor privately promised his endorsement to three candidates but "sold" it to Hayes because of a $300,000 campaign contribution from Hayes' union.

Too many observers are looking at this race as a measure of the mayor's "control." What they will find, as the black community will, is that there is nothing wrong if the lid is not clamped on all the time.

Unity really is more than skin deep. ■

July 23, 1983

The second annual boycott is on

ChicagoFest is surely cursed. The mayor dropped it from the city's agenda, for this year at least, because of costs. There were reports that the city lost $1 million on it last year, but the bookkeeping has never been verified.

A deal by a group of private investors who wanted to continue it at Navy Pier fell through because of the mayor's objections to the promoter, Festivals Inc.

Then when it was announced that the event would be sponsored by the Park District in mid-August in Soldier Field with Festivals as the promoter, civic groups objected to the traffic congestion the fest would create, and later the schedule was found to conflict with the $35 million National Hardware Show, second largest trade show in town. That problem was resolved by scheduling the fest closed for three days during the hardware show, and it is now scheduled for Aug. 10-14 and Aug. 18-22.

And the curse goes on. The Better Government Association has charged in a suit that Festivals was merely a fund-raising auxiliary for former Mayor Jane Byrne and that she transferred money to Festivals without council approval from a secret slush fund.

With all of this against it, it was not surprising when the second annual black boycott of ChicagoFest was announced this week.

The catalyst for last year's boycott was Byrne's capricious appointments to the Chicago Housing Authority. Black attendance at the event, usually about 14 to 17 percent, dropped to less than 1 percent, and many black entertainers canceled.

The reasoning behind this year's boycott is similar—that many white politicians continue to disregard the black community.

Yet this year there is a complicating factor in such a direct action by the black community: It has elected a black mayor, and it did so, coincidentally, from a spark lit by last year's boycott.

The election of a black mayor did not automatically bring a greater regard for black Chicagoans; Byrne is gone, but little else has changed. Indeed the insults have grown worse and the politics more sinister by the "Cabal-o-crats," as Slim Coleman, an Uptown community activist, labels the mayor's opponents. A boycott will put the mayor in an awkward position, but the black community is so worked up that it had no other choice.

The "Citywide Coalition to Boycott ChicagoFest" was announced by Robert Starks of the Task Force for Black Political Empowerment. It includes 20 other groups, including the Council of Black Churches (representing 300 congregations), Chicago Black United Communities, the South Austin Community Coalition, United Black Voters of Illinois and the Greater Roseland Community Organization.

It should be plain to everyone, black or white, that ChicagoFest is now just another battlefield in the city council war. While attention has been focused on City Hall and three courts, the brushfire has spread in every direction, including Springfield.

ChicagoFest is no longer ChicagoFest. It has become "EddieFest." One can pick either Eddie—Ald. Edward Vrdolyak (10th) or parks Supt. Edmund L. Kelly. The third Eddie, Ald. Edward Burke (14th), is only marginally involved, but he is never far from the spotlight and surely will find a way to increase his role.

Kelly accepted the Festivals Inc. proposal not so much to save the fest or to make a quick million dollars for the park district as to needle Mayor Washington. Kelly's rescue effort is another round in the mayoral campaign tiff that began when he and his 47th Ward workers made their once-in-a-lifetime defection from the Democratic party to work for Republican Bernard Epton. This point and the recent federal lawsuit on discrimination in park services and hiring could not be overlooked by the black community.

"The park district is the most glaring symbol of racism," said Starks, a professor at Northeastern Illinois University. "It would be self-degradation to help maintain that machinery. There is no guarantee that the money the park district collects will be redistributed to black and Hispanic areas on an equal basis." He said the coalition is seeking Hispanic support.

"This boycott won't injure the mayor or the city. It will enhance it because it will help to shift the economy away from downtown back to the neighborhood festivals where local vendors get some help. This boycott makes political and economic sense. Why should we spend money in a time of hardship? We have no money in the black community and no jobs. We'll do more good by attending those free neighborhood festivals. Why should we fatten the coffers of our enemies?"

The mayor cannot and should not support the boycott because he is the mayor of all the city. He cannot and should not aid and abet divisiveness, though Vrdolyak feels no qualms about spreading hatred by saying the mayor has a scheme to blacken the city.

Whether the mayor can turn down the volume is anybody's guess. The support he gets won't always be the support he needs. However, the mayor has done the most diplomatic thing he can do. He has wished Ed Kelly well. ∎

August 6, 1983

Spoils of war, Chicago style

The city council dispute seems to spoil everything it touches, and it seems to touch everything these days.

Up is down and down is up in this town since Mayor Harold Washington's election. The old guard now are the "reformers," putting the screws to the reform mayor. The very people to whom reform was a curse now are championing causes they once viewed as poison. Otherwise, would they have outlined rules on distributing Community Development Block Grant funds, or on accepting campaign contributions from those with city contracts?

Aldermen who have not cared about budgets except to pass what was waved before them by past mayors suddenly are expert financiers, carrying on about allowing enough time to study the budget, about the public's right to know—a public they have disregarded until now.

If Mayor Washington were to announce that the sky is blue, the "29" no doubt would pass a bill proclaiming it orange. He would, of course, veto it. His loyalists would, of course, foil an override. The whole matter would end up in court.

The feud complicated deliberations in Springfield. In the school property tax fight, the Chicago delegation split along racial lines and it was the Downstaters who helped put over a tax that affected only Chicagoans. Even in working toward the common goal of killing the RTA* subsidy, the sides had divergent interests—the mayor's legislators trying to preserve his power, the legislators tied to Ald. Edward Vrdolyak (10th) protecting their patronage and RTA Chairman Lewis Hill.

Here at home, the very people who had fought the Shakman decree now are its defenders. No sooner did the mayor say he would not honor $8 million in back pay to city tradesmen than Ald. Edward Burke (14th) jumped to their defense. When the mayor requested TV time, the opposition couldn't bear not being stars, too. The Vrdolyak faction has not even been able to resist making issues of garbage pickups and the mayor's inauguration bill. And ChicagoFest is a can of worms best left untouched.

---

*Regional Transit Authority

The motto seems to be, if it will embarrass or compromise or merely taunt the mayor, do it. For his part, the mayor has not helped by being too quick-tongued, resorting to insults unbecoming his office.

Who is to blame? Everyone and no one. No side has a monopoly on truth or the public interest. These are warring politicians, after all. Besides a few zoning or contract decisions left unsettled, it has not hurt day-to-day city business.

But can the city stand four solid years of hand-to-hand combat? Amazingly, the combatants find common ground on this question. They say the feud isn't all that bad, despite the verbal sniping, and that no permanent damage will be done. To hear them, it's all just "politicians will be politicians." And everyone thinks the end result will be a real governmental body.

To Ald. Roman Pucinski (41st), chief negotiator for the "29," the real tiff has concluded—and his side won: "I've seen no evidence that city functions have been hurt. Only some pride and some ego. The committees are conducting business in an orderly manner. The question is does the mayor really want an accommodation? The administration is becoming more and more identified with confrontation and turmoil."

Freshman "29" member Ald. Patrick O'Connor (40th) said: "I think the council would be more than happy to put most of this behind them right now, but the politics of the situation won't allow them to do it. There might be some animosity, but I think the public gets an overly dim view. Most of the aldermen are quite friendly at the ward level. [Former Mayor Jane] Byrne had her fights when she came in. It's just a stage where we have to get comfortable and work with one another and then it will be over."

As for the mayor's side, press secretary Grayson Mitchell says damage will be "minimal to slight." Already, he says, to call it the 29-21 rift is too simple. "The more we move along, we will have a different constituency for each piece of legislation. The lines have gotten blurred. Even during the hectic days of May, what was portrayed about the feud was not that serious.

"In the long term, it's not helping the racial problem, but as I watch the mayor move among the people I don't see animosity comparable to some of the things said in the council."

But one "21" member is concerned nonetheless about the racial matter: "We could have begun to make some substantial progress in race relations. And that keeps us from dealing with all the other problems—education, housing, poverty. It isn't like he could turn it around. It's a long, long goal. But we haven't taken the first steps forward and probably have taken a few backward."

He also worries that the tiff could damage the city's image with rating agencies or businesspeople looking to locate here, and lastly, that the mayor is appearing not to get anything done. "What bothers me is the opportunity costs, the failure to move ahead in so many other areas because the mayor is kept busy reacting and can't do what a mayor should do."

For all of the talk about underlying calm in the council circle, the outward appearance of venom and chaos is what is being accepted. Even much of the citizenry, the audience that the aldermen play so well to, must share the disgrace. The uproar shows no signs of abating and just might grow. It has been a sorry, base and ungentlemanly spectacle. ■

October 2, 1983

A corner-tavern
fight in the council

One of the rawest, rowdiest city council meetings in the history of Chicago took place Wednesday, Sept. 29, 1983. In it Ald. Edward Vrdolyak baited Mayor Washington by looking up at the mayor, his hands clasped as though in prayer, and saying, "Please, Mr. President, point of order please."

"You are improving by putting 'please' in front of what you say," the Tribune *reported Washington as replying, "but you haven't gotten there yet."*

"To someone of your gender I should say 'pretty please,'" Vrdolyak said, his roice rising to a falsetto.

Washington angrily retorted: "You're about to get a mouthful of something you don't want."

Even for the Chicago City Council, this was not business as usual.

That does it.

Anyone who gives me that high-brow analytical garbage today about how the city council brawling will lead to a polished, astute, deliberate, representative legislative body will be met by icy silence.

Last week's exchange in the council chambers between Ald. Edward Vrdolyak (10th) and Mayor Harold Washington was as low-brow, as corner-tavern as this fight has gotten. Anyone from any ward should be offended.

For all of his millions, Vrdolyak still must have enough good old-fashioned South Side dirt beneath his fingernails to recall how such a remark involving sexual innuendo used to be settled—with fists in the alley around the corner.

Ald. Edward Burke (14th) remembered, and he surely has no dirt under his fingernails. He yelled to the mayor, "Come on down here on the floor."

The mayor shot back, "Come on up," before calling a recess for five minutes.

Although Vrdolyak, who instigated the incident, and the mayor, who fed it with his response, tried to laugh it off later, they meant every word. There was nothing funny about it. Nothing.

Aldermen sitting guard in front of their precious committee office and changing the locks on the door is funny. So is calling a mayoral aide to testify about the mayor's filming a movie with high school students in council chambers. But last Wednesday's exchange did not tickle my funny bone, as it did for some tittering aldermen.

If some people would stop laughing long enough, they could see the implications of this: The city is in for a bloody four-year war. These people are not playing. Their antics will provide great news copy, but in the meantime every Chicagoan is going to be living on edge.

It has been said over and over that this is the way governments operate everywhere, so why the big deal about the council fuss? Chicagoans have been drugged by tight-fisted control for too long, this argument goes; members of Parliament rail at each other all the time (and so do aldermen).

This theory would be acceptable except for one prime fact: This is happening to Chicago's first black mayor. Race is going to be read into it, and you don't have to be black to think so—to know so. Stooping this low is unforgivable.

There is a deeper and dangerous psychological factor at play in the council wars, especially when the fighting gets this dirty. Any reform mayor would have had a battle on his hands, but Mayor Washington's foes are emboldened in their sniping because of his color. That is the way it is in this world. Whether whites can see it or not, or admit to it or not, they are ingrained by this society with a superior attitude toward blacks that is as natural and reflexive and uncontrollable as sneezing. That means that a black mayor is fair game for the most vile public insult, as Vrdolyak showed.

The very office of the mayor should demand some respect. His foes respect the office all right; they respect it so much they don't want to give it up. And to have to give it up to a black man—one with brains and political panache, at that—makes them break into a sweat. That is what binds many in the "29."

The council is still dotted with crooks and hacks—on both sides—who suddenly became "legislators" after Washington's election. They probably called Mayor Jane Byrne a shrew, or worse, in her early, feisty days, or called Michael Bilandic a wimp. But it was done behind their backs. (Sexism against Byrne is yet a valid topic.)

Vrdolyak's remark is sickening for another reason. It is the kind of reprehensible locker room blather that is disgusting in that setting and entirely out of order at a public meeting.

The council battle, even in its tenser moments, has been informational—voters who only suspected their elected officials of being dolts have been given proof in some cases.

Still, citizens with any decency and courage, whether "29ers" or "21ers," should press for an end at least to the cheap shots while we're on the road to this brave new world of legislative sophistication. ■

October 30, 1983

Washington's electrifying elocution

Mayor Harold Washington either needs an interpreter or he needs to have his mouth washed with soap.

Yet for all the flaps about his public statements, you cannot deny that there is a cadence, a flair in his elocution that has been missing in the last two mayors. Whether you like or detest what he's saying, not since Richard J. Daley has there been a more "quotable" mayor. Daley was quotable by mishap, Washington is by design. He revels in using language to jest, to fence, to demolish. When Washington called state legislators "antediluvian" during last session's tax fight, he sent an awful lot of people to their dictionaries. And "scurrilous" and "spurious" are part of his theme song.

He would be great in a pulpit or at a college lectern. The problem is he isn't a preacher or lecturer, he is a mayor, and what he says is often inappropriate for his position. The famed "doo-doo" remark, in describing a proposal by the council opposition, is one example.

Another example of how his language gets him into trouble is the varying interpretations of his off-the-cuff remarks about whites in the media not understanding him. Every politician is required to have a spat with journalists. The mayor was on target about the cultural unfamiliarity; but that would apply to blacks about Ukrainians, too.

Everyone has private mannerisms, phrases and habits they display at the family dinner table but would not display at a dinner party. Public figures especially have to put their personal style aside. To put it bluntly, the mayor should know better.

And the element of race that he must be continually aware of should make him think twice. He should keep this in mind in particular before black audiences, even knowing there are certain things they want to hear from "their" first mayor, because of the larger audience that eventually will hear or read his words. It's a quandary that his tongue gets him in trouble as often as it does because any black person who has succeeded at anything in this world should be well schooled about putting on a social face.

Beyond this, however, there really is a cultural failure to communicate, a literal difference in use of language between blacks and whites that is based on more than dialect or slang. It has been analyzed in a book, *Black and White Styles in Conflict,* by Thomas Kochman, a University of Illinois at Chicago professor of communication and theater. Reading it just might help blacks and whites in the media in understanding the mayor.

Through years of observation of interaction of black and white students in the classroom Kochman shows how language compounds racial divisions. Among his data are: that interruption of another speaker is unacceptable in debate among whites, yet perfectly all right among blacks; that if the volume of debate rises, whites perceive a threat, while blacks just see an exciting exchange; that in white culture to go so far as to voice a threat means that the next step is carrying it out, while just voicing it is a sufficient release for blacks; that whites do not mind direct personal questions on first meeting, but blacks do; and that a white wrongly accused will rise to defend himself, while the black view is that to protest too much affirms the guilt.

Kochman's ideas may seem like so much psycho-sociological pap; whites could see it as an excuse for black behavior, blacks could see it as perpetuating the stereotype about being loud. But he offers enough of his own and other researchers' evidence to make a convincing case. One of Kochman's theories is especially applicable to the varying interpretations of the mayor's "white media" remark. Kochman writes: "Accusations or allegations like 'Men are sexists' or 'White people are racists' are understood by white people to be categorical; all individuals who fit the generic criteria . . . feel themselves accused, whether they are guilty or not. Consequently if those making the statement do not intend it to be all inclusive, they are expected to qualify the statement at the outset. . . .

"Among blacks, accusations or allegations . . . are general rather than categorical; they are not intended to be all inclusive. Furthermore, the determination of who is to be included is not the responsibility of the person making the statement but of those whom the statement might conceivably describe. . . .

"Because *all* whites who fit the generic criteria feel themselves accused—not just those who are guilty—those who regard themselves as innocent will demand redress from the accuser. . . .

"Within the black cultural perspective, however, there can be no inadvertent hits; for people to admit that they feel accused is, by that fact alone, to acknowledge their guilt."

Kochman's theory was proved at a City Hall press conference in which reporters pressed the mayor for the most picayune specifics as to which whites in the media he was accusing. They all felt accused.

But enough talk about talk.

With all due respect, Mr. Mayor, please "hush yo' mouf." ∎

November 16, 1983

Robinson's brief
CHA honeymoon

The rice hasn't landed at his feet yet, but the honeymoon is over already for Renault Robinson, chairman of the Chicago Housing Authority.

The malfunctioning elevators remain his most serious calamity, but the list of other failures is long. Robinson has dueled with CHA commissioners over a $14,000 car, and one commissioner has resigned. He has riled community groups and aldermen about keeping secret the sites for scattered housing. Tenants are threatening a rent strike. And the federal Department of Housing and Urban Development has sent in an overseer for the first time.

It has been an eventful few months for Robinson. But as much as he has botched it so far, it would be premature to toss him out. When the time comes, Robinson, the mayor and everyone else will know it.

This is not to make excuses for him. If one were trying to make a case against him, steering the purchase of his automobile through the board would be enough.

His irresponsibility with regard to tenants is damning indeed.

When he was named, Robinson was seen by tenants as their salvation. They were positively delirious, hugging and kissing him. He was a man of the people after all, so everything would fall into place. But it did not.

First, the man of the people wanted a proper auto. "Take the bus like we do, brother," was the advice of some angry tenants.

Now, one should not begrudge Robinson wanting a car, even though he begrudged his predecessor having one. The offense came in the way in which he went about getting it, which was buying it first and asking for the allowance later. And it was none too prudent to chastise in public the two commissioners who voted against it the first time, resulting in a tie vote that temporarily shelved the idea, and then wishing them a swift exit from the authority. One, Patrick Nash, did just that. It was bad form on Robinson's part.

But the elevators are the critical issue. A CHA spokesman said the firm now trying to break the elevator curse will have at least one car in each high-rise building in good working order within 30 days. Promises, promises.

The lesson in all this is that salvation doesn't come in any particular color.

Yes, Robinson does indeed have a special understanding of being black and poor, but that does not necessarily lead to the reasoning that these traits make him a more responsive chairman. What is evident in the CHA battles is that both sides are learning to operate in the real world.

The growing demand for black officials to deal with the complaints of black citizens is not always the best or fastest way to bring about change, as angry CHA tenants are discovering, in spite of the historic dearth of such officials. Being black and making mistakes are not mutually exclusive.

At one board meeting commissioner Leon Finney reportedly chided residents, saying, "I didn't see them doing this to former chairman Charles Swibel or Andrew Mooney."

Could it be there is a double standard, a different set of rules by blacks where black officials are concerned? It is not fair of tenants to expect the world of Robinson because he is black, or to expect that he would not want a car like any other official. But neither should he, or Finney, expect special dispensation from tenants because of color. It is a healthy family spat, and there is no disgrace in it because the white neighbors are eavesdropping.

Some of these problems were not of Robinson's making; he may well be swimming as fast as he can. They were the making, or inheritance, of white administrators who were lambasted too, sometimes more harshly. But the problems are also the result of some tenants' indecencies. There is enough blame for everyone.

It is assumed most tenants wanted Robinson. Now they have him. And while they have every right to grouse, to organize rent strikes or whatever, they should be mindful that the choice was made with their initial blessing and, I think, in their interest.

As for Robinson, he has quickly discovered the difference in trying to tell someone how to run the agency and actually running it. He will sink or swim in short order. But first things first—he had better get the elevators running. ■

November 27, 1983

The real secret weapon of the GOP

The not-so-secret weapon of the Republican party may be Edward Vrdolyak. But the best-kept secret weapon is Harold Washington.

He has brought a resurgence to the Grand Old Party that should make Ronald Reagan both grateful and envious. What power Washington must possess, to have gotten tens of thousands of stalwart Democratic voters to defect to the Republicans last April, including many aldermen and Park District Supt. Edmund L. Kelly's "Dem-or-die" 47th Ward machine.

Washington even moved Jane Byrne to flirt briefly with the idea of converting after losing to him in the party primary, and he might be the inspirational force behind former police Supt. Richard Brzeczek's switch to the GOP in his current bid for state's attorney.

And now Washington even has the Cook County Democratic party chairman himself reconsidering his political loyalties. It was revealed last week that the mighty Vrdolyak trembles so at the thought of Washington that he actually went to the White House last summer to get help from the opposition.

Meeting with White House Chief of Staff James Baker and Political Director Edward Rollins, they talked about the career plans of presidential candidate Walter Mondale. Vrdolyak reportedly offered to get Mondale an early endorsement, then to discourage his faithful precinct workers from getting out the vote so that the president would show well. It was a classic move by "Fast Eddie," wheeling and dealing more nimbly than usual, until he got caught.

One motive behind this scheme may have been to "fix" the national Democratic party for having had the audacity to come into town to help Harold Washington's election to the mayor's chair when even true blue (and white) Chicago Democrats knew better. There also was the matter of a little stipend, just to keep up a Chicago tradition. And that's where the deal was squelched.

The Vrdolyak caper was not just politics, although he is a political creature through and through. There is something other than the council power play driving him, something other than an attempt to make a few bucks, and certainly something other than the interest of the party.

That same something drove Chicagoans who have been Democrats since birth—and who probably will be in the afterlife, given the city's legendary vote padding—to turn away from Washington last April.

What is so awesome about Harold Washington's presence that he turns Democrats to Republicans, as the mythical Medusa turned people who looked upon her to stone? Could it be something about the way Harold Washington *looks,* too?

Face it, Chicagoans, there *is* something about the way Washington looks. And you only get one guess as to what it is.

That Harold Washington is one sharpie, recruiting so many white people for the GOP, and all in one year.

And white is apparently what the Republicans want. At the recent meeting of the Republican Governors Association members were urged not to waste their time to pursue the black vote, but to go after Hispanics, Asians and white ethnics. Illinois Gov. James Thompson told the gathering his black votes last November were "inconsequential." That is, inconsequential in number, not in importance, he quickly recovered.

But Mayor Washington is one black person who must be of consequence to the GOP, with his effortless drive to increase their rolls.

If you didn't know better, you'd think Washington had beat even "Fast Eddie" to the Republicans and cut a deal. You'd think he is being paid not to change the way he looks so that more white Democrats will defect to the GOP. But he is kindly providing his skin color free of charge.

Or maybe Washington is paying off the folks at the White House to ensure that the president and his party continue to make inane statements and look convincingly contemptuous of black voters. But they usually provide that for free, too.

The possibilities are infinite. So too is Vrdolyak's luck and control over the local party, it seems. After the plot was revealed, Vrdolyak's supporters defeated a motion to censure him, not knowing a double-cross when they see one, or not caring so long as it's a double-cross of the right color.

The Republicans are welcome to the lot of them. ■

December 4, 1983

The county
Democrats' Titanic?

"It is a terrible, horrible, lousy thing when we put color first instead of qualifications."

That bit of profundity came from no less a defender of liberty, equality and fraternity than 10th Ward Alderman and Cook County Democratic party chairman Edward Vrdolyak after the party's slatemaking session last week. The outcome of that session was a county ticket that tossed in a few blacks for show but for little political substance.

It was denounced by black ward committeemen, who hustled off to try to draw up their own slate within the two-week filing deadline for the March 20 primary. That action, of course, will be called playing on race, as if the guitar had not been strummed already.

Why is it that ethnicity was fine in the days when the ticket had its quota of Irish, Italians, Germans, Poles, or whatever, but not now when blacks want in? Suddenly, it's qualifications that count. Come on, we're talking tradition. Except that blacks know all too well how traditions are disavowed in a split second when they begin to take advantage of them, "qualifications" or no.

In the scheming of smoke-filled rooms, last week's slatemaking machinations will take some time to fumigate. But the truth about who did what to whom doesn't have to be told for you to surmise that there are an awful lot of old-style politicos caught in their skin color who would gladly make a deal except for the racially charged times in this city. What do you do if you're a committeeman, white or black, who is used to playing along and getting enough to take care of your people, and suddenly you're with one faction or the other by birth?

Lots of black committeemen are finding out that they have had limited partnerships in the party. Ald. Wilson Frost (34th) is one. He got the slatemaking session going by seeking the recorder of deeds office, and many in the black community wondered briefly if he was betraying the mayor. But by the time the slate was drawn, Frost was absent from it and looking strangely like a tragic figure again at the hands of Vrdolyak, who has been described as an old buddy of Frost's. With friends like that . . . .

Why would Frost want to be recorder of deeds? Remember, Frost is someone who has played poker with Vrdolyak before and won, when he relinquished claims on the mayor's chair after the death of Richard J.

Daley and was chosen Finance Committee chairman. This year circumstances and skin color have made him an outsider. He had a rough reelection against a newcomer and lost the Finance Committee. Maybe he wanted someplace to hide where there are 300 jobs to be dealt out—and a way to be dealt into the game again. Now that's tradition.

Frost defended himself Friday, saying he wanted the post because of "the principle and the symbolism of it." He said blacks were promised the post before, four years ago.

But he apparently wanted on the ticket without assuring that he would support the full ticket. You could ask what brand of loyalty that is, except that last April other members of the regular Democrats were pretty selective about whom they supported, and party affiliation made no difference.

What on earth happened between Frost's incredible announcement and the finale?

"We [blacks] were undercut," a still-simmering Ald. Timothy Evans (4th) told me. "It's evident these people think that a black mayor and black voting power are just a temporary thing. They don't think Harold can keep up the momentum from his election. They think they're going to retake everything.

"I wouldn't want to promote talk of a third party, or a black party," said Evans. "We're Democrats, and blacks have been consistently loyal Democrats. We're just talking fair, and the party ticket isn't fair—to blacks, women or Hispanics."

Evans emerged as one of the slatemaking session's orators, calling the ticket a "replica of the Titanic." He could prove right. You can dismiss an alternate slate, or you can remember the lessons of last February and April, with its devastating black vote, a vote that should never be taken for granted again, even if it turns up short on occasion.

The county campaign involves different geography, but it already is becoming as foul and divisive as the mayoralty. ∎

December 11, 1983

Unequal cultures,
unsavory pasts

If mayoral aide Clarence McClain, a convicted panderer, had become a minister or were running a community center for troubled children, he would be the subject of feature stories on the worthiness of rehabilitation. Instead, he is aiding the mayor in making political and governmental decisions and is being soundly—and rightly—blasted for it.

At the Chicago Housing Authority, Michael Buford, 39, the brother-in-law acting chairman Renault Robinson put on the payroll, has an arrest record for robbery from his days as a teen gang leader. And now the police records of staffers in the Department of Neighborhoods are being revealed, including the record of acting commissioner Joseph Gardner, who has a 1978 conviction on a gun charge. One staffer described as McClain's chauffeur, Nabors "Jake" Miles, has a record of arrests on charges of assault and contributing to the delinquency of a child. A first deputy has a conviction for defrauding the state unemployment compensation program; another aide was convicted of disorderly conduct.

It is impossible to dismiss these records simply as past mistakes; some of the indiscretions are unpardonable. But they must be examined more astutely. The employees in question have families to protect and reputations they have tried to rebuild. They should not be used by either faction as political darts or to whip up cries of racism, though you can almost hear, amid the inquiries, "See what *those people* are like."

A public employee's record should be disclosed if it shows serious indiscretions and if the employee holds a fairly high-level position. Disclosures of this kind have occurred in past administrations, and this may be only the beginning of revelations about the Washington administration's black and white members. Yet it is not enough to say that better people should be hired. Among blacks in particular, even the very best and the brightest in any field run a greater risk than whites do of having been suspected or accused of a crime, and certainly of knowing someone who has. This explains why the mayor's own transgressions were embarrassing to some black people but were not enough to keep them from voting for him.

Stop 10 black men and 10 white men on the street and you are likely to prove this theory by inquiring solely about traffic violations. The reason for the discrepancy is not that blacks are worse people, or more dishonest, or more prurient, as the twisted mentality of bigotry maintains. The reason is too often this very negativism, which accuses and tries blacks instantaneously. On the other hand, let's not be Pollyannas: The reason can also be that someone is just a guilty good-for-nothing.

Still, the social factors behind the disproportionate black contact with the criminal justice system have to be acknowledged. I am not offering the old excuse about poor, disadvantaged, one-parent, aimless youth being let off because of their pathetic life circumstances. Yet, if you have any sense of fair play, you have to admit that those circumstances must somehow contribute to delinquent behavior.

If criminal infractions seem less relevant to blacks, it is not because blacks find them excusable, or see everyone as redeemable. Indeed, blacks can be most harsh concerning punishment because they are victimized by crime more often and know its cruelties better. But they also understand what may have driven someone to commit a crime. They know that a suspicion is sometimes as good as a conviction where someone black is concerned. So they give the benefit of the doubt, knowing that the accused black frequently has not been afforded it. This negativism presumes that a black victim or witness is less credible, too.

A police officer may stop a black kid and haul him in for hanging out, but he will just shoo away a white kid or take him home. The black burglar who gets caught in an industrial plant is dealt with more harshly and appears more menacing than the white president of the firm who is caught defrauding investors. (White-collar crime really is white.) A black woman, dressed impeccably, is more apt to be suspected of shoplifting in an exclusive store than is a white person who is dressed sloppily.

But these are hypothetical examples. The city employees under fire have been involved in the real thing. I enter my plea on black versus white criminality not to apologize for these specific cases or allege that the city workers were falsely accused or were victims of discrimination. I only wish to explain that the fact of different circumstances requires different judgments about people's pasts.

The futures of these men in city government will have to be determined case by case. The mayor and McClain (no relation, for the curious) can socialize and consult as much as they please, but the mayor should not have McClain in the environs of City Hall acting as liaison in official matters.

The worst crime against Buford is being Robinson's brother-in-law. Hit Robinson on that; don't knock Buford for youthful recklessness going back 20 years. There seems no reason why Gardner cannot run the Department of Neighborhoods, or why Miles cannot drive a car, though Miles' and McClain's offensives are most repulsive.

There may be reason for concern if the convicted defrauder has a job with the chance to defraud again, but isn't that prejudgment unfair? The disorderly conduct charge is not worth addressing; a black person buying chewing gum at a newsstand can be picked up for that.

This furor is ultimately a clash of two separate and unequal cultures finally meeting head-on as equals. And, unfortunately, the collision is in the very public halls of government. ■

January 8, 1984

Harold Washington, gladiator

Harold Washington was elected mayor of Chicago, but his greatest role has been as gladiator.

He has been fending off the lions in the city council. His election put him into national prominence and pitted him against President Reagan and against his own national party. He has even done battle with his key black supporters, in the 1st Congressional District race. And he will be dueling doubly in the March 20 primary, attacking with one hand the issue of Jesse Jackson's presidential candidacy and delegate selection to the national convention and, with the other, his nemesis Ald. Edward Vrdolyak (10th) and the Cook County Democratic party in the ward committeemen races.

Through it all, Washington has found time to be mayor, and to be a good one, I think. Were it not for the manic racial character of this town, people, especially whites, might be able to see the uncanny irony in this fact: Harold Washington has emancipated them and given them good government. What they had before was no better than Moscow's Politburo, with the party and government as one. Now the party and government are not one.

Therein lies the distinction Chicagoans must learn to make, and therein lies Washington's occasional undoing. Washington's job would be much easier if he were both party and government. But he is not.

As a mayor, Washington has opened up the business process of this city with the Freedom of Information Act; taken on labor on the prevailing wage; tossed out thousands of payrollers; involved bright, responsive, hard-working, multi-ethnic people in the management of this city—people who have expertise beyond hiring their relatives (not that they or the mayor are pure in that regard).

Most recently, he gave Chicago a real budgetary process—with the able hand of already-missed David Schulz, the departing city budget director. No matter what the bottom line was or which department was being saved or punished by the numbers, the fact remains that no mayor had ever thought enough of the brain power of the aldermen to give them a full month to review the city's finances. And then, of course, given the extra time, the opposition ungraciously whipped out an alternative budget.

Washington is mayor, but can he also be a "boss," even of only a small faction of a party?

He is certainly trying in the coming ward committeemen races. But if the mayor is a different kind of mayor, he is proving to be a different kind of boss, too. He will never be "boss" in the Daley sense for more than reasons of color.

There is a difference between a boss and a leader. The leadership Washington displays in government only seems lacking when translated to the party. His campaign offices are busy enough, and he will be supporting a cadre of black, white and Hispanic candidates on and off the county ticket and in ward races.

The criticism of disorganization that plagued Washington before his election and during the early days of his administration are being repeated about Washington as party leader. Can the Washington who gathered the popular vote gather together a bunch of politicians? His fiercest battle in the arena may be this one with a two-headed local party.

When the regular party's county slate was rejected by angry black committeemen who stalked out, their threatened alternative lineup never came together. It was doomed by old-line black politicos vs. born-again Washingtonians vs. slighted suburban black party members—and may never have had the mayor's blessing anyway.

The infighting and many challenges now in the inexplicably convoluted petition filings for ward committeemen also are making his "organization" appear inept.

The odds seem against him because of the disorganization, because he is fighting on too many fronts and because his opponents are in their own right formidable (and whatever disorganization they have never seems to be played up publicly).

The disparity between Washington the disorganized candidate who became a quick-study mayor and Washington the seemingly disorganized party leader may prove not so great.

Before turning thumbs down, remember that Washington the gladiator knows well the jaws of the lion. ∎

March 4, 1984

Is Navy Pier up
Swibel's sleeve?

One of the first political lessons anyone learns in Chicago is: There are no coincidences.

And there certainly are no coincidences when Charles Swibel is involved.

So when Swibel's periscope was sighted in the waters off Navy Pier, it was not a supernatural occurrence. Swibel is always there when he needs you.

Reports that Swibel had a plan for Navy Pier surfaced only after a special joint session of two city council committees (Special Events and the World's Fair and Ports, Wharves and Bridges) scuttled the mayor's request for continued negotiations with Rouse and Co. developers on a $277 million shopping complex at Navy Pier. The reports surfaced and submerged so speedily they hardly caused a blip. But there had to be something on that radar screen.

Mayor Harold Washington and Public Works Commissioner Jerome Butler had asked that the deadline for talks with Rouse be extended from mid-February to June 30. The committees said no in a 15-5 vote weighted by the opposition-29 bloc. The committees weren't voting on money or blueprints or any such tangible matter, just on whether the mayor should keep negotiating with Rouse.

Of course, many of these aldermen lined up behind Jane Byrne three years ago when she proposed turning the lakefront white elephant into a shopping bazaar. They would never have voted to muzzle her, even when she had nothing to say; and there wasn't much to the plan then except Byrne's noted grandiosity. But it looked and sounded good because Rouse and Co., from Maryland, has an impressive list of similar developments. In Milwaukee, Baltimore, Boston and other cities, Rouse helped replenish urban vitality and revenues.

Ald. Edward Vrdolyak, who led the charge against Mayor Washington's proposal, called the Navy Pier plan a "pig in a poke." That was true under Byrne.

Lately, though, there seemed to be something of worth wriggling around in that poke. It still is an iffy proposition, just because of the cost of renovating the building and grounds. But it is certainly worth pursuing, and it is the mayor's right to study ways to ensure the economic future of Chicago.

The mayor himself took a long time in deciding to back the plan; he was asked about it often during the campaign and was noncommittal even after taking office. But once he was convinced of its worth, Robert Mier in Economic Development, Liz Hollander in Planning and Butler, a Byrne holdover, got to work.

They actually had begun to find common ground with Rouse, although the city had missed promised deadlines on an agreement. There was a tentative plan for $40 million in UDAG (Urban Development Action Grant) funding, which would have saved city money; the plan fell through, but it showed that officials were thinking and moving. In late January, the mayor met with Rouse in Washington and received a promise from the company to help finance neighborhood projects and to allow space for local entrepreneurs in the Navy Pier bazaar. Rouse has made such concessions to municipalities before.

The deal was in the formative stages, but the anticipated $15 million in revenue and Rouse's track record were making the risks seem worth taking. Even the State Street and Michigan Avenue merchants, who have the most to lose if Navy Pier works, reluctantly advised continuing the talks.

Now enters Charles Swibel, who is certainly familiar with the real estate development business—at the high end, given his involvement in Marina City condominium dealings, and at the low end, with his 20 years as head of the Chicago Housing Authority. Navy Pier is a considerable piece of property for anyone to take on, but Swibel could turn it to some good use for everyone to share in, especially some cronies on the 29 side.

No sooner was the committee vote tallied than it was disclosed that Swibel had a brilliant idea for Navy Pier in which the Ohio millionaire De-Bartolo family, one-time prospective buyer of the White Sox, would take Rouse's place. Swibel, it seems, made the offer two months ago to Ira Bach, the mayor's director of city development. (I am not above thinking there is no coincidence on the administration side in revealing this conversation *after* the committee vote.) The DeBartolos denied that Swibel represented them or that they had plans for or interest in Navy Pier.

It is highly likely that Swibel had something up his sleeve. And it is a sure bet that the vote against continued negotiations with Rouse had a lot to do with whatever it was. ■

March 28, 1984

County Hospital:
hope for the poor

Cook County Hospital is a hellhole.

Cook County Hospital is a life preserver.

The grande dame of Harrison Street is much maligned. But it seems dishonest for those who have never suffered with her to be so quick to denigrate her.

All most people know of Cook County is that they never want to go there. And it seems that with the never-ending fiscal crises, the disregard for its staff, the patchwork rehabilitation, some would mercilessly write off County and the thousands of indigent for whom there is no other harbor.

While the horror stories at Cook County are not overstated, the good that goes on there is too often understated.

Until I was an adult, I had no idea that doctor's offices had comfy cushioned seats, magazines and Muzak, or that in other hospitals privacy was the norm. Whenever anyone sneezed in our household, she was bundled up and deposited into the caldron of humanity at Cook County. There was no need to explain why we always drove by other hospitals to venture to the West Side. The reason was the same then as it is now: Other hospitals do not want you if you do not have health insurance or instant cash. Better to go to County on your own than to be "referred" there (the less polite word is "dumped"). A society that discriminates among the sick is itself diseased. But such is life and death at Cook County.

As a child I sat in the emergency room on backless pews, feverish and congested, for four hours because the form that was filled out upon arrival was inevitably lost; the promise to be called shortly was met somewhere within the next two hours.

It is the hellhole where my sister lay motionless for days, the doctors fearing polio but diagnosing some mysterious virus. It is the hellhole where my mother was revived from a diabetic coma and returned home three dress sizes smaller. Too young to visit her, I remember standing on the sidewalk below and waving to her as she leaned against the window.

What went on on those upper floors was a mystery to me—until the next year, 1964.

In March it was the broken leg, and an overnight stay in a crammed ward where one woman's groans finally were silenced by a resounding "shut up" from her fellow patients. By fall it was chicken pox at 13 and a week's stay in the old contagious wing. I know Cook County Hospital, knew her in her old disgrace.

There are those who do not know her. They do not know the bizarre expressions of love that are exchanged by a sobbing couple after one has shot or stabbed the other, and the accompanying police officers who stoically set about the required paperwork, having seen this movie before. They do not know what it is like to be in pain and lean up against a wall, or to wait an hour and a half for a prescription at Fantus Clinic—"Fantasy" Clinic, as every patient mispronounces it. They do not know what it is like to be condescended to by a doctor or nurse with a foreign accent or to demand respect and attention with a desperate shriek; Cook County has never been a place of silence.

All they know is that they don't want to go there, don't have to go there. They do not understand that there are people without a choice, or for whom the choice is made, without their consultation, in another hospital's emergency room.

Of course there are those who do care and who want to save County. But the question is money, always money, and whether anyone cares enough to spend it on the poor.

The Cook County Board knows the need, but it also knows the cost, about $300 million to replace the old building. There is no doubt that the hospital should be sustained, whether in a new building or a series of more accessible satellite facilities.

Cook County may always be a hellhole to some, but to the poor, that hole is the middle of the floating life preserver. ■

April 22, 1984

Crimes against free expression

The 1969 raid on the Black Panthers, mentioned in paragraph eight, was led by then-State's Attorney Edward Hanrahan. It resulted in the violent deaths of Panther leaders Mark Clark and Fred Hampton, and the demise of the political career of Hanrahan, who was voted out of office in 1972.

Let us now hail no ideas. That's no ideas, not new ideas. No ideas is what President Reagan's administration is about.

Of course, he and his loyalists have ideas aplenty. It's just everyone else's ideas that they want to stifle.

He and his administration have crept up on free expression, intent on strangling it. Their actions are regressive and dangerous and, though they can't see it, un-American. The free flow of opinions is this nation's very reason for being. It has worked amazingly well for more than 200 years. But Reagan would quash it.

The gagging has been carried out in stealth and with such effectiveness that most people probably have not noticed that the Constitution is being debased. There is a Reagan view of the world, and everyone ought to share it. It's the reincarnation of "Love it or leave it."

This administration's disregard for rights was fully unmasked last week in the president's directive on terrorism. Though the details were not told, the rules reportedly include more (and presumably more unfettered) intelligence gathering and reprisals to protect U.S. citizens on the domestic and foreign fronts.

Secretary of State George Shultz, showing he can stand as tall and hang as tough as his boss, said the intent of the directive is to show an "active defense" that might entail "preventive or pre-emptive action." It's the tired old "national security" excuse for everything from bashing heads to exploding cigars to who-knows-what. This administration is out looking for something in which to interfere. Where is Salvador Allende when we need him?

Obviously, all nations hope to thwart or to punish terrorists. The consistent and frightening signs from this administration are that an "active defense" may be applied, or rather unleashed, domestically after years of trying to reverse the abuses of infiltration during the protest movements of the 1960s.

The terms being used previously applied to nuclear war strategy. What was the 1969 raid on the Black Panthers on the West Side but a "preventive or pre-emptive action"?

But the missive on terrorism is just part of a pattern that reveals the administration's alarmist and paranoid tendencies.

Remember, this is the administration that wanted to plug its leaks by requiring lie detector tests for more than 2 million "randomly selected employees" in the civilian and military services and another 1.5 million workers with government contractors. Those who refused could be subject to "adverse employment action," a nice bit of euphemistic double talk.

Another part of that brilliant plan was to have 100,000 federal employees sign secrecy agreements requiring them to submit anything they wrote concerning intelligence, even after leaving office, for prepublication review.

At a hearing on those proposals last year, former Undersecretary of State George Ball warned (or was it prophesied?) that "we should be very careful in our obsession with the Soviet Union that we don't imitate their methods and become much more like them."

There is still more evidence of this administration's police state mentality.

It reversed domestic spying rules for the FBI last year, rules that were clamped on because of overzealousness during the 1960s and '70s. The changes would authorize infiltration and other extreme measures now in a period that is tranquil, indeed comatose, compared with those days of sit-ins and marches and university building takeovers.

And capping the list of crimes against free expression is the news blackout on the invasion of Grenada. There is but one reality, Reagan's reality, and it is one-dimensional.

This flag-waving administration ought to review its American history and the role dissent has played in helping to preserve democracy. ■

April 25, 1984

Olive branch? Sez who, buddy?

In one of her rare satires, Lea uses as a vehicle "Chicago Week in Review," an intelligently packaged public television program hosted by attorney-journalist Joel Weisman.

[Mayor Harold Washington and Ald. Edward Vrdolyak have extended olive branches, but neither has reached for the other's offering.]

ANNOUNCER: And now "City Hall Week in Review" with your host, Knowall Wiseman.

WISEMAN: Good evening and welcome to this very special edition of City Hall Week in Review. Tonight we're going to discuss whether the city's blacks or the city's whites started the political mess we're in. We'll also compare the IQ scores of the two aldermanic factions in the council. And last, we'll explore whether those new experimental lift garbage cans in five wards are what's causing a mysterious outbreak of dyspepsia among precinct captains.

Our guests are Mayor Harold Washington . . .

(Washington looks to camera, smiles)

. . . And 10th Ward Ald. Edward Vrdolyak, leader of the majority 29 bloc in the city council and newly re-elected Cook County Democratic party chairman . . . (Vrdolyak looks to camera, smiles.)

. . . Together for the first time, here on this show. (Thinks to himself: Eat your heart out, Jacobson.*) To get started, gentlemen, you first have to turn your chairs around and look at each other.

(Neither Washington nor Vrdolyak budges.)

WISEMAN: Come on, guys, turn around. At least turn around and admire this funny custom-made trapezoid table we have in order to give everyone around it a chance to be a star, especially those newspaper and radio people.

---

*Walter Jacobson, a popular, controversial Chicago television news anchor.

(The chairs begin to swivel, then stop. Waiting for the right moment, both politicians turn around to the table simultaneously.)

VRDOLYAK (showing surprise): So you're Harold Washington! You raced off so fast from the council your first day on the job last May, I hardly remember you. Hardly seen you since (devilish smile).

WASHINGTON: Why you scurrilous . . .

WISEMAN: Mr. Mayor, you'll have to save that kind of talk for the council. I think we ought to remind our viewers that this is the first time the two of you have gotten together, not just on this show but for the first time ever since your election. I figured if Cronkite could do it with Begin and Sadat, so could I. Let's start with you, Mr. Mayor, what do you think about the racial . . . ?

WASHINGTON: I'm getting tired of that question. I said I was going to be the mayor of this city, all of this city, and I am. I say that unequivocably. What I want to get across to the people of this city is that I turned my chair faster than Fast Eddie did tonight.

VRDOLYAK: You did not.

WASHINGTON: Did, too.

WISEMAN: Look, we only have a 30-minute show. And I've got to squeeze in all the questions I brought up in the opening. So quit it already. Ald. Vrdolyak, what about that "it's a racial thing" statement? Wasn't it the first salvo in this battle?

VRDOLYAK: That's past, gone. I want your viewers to know that I offered to meet with the mayor no less than 433 times just in the last week. And even though I said I'm not going to negotiate in the media, I got 433 stories about my extending the olive branch and turning over a new leaf and becoming Nice Eddie. Tonight is my big chance to show my new image, and you have me seated for my worst profile.

WASHINGTON: The media never understand me or my culture. I made the offer—first—and a total of 527 times, but the funky media only reported it 5 times.

WISEMAN: Mr. Mayor, just what do you mean when you use the term "funky"?

WASHINGTON: See, you're what I mean. You don't understand me.

WISEMAN: Let's turn to another subject, the . . .

VRDOLYAK (jumping up from the table and pointing his finger at Washington): He kicked me! He kicked me! Did you get that on camera? The mayor of the City of Chicago kicked me in the shins, right here on the air.

(Washington lunges across the table.)

VRDOLYAK: Hey, bub, don't muss my bulletproof vest.

WASHINGTON: I knew this was going to happen. I should never have agreed to this. You scurrilous, spurious, antediluvian, doo-doo, funky low-life . . .

WISEMAN (ever composed): Speaking of low, we're just about out of time. We'd like to thank our guests, Mayor Harold Washington and Ald. Edward Vrdolyak, for their joint appearance . . . Hey, no fighting on the table top . . . Good night. ■

May 2, 1984

And we will all sink together

Blacks are talking a third-party county election challenge and ethnic whites are setting agendas and becoming overnight Republicans. But we will all be naysayers when the national media point out Chicago's race problem.

What race problem? There wouldn't be any race problem, every side insists, if "those" people would just do right or go away or try togetherness. Integration won't have a chance here before it's buried, and few will even lament it.

It doesn't matter now which side started it, or is keeping it up, for when it is finished everyone will sink together.

In the midst of this insanity, voices of reason are drowned out. Last week some 100 business, union and civic leaders issued a "Chicago Covenant" to stress their concern "about the injection of racial antagonisms into politics and the struggle for neighborhood improvement which is fragmenting and polarizing the city along racial and ethnic lines."

The covenant begins, "We, the undersigned, are citizens who love Chicago and believe in its future." It is bolstered by such names as Warren Bacon, executive of Inland Steel Corp.; Edwin C. "Bill" Berry; Rabbi Herbert Bronstein of the Chicago Board of Rabbis; Gale Cincotta, National Peoples Action; James W. Compton of the Chicago Urban League; Msgr. John Egan of the Chicago Roman Catholic archdiocese; William Lee, Chicago Federation of Labor; John McDermott, the *Chicago Reporter* newsletter; Rev. Jorge Morales; Rev. Kenneth B. Smith, former school board president; and Rabbi Arnold Wolf, Temple KAM.

It continues: "We respect Mayor Harold Washington as our chief magistrate and call on all citizens to give him the respect and cooperation which he and his office deserve.

"We also call on the mayor, the chairman of the Democratic Party, members of the City Council and all community leaders to set a good example by addressing the serious issues facing our city with dedication and civility."

The sentiment of the covenant is admirable—and futile.

For meanwhile, the jousting goes on in the city council. The majority bloc will stand firm against allowing Mayor Washington to buy even a new push broom for the next three years, so that when he tries to point to his accomplishments, they can gloat that he has been ineffective. And they, of course, will have been far too effective.

The mayor would rather be combative than mayoral, and given the obstreperousness of the opposition, it is hard to blame him. But good government will indeed be good politics, if he gets his staff's agenda together.

White ethnics are holding conventions to formulate an agenda, as if the agenda hasn't been theirs for all of history. What is it the white ethnics fear? Is their garbage not being picked up; aren't their streetlamps on? Just how many blacks have moved onto their blocks since Washington's election? Their concern is neighborhoods, and so is Mayor Washington's. But they find it inconceivable that a black mayor could treat them fairly, given that blacks were mistreated at the hands of white mayors for so long.

Many blacks talk loosely of a third party, overlooking that they could not defeat bad apples in some predominantly black contests for committeeman and the legislature in the primary; that Cook County's population does not break down like the city's; or that there are some internal community problems of crime, education and respect that need to be tackled—and to discuss them is not antiblack.

But curses on any outsider who would dare say Chicago has a race problem.

What race problem? ■

May 20, 1984

Confirmation
mischief of little men

The confirmation hearings of city appointees are becoming a modern-day Inquisition.

The city council Rules Committee vote against Ald.-designate Dorothy Tillman last week means the people of the 3d Ward soon will begin their second year without representation. Former Ald. Tyrone Kenner was convicted of bribery and mail fraud last June. Tillman was nominated in December and has been grilled and delayed ever since.

While she has waited, none too patiently, a black businessman named Edward Gardner of Soft Sheen Products is voluntarily paying her $26,000 aldermanic salary and ward office rent that was in arrears—a problem she might not have had if she were a full-fledged alderman with a budget. That should be some indication of the black community's faith in her.

In March, she won the ward committeeman race with 61 percent of the vote, which probably is a bigger mandate from her constituents than most of the aldermen opposing her received. A galvanizing activist and organizer, Tillman surely knows her constituents better than most aldermen know theirs.

But the only evidence against her has been the bruised feelings of Ald. Bernard Stone (50th), who claims she called him a bad name during her school protest days. Poor Bernie.

And then there is Cultural Affairs appointee Fred Fine, 70, who is being baited about his Communist party membership in the 1950s. The ghost of Joe McCarthy doesn't belong in hearings on the arts.

And on and on it goes. There are so many appointees to city departments and boards and commissions waiting now that they'll have to take a number to be served. No doubt the council majority is hoping the wait will span Mayor Washington's term in office.

An administration spokesman said that, at last count, these appointments were on hold: Board of Health, Dr. Quentin Young; Department of Purchasing, William Spicer; Board of Municipal Investigations, Raleigh Mathis; Chicago Park District, Dr. Margaret Burroughs and Walter Netsch; and the City Colleges Board of Trustees, Dr. Shirley Buttrick, Carmen Rivera-Martinez, Tommy Briscoe, Ronald Grzywinski, Rev. Albert Sampson and Rev. Jeremiah A. Wright Jr.

Also, the Chicago Police Board, Robert Hallock, Nancy Jefferson, Norval Morris, David Rivera and Aurie Pennick; Personnel Board, Warren Bacon; Chicago Public Library Board, two confirmed but three remain, Carmelo Rodriguez, Dorothy McConnor, Dr. Cannutte Russell; Chicago Regional Port Authority, Garland Guice; Plan Commission, Walter Clark, Marshall Holleb and Laurina Esperanza McNeilly; Chicago Board of Education, Dr. Frank Gardner and attorney Joyce Moran; Cable Commission, Arnette Hubbard, Lilia Delgado, Robert Mann, Mark Jones. The school board and cable panel have had hearings.

And last but hardly least is the Public Building Commission. A certain person by the name of Harold Washington has not been afforded the respect of past mayors in getting an automatic seat on the panel that oversees all the public buildings in his own domain. The Rules Committee that is trying to frustrate Tillman has had its hands in this one since October.

No one is suggesting that every name submitted be approved. There will be legitimate questions of competence or conflict of interest, though more than likely the questions will be invented. To be fair, a few of the delays are in committees headed by Washington allies, and some appointments were quite recent. But the council majority's skulduggery is the issue.

Meanwhile, the business of some boards is going on with hacks whose terms expired years ago. And there are charges that the shenanigans go beyond delaying hearings; many sitting appointees with expired terms have loyalties to the 29 majority-bloc alderman and allegedly are being instructed to miss meetings so there will be no quorum.

The mischief on confirmations offers a fine lesson in what a little power can do to little men. ■

May 27, 1984

Trifling with the city's stability

Politics, my eye.

The legal maneuvering last week to dethrone the mayor was not just a sample of Chicago's intriguing mode of government. The move by Ald. Edward Burke (14th) was pure provocation, a laboratory specimen of racism.

When Burke filed a lawsuit alleging the mayor was not the mayor, he was inciting more than a council floor fight. The standing and stability of the City of Chicago should not be trifled with.

The mayor apparently did not file his financial disclosure statement until last week; the deadline was April 30. The required forms also were signed by his secretary, not him. Burke gleefully proclaimed the mayor had forfeited his job by state law because of these errors. The administration said it was a "snafu."

Snafu or not, the mayor should have had the statement in, if not on the dot, certainly sooner than three weeks past the deadline. But the response to this laxity should have been a slap on the wrist, from some "authority" other than Burke; it did not have to become a slap in the face, of the mayor and the black community.

Harold Washington surely recognizes after a year of experience with the council majority that if his suit coat is missing a button, the 29 will twist that to his detriment. Unfortunately, his response is going to have to be owning a lot of buttons and thread. In government, that translates into having an impenetrable line of defense: a solid plan, a quick idea, an airtight legal argument, a wily staff, an unimpeachable spokesman or two, a direct communication link to all communities, a strategist who can anticipate the unthinkable, a capable council diplomat, a capable council cutthroat and at least one detail person to ensure against these minor snafus that become major imbroglios.

The mayor does not have all of these, sometimes because of the opposition's obstructionism; for example, the loss of an advocacy Department of Neighborhoods in the budget battle severed some new links with communities. But oftentimes the mayor's own stubbornness has foiled him; his allies complain that he does not seek their counsel.

He has, especially in recent weeks, responded affirmatively to criticism that he temper his remarks, reach out to business and fearful neighborhoods and just run the city as best he can with these mad dogs nipping at his heels. Yet the 29 have scoffed at such appeals, shamelessly speeding ahead with their plunder of what is left of the city's reputation and good will. It's tough to be magnanimous in the face of bared fangs, but the mayor will have to try. Ald. Edward Vrdolyak (10th) is more likely to cry "sic 'em" than yank in the leashes anytime soon.

All the hugging and talk of Democratic unity is so much folderol. But there is a city to be managed, and it will take the mayor and 50 alderman to do it.

The mayor will never change the hard-core obstructionists, who are most of the 29; these are white men of the old order politically and socially, who have yet to recognize Washington as a human being, a black, a man or the mayor. But magnanimity might work on a few of the more thinking members, who ought to be downright embarrassed.

The wonder in all this is, where are the voters in the wards of the 29? Maybe they would destroy the city to save it. No one is asking them to let the mayor live next door, but they surely see the viciousness in the assaults on the mayor's command and in the opposition to Dorothy Tillman, who is being toyed with on her 3d Ward aldermanic nomination. (She was another intended victim of the council chaos last week; discussions on the World's Fair, community development block grants and other city business were just in the way of Burke's sniping.)

Other cities with black mayors function, even flourish. To those who intimate that Washington is not like those other "good little colorless and inoffensive" black mayors, take note that the bare-knuckles brawling that resurfaced in the council proves our elected representatives are unlike any other city's, too. ■

CRIME AND PUNISHMENT

If the old saying that a conservative is just a liberal who has been mugged is to be believed, Leanita McClain might best be described as a modern urban conservative on crime issues. Early in her career she was the victim of a purse snatching while covering a feature story at a public housing project. Later she was robbed at gunpoint in San Juan, Puerto Rico. Growing up in housing projects, she knew the victims and perpetrators of violent crime firsthand. As a result, her view of urban street crime presented liberal ideals tempered with modern realities. She sympathized with the need to prevent crime by improving opportunities for inner-city youth. She also knew police brutality was more than a myth and felt corrupt police should constantly be screened out. She also supported in her columns the need to provide legal help to those who cannot afford it and rehabilitative service in prisons for those who need it and will use it. But, as McClain shows in writings about black street-gang leaders and other notorious characters, she realized that some people are beyond rehabilitation and deserved nothing more than removal from law-abiding society.

Having grown up in some of the lowest income, highest crime areas of Chicago, she offers a view of the roots of street crime that is based on firsthand knowledge. And she had little sympathy for criminals who grew up with the benefits of good homes and schools. They had much less excuse, she felt, than the vile street-gang leaders of the inner city. Yet they were much less likely to be severely punished.

Crime was an important issue to McClain because it played a major role in the deterioration of cities, the exodus of commerce and the destruction of human lives, particularly those of poor minorities. At the same time, there were few issues that frustrated her more than the way those who had the greatest ability to improve the situation seemed to persist in making it worse.

September 28, 1981

Atlanta's victims on
my mind

The ribbon was frayed and unsightly, but I could not bring myself to remove it, not just yet. The fraying, broken threads, evidence of last spring's assaulting winds and rains, are as symbolic as the ribbon itself. They show how much time has passed, how worn everyone has become, how difficult it was to unravel the case of the 28 murdered black young people in Atlanta.

It had been months since I'd reached for a raincoat. The black, green and red ribbon, worn in sympathy for the suffering families, was still attached to the collar.

Hundreds of lapels and coat collars throughout the nation displayed the ribbons earlier this year, some simply green, others green and black, still others in red, black and green. They all had a common purpose, a common good. The Atlanta Braves even wore green tape on their batting helmets. Actor Robert DeNiro had a touch of green on his tux when he accepted an Oscar.

Many churches raised money for the families of the slain children by selling the ribbons. Some were fashioned into ingenious petaled creations, imitations of the real flowers that have decorated many a chapel and gravesite in Atlanta since the killings began in July 1979.

The tricolor ones, red for blood, black for skin color and green for the earth and life, symbolize the Pan African or black nationalist movement, and, in the sixties, were unlikely to be worn by anyone who did not also bear a stern face and a clenched fist. But the colors gained new meaning with the Atlanta tragedy, and the color of the person wearing them was insignificant.

The ribbons flapped in the unrelenting chill last spring as Chicagoans looked up for any sign of a delayed summer, for a burst of sunshine, as a break might occur for investigators in the Atlanta tragedy. But the ribbons would not be shed before the coats would be. The coats went into the closet for the season, but the Atlanta case dragged on.

It dragged on until it became more than a crime story. In fact, it often became an "event," and the true import of the story became blurred. A great many "happenings" began to swirl about the case, some well intentioned, others ludicrous, insensitive and sensational.

There were marches across the country, celebrity benefit concerts and charges that the police weren't trying hard enough, that no one cared because the children were black.

More than $1 million in federal aid was sent to the special police task force. Mayor Byrne sent $10,000 of her own money. And 5,000 people attended a rally in Washington.

A parade of psychics entered the picture, each with his or her own composite psychic sketch of the killer. There was debate over the killer's race—the hunted suspect was a long-haired, mustachioed black man one week, a long-haired, scar-faced white man the next. Or was there more than one killer? The FBI offered a "psychological sketch" of a middle-aged "gentle" man with feminine tendencies—or possibly a woman.

Sociologists talked about the wayward "street child" and others suggested that some of the children were deep into the sordid side of street life, as if their loss would be any less significant. Special activities were organized for kids for the summer.

Psychologists were quoted about the stress on Atlantans and the nightmares of the city's children, and a distressing letter from a 10-year-old, published in papers nationwide, beseeched the killer: "If you like killing kids and it makes you feel good and happy, then you could be sick or something and there are people who could help you."

The vigilante Guardian Angels group flew to the rescue from New York. Residents of a low-income project where a few of the victims lived formed their own vigilante group and were arrested on arms violations.

One of the mothers declared that the killings were being committed by a cult, another said she suspected some of the other parents. Many of the families began to charge the media for being "quotable" and ethical issues muddied the case even more.

Then, incredibly, activist Dick Gregory suggested that the children were being used in experiments to manufacture an anti-cancer drug. And lastly, television is producing a docu-drama on the subject.

It has been a grim, curious, touching, story that seems neverending. Thankfully, no more names have been added to the list. But will the upcoming trial of Wayne B. Williams, the 23-year-old photographer charged in only two of the slayings, really tie up all the loose ends?

The nation's consciousness is as battered by this agonizing tale as the ribbon on my coat, but its scars cannot be removed as easily. ■

February 1, 1983

Grandma, get your gun

The antigun contingent should meet Dorothy and Li'l Pete.

Dorothy, an arthritic but busy grandmother, never goes anywhere without Li'l Pete, her trusty .38. And if the people of such places as Morton Grove, whose gun ban recently was upheld, had to trudge from the bus stop to get to Dorothy's home in a South Side housing project, day or night, they just might change their minds and adopt a Li'l Pete themselves.

They might think twice, too, if their financial transactions were conducted in a dingy currency exchange, probably no bigger than their family rooms, that is a marvel of security hardware. The doorway often is obstructed by the local young men who, having no jobs, keep bankers' hours on the walkway.

Instead, most suburbanites have the luxury and security of a friendly neighborhood bank or S & L with friendly Muzak and friendly guards and friendly tellers who bid everyone "have a nice day." Not to mention convenient mail and drive-in service and shiny computerized money spewers that would be foreign to Dorothy's neighbors, many of whom have never had checking accounts. Their tight monetary policy is cash or money order.

That Social Security check is all Dorothy has, and she isn't about to let some young punk get away with it without a fight, whatever the consequences. Dorothy and many others like her, if their checks survive the mailboxes, have devised security systems as elaborate as the currency exchange's—carrying an empty handbag, sewing a hidden pocket in a coat, or the old-fashioned tucking into the bra or stockings. They often travel in groups for safety, or have to wait for a relative to transport them by car to and from the door, and occasionally leave their money in the relative's care altogether.

Thieves know better than the government when and how its check system works. Most of Dorothy's neighbors are on some form of public assistance, and they stay home on the day the checks arrive. Even though the funds from the month before might have run dry, they'll wait a week or more to cash the new one to avoid the rush on purse snatching.

Dorothy has heard the fuss about handguns. Yes, they were meant for nothing other than killing another human being. Yes, they are a leading cause of domestic homicides. Yes, there are unfortunate accidents with children. Yes, it is easier for criminals to get handguns than for honest citizens who go through waiting weeks for a state license and the three days' "cooling off" period to pick up their gun after purchasing it. But, no, Li'l Pete stays put.

The people of Morton Grove have put their faith into a handgun ban. She puts her faith in Li'l Pete. A ban may work in Morton Grove, but it won't work in her neighborhood. And neither will the city's gun law.

The U.S. Court of Appeals upheld Morton Grove's law last month, giving more ammunition to both sides in the handgun issue. The ordinance forbids residents of Morton Grove to own handguns except for antique gun collectors, licensed gun clubs and the military and police.

The court, in a two-to-one decision, said the law was constitutional, although it may not "promote peace and security for its citizens."

Judge John Coffey, in a pointed dissent, said, "Morton Grove, acting like the omniscient and paternalistic 'Big Brother' in George Orwell's novel, '1984,' cannot in the name of public welfare dictate to its residents that they may not possess a handgun in the privacy of their home."

There are, no doubt, more than a few decent citizens who have been turned into criminals by default since the Morton Grove law was enacted, as Dorothy and others in Chicago have been since the city's new law passed in April. At least Morton Grove had the guts to impose a ban; Chicago's convoluted new law is a roundabout and feeble facsimile. Every time Dorothy steps from her door, for example, she is breaking the law that makes it illegal for anyone other than a law enforcement officer or guard traveling to and from work to carry a gun.

To control handguns or to ban them? As neither is 100 percent workable, the first option, with some semblance of cooperation between law enforcement and the average scared citizenry through registration, is best. Since every handgun everywhere is never going to be collected, people should be made to understand their power and awesomeness. That alone might lead to voluntary submission of handguns.

The city might have done better to start an education and registration drive, which it is pretending to do now. By Feb. 3, every registered owner must re-register all guns, not just handguns, even those people who registered in a hurry in April (there had been registration since 1968). People should go to their police districts to register properly, with applications for each gun, photos for each gun and one for police files and a $5 total fee regardless of the number of guns—but remember, don't carry the gun with you or you're breaking the law.

Yet anyone who failed to register a handgun before the April 9 deadline or who has purchased a handgun since, because they could not register it because of the new law, already is in violation and faces a $500 fine or six months in jail. Those who want to buy guns of any kind may still do so, but no unregistered handgun can be kept in the city.

Confused?

Dorothy isn't. She and Li'l Pete, as usual, will just mind their own business. ∎

June 18, 1983

Standing square on dope

"Did you hear about Belinda?" asked Penny, one of those old high school friends you run into in theater lobbies and restaurants every two months or so.

Penny's voice was ominous and her fingernails clamped tighter and tighter into my forearm.

"She's dead," Penny said.

The ensuing "how" and "when" had no answer.

"No one knows," Penny said.

We determined to find out. We were sorry when we did.

Belinda (I've changed her name to avoid causing anyone pain) was one of the best-dressed, most outgoing and flamboyant girls in the class of '68—yearbook and newspaper staffs, honor society, science club, student council, Girls Athletic Association. She died while free-basing, according to reluctant sources.

Free-basing, made famous by the 1980 fire mishap of comedian Richard Pryor, involves smoking a concoction of ether and cocaine in a pipe. Belinda, an asthma sufferer, clogged up her respiratory system somehow and choked, or so the story goes. With Pryor, the ether reportedly exploded and set his shirt afire, resulting in third-degree burns.

While Belinda got a hurried and secretive funeral, Pryor got an additional routine out of his encounter with tragedy. "What's this?' he asks, lighting a match onstage and bouncing it through the air. "Richard Pryor running," he answers.

But there is little humor in what has become of the children of the sixties. As they graduated, so did drug use. You used to be "square," to revive an expression that now seems ancient, for not smoking pot. Curses to the party poopers in the circle who passed along the reefer without taking a drag, who ate pretzels all night because the brownies were laced with marijuana, who were not daring enough to try LSD.

Now marijuana is a common household item, right next to the lettuce in the refrigerator vegetable crisper. A midnight smoke before bedtime or a few puffs before sex are essentials to many people, most of whom surprisingly are still prudish enough in their approaching midlife to keep it from the children. But there are those who don't even keep it from the children.

Soon, snorting cocaine will be just as common, if the price of this high-priced high ever goes down. It's nearly impossible to powder your nose in the rest room in some Rush Street spots because of the white powder that some people are snorting. They do "lines" (the pharmacy-neat laying out of a row of cocaine) atop the metal cigarette machines.

Their offers to strangers to pay up and join in are as distressing as the old image of the pusher at the schoolground fence. The shimmering ambience makes the practice no less grimy.

Because of the generational kinship, those who do not indulge are unsuspectingly drawn into the sport. They are accepted spectators because of the participants' presumption that a shared age brings with it a shared morality. And this is causing an intrageneration gap.

What do you do when a party guest disappears into the bathroom and leaves that funny cigarette aroma behind? Or when another guest boldly lays out rolled cigarettes amid the cheese and crackers? This is carrying a "Bring Your Own" invitation a bit too far.

And reprimand is met with a standard retort: After all, everyone's doing it, so it must be all right. Everyone *is* doing it, so much so that to denounce it publicly can be an unintentional insult to everyone within hearing.

Why is it that those who do not indulge are left feeling ashamed, accused of moral holinesss—and seldom believed? For these intolerants, who remain "squares," who do not share the permissive attitudes of their contemporaries, the scorn and taunts are sometimes as great as any peer pressure suffered during the teen years. Obviously, given such widespread drug use, so too is the lack of will to refuse to go along.

But many "squares" still do stand square on the issue. "I've made it clear that no one brings any of that stuff into my house," said a friend who is now married to a lawyer, has two children, a dog, a mortgage and all of the rest that our generation scorned, not perceiving that time and money would make them the norm. We did not expect that drugs would be the norm, too.

"I won't tolerate it. I don't understand it. Why do these people with money and good jobs and fancy vacations need it?"

Why indeed?

Penny and I would like to have asked Belinda, asked her if she thought about her little boy whenever she did this.

Now all we can do is ask each other why and plan a reunion before we lose anyone else. ∎

September 28, 1983

Legal services for poor in jeopardy

The Reagan administration has tried to throttle, starve and dismember Legal Services Corp. Now it has resorted to sheer humiliation and harassment. It has gagged the nine regional offices of the "poor people's law firm" from contact with the media and elected officials. In addition, it has proposed changes in eligibility that will drop more poor people through the safety net.

As usual, the ultimate goal is to rid the nation of this public service, to deny the poor due process of law. There are even fears that its conservative detractors, having failed to kill it, will recycle it into "Judicare," a concept that would pay private attorneys to represent the poor, an approach similar to school tax vouchers.

Since his election, the president has schemed persistently against the agency, arguing that it is too costly, that the states should decide whether to use their block grants to fund such programs and that with its class action suits it is a thorn in the side of the very government that funds it. Fortunately, Congress is not as heartless and has saved it, sometimes just barely.

The president's first assault on the agency was to turn over its board of directors to a pack of conservative wolves in sheep's clothing. Their mission was to dismantle, not salvage, the agency.

But this backfired. They were found last December to have billed the agency for $156,000 in consulting fees, double those of the year before. With typical White House logic, the response of presidential counselor Edwin Meese was that there would be no such controversy if the agency did not exist. The General Accounting Office investigated this fiasco and has exonerated the board, but the embarrassment is lasting.

And of course every year the president has asked that the agency be eliminated. Last year it was rescued again, but the budget was trimmed by about 25 percent, from $320 million to $240 million.

In the last two weeks there has been a new barrage: the gag order; a change in eligibility rules that will cut still more clients; and GAO allegations that the corporation misused public funds by lobbying to save its own budget—a revelation conveniently timed just as the reauthorizing legislation is before Congress.

The eligibility rules, which could take effect today, will hurt the elderly, handicapped and unemployed the most. They would maintain the eligibility of people with incomes no higher than 25 percent above the official poverty level, but then require that other government benefits that were formerly excluded be counted, plus the income of everyone in an applicant's household. Battered women could not be aided unless they lived in shelters. And last, they would deny service to anyone who had more than $15,000 equity in a home, which omits a good portion of senior citizens.

Obviously these are not the most pleasant of times for attorneys in the program. "We're under siege," says one with four years' service. "What it boils down to is that we are going to spend more time checking into the eligibility of clients than representing them. It's going to get more stringent than public aid."

Sheldon Roodman has taken the federal beatings in stride as executive director of the Legal Assistance Foundation of Chicago, the independent, nonprofit corporation that is chief conduit of Legal Services Corp. funds in the city, where an estimated 30,000 could be served.

Roodman, chief for six years, has had to eliminate 25 of some 100 lawyers and one of seven offices as resources shrank. "We are merely giving advice to some people now, telling them how to represent themselves in court when we would have actually represented them," he said.

He defends the agency's purpose with zeal: "There has been an enormous expansion in the rights of the poor, and it has been the full-time professionals in neighborhood offices who have made this so effective. It is hogwash to believe that lawyers in private practice on a voluntary basis could replace the services being provided. That was the reason for legal services in the first place, the poor were not being given access to our system of justice."

At issue really is a clash of philosophies. The administration holds that legal services lawyers are all do-gooder lefties. That is a compliment, considering they aren't getting rich at $17,500 to $29,000 a year.

The Reagan philosophy is simply callous. He seems to think anyone who can't pay $200 an hour to a lawyer with a fancy mahogany-paneled office doesn't deserve any lawyer. ■

November 2, 1983

Money won't stop
street gangs

Evanston is a suburb on the North Shore of Lake Michigan. Unlike its sister suburbs in the area, Evanston has a substantial black population.

For every "E" on my report card father used to give me 50 cents.

Was I ever cheated! That was small change compared with a proposal put forth by the Evanston branch of the NAACP to have the city identify the 100 worst gang members and pay their families $100 a week if they turn good.

For me, good performance was expected, payoff or no. And I understood the reciprocal arrangement, that there would be unpleasantness from my father's right hand had the grades not been good. So too should it be with the kids in Evanston.

The NAACP's proposal was a serious one, but fortunately it has not been taken seriously. It was one of three ideas, each one as absurd as the others, to help Evanston politicians and community workers find ways to tackle this "urban" problem that has found its way across Howard Street.*

The NAACP's suggestions should be an embarrassment to the group. This is a classic case of wanting to toss money at a problem but ignore the cause of it. The family that cannot discipline a child is not going to be able to do so any better with an extra $100, no matter how many circus tickets or other extracurricular activities it might provide. Enough studies have shown that family instability is the prime contributor to gangs. A hundred dollars isn't going to stabilize a family or help parents do what should come naturally.

There are of course good parents with bad kids, but paying even them won't make their kids better.

On the other hand, will penalizing parents make for better kids? Evanston Mayor James Lytle has a counterproposal to fine parents $500 and six months in prison if teenagers violate curfew or alcohol or drug laws in the parent's home.

Howard Street is the boundary between Chicago, a city long identified with gang activity, and Evanston, its middle-to-upper-class northern neighbor where the problem was not known until recent years.

Money, either as reward or punishment, will not root out the evil of street gangs. But both proposals at least recognize the real problem, parenting, though they have not found the right answer.

Specifically, the NAACP proposed that the $100 subsidy be "awarded to any parents who will insure that their previously disruptive child (those who have been identified by the police department as the main 100 youths who are gang members and who are destroying the tranquility of the community) conducts himself or herself in acceptable social standards."

Unacceptable social behavior was quickly righted in my childhood with a stern look because the next phase of disciplinary action was too painful to think about, much less test.

The NAACP also would require parents to attend a monthly workshop covering the subjects of employment, parenting, developing human potential, human development and positive thinking.

This part of their idea doesn't seem quite so ridiculous, given the numbers of gang members and just plain aimless and lonely kids at all income levels, but is it the government's responsibility to teach people to be parents? Evanston's only obligation beyond human relations is to use that $100 a week on supervised activities, or on facilities and equipment. Saving the family should be the business of the Evanston NAACP, through counseling parents and children about their responsibilities to the greater community.

The NAACP also suggested earlier curfew hours and a $50 fine if parents fail to receive a city permit to hold a party for youths under 18. The permit allows no more than 30 youths for each bathroom in the house. (Thirty youths per bathroom? What about half-baths?)

Such ideas did not need to be suggested to parents in times past. If father said to be in from a date at midnight, then a minute after was pushing it. The only permit needed to keep parties under control was the group of mothers making potato salad in the kitchen who peeked in on the dance floor every quarter hour.

What the Evanston rules are talking about is plain, old-fashioned discipline, and it shouldn't have to be bought or sold or bargained for between city government and individual families or between a parent and child. It should be expected, and the expectation alone should be enough incentive.

Times have changed, of course. Drugs, drinking and teen sex have all confounded approaches to child-rearing, but they have not made it impossible. And there is sympathy aplenty for the woman heading a household, living on tight finances and in fear of her six-foot baby boy and his pot-smoking buddies.

But only an investment of human capital will solve this social ill. ■

March 21, 1984

Police and the
dynamics of fear

"Why did you have to pull up so close to *him?*"

This question was put to me by two passengers in my car on separate occasions last week as I stopped behind a police squad car at a traffic light. It was asked with visible fear.

Why was even the nearness of the police so dreaded? And why is such anxiety triggered automatically in the black community?

Then came the warnings: The police might jump out and drag us from the car, take us in to be strip-searched, charge us with all manner of crime, and it would be our word against theirs. The tale built into a thriller.

These nervous warnings seemed in contrast to the attitudes of defiant blacks in Miami last week; that city had its third disturbance in four years after a police officer was acquitted in the 1982 killing of a black man. Yet beneath the surface there is a link between the inordinate fear of police expressed in Chicago traffic and the inordinate belligerence of a Miami rock thrower.

Last week, Miami policeman Luis Alvarez, pleading self-defense, was acquitted in the shooting death of Nevell Johnson, 20, on Dec. 28, 1982. Johnson had been stopped on charges of carrying a concealed weapon, and his death ignited a three-day riot that left another man dead and 26 people injured.

After the verdict, people took to the streets again in Miami's Overtown, Liberty City and Coconut Grove sections, yelling, "They let whitey go." A thousand police officers were mobilized; violence was not nearly as bad as in previous years, but at least 20 people were hurt and about 500 arrested.

It does not require analytical training to connect the dynamic in the emotions of paranoia and aggressiveness directed at police in cities hundreds of miles apart, or to wonder why they are so spontaneous. But understanding them requires more than the easy explanation of racism, even when all-white juries, as in Miami, may deserve condemnation. These emotions are aimed daily at whoever is in uniform, and so black officers get it as much, if not more, because they often are seen as traitorous.

These emotions, fear and belligerence, are not the polarized extremes they seem, but are hardly separated; the line between them is microscopic, like that between love and hate, genius and madness. The difficulty is in predicting which emotion will surface and under what circumstances. And these emotions rule the police as much as they rule the community.

The environment in which the black community and police interact is like that of a prison. But many people refuse to draw this analogy because it is simpler to dismiss black behavior and endorse police behavior. Black people are just that way, the detractors would say, and be done with the topic. Cops are just that way, many in the black community would say with the same quickness and error. If blacks do not like to be painted in such a fashion, then it is unfair to do so to the police, who see the most horrid of what is already deplorable in every community.

Within this psychological and socioeconomic prison that walls in a good part of the black community, everyone and everything foreign is an enemy.

In a jail, the guards relinquish their freedom for so many hours; so do police on duty. Police are an occupying army, sent by those in authority (whom the inhabitants cannot reach) to sweep the mine fields. So the police officer is society's proxy—and its patsy, in the very way the community is.

And like news from prison, news about the black community and police is of two kinds—the inmates' cruelty to each other (black-on-black crime) and to guards. Otherwise, there is little news deemed worthy of coverage. The prison/ghetto, the inmates/residents, the guards/police are best left unmentioned.

As society would keep this culture generally out of its sight and mind, so it wants no part of the police or the black community's tales. And when this untidiness encroaches upon the conscience of "civilized" society, in riots, in mug shots on newspaper front pages, or, worst, in crimes committed in the "civilized" zone, even then the command to police is to get the problem corralled, get it out of sight again. There is no thought of what could be done about such conditions or behavior.

There is no thought in any of it, no rationality. There is just reaction—or too often overreaction, whether in a motionless car in Chicago or outside a ransacked store in Miami.

And the two emotions will continue to feed upon each other and build until they defy containment. ■

March 25, 1984

Justice by castration is disgusting

From a female point of view, sentences of life in prison faced by four men convicted in a gang rape in New Bedford, Mass., hardly seem sufficient.

Two other men were acquitted in trials on charges that they raped a woman atop a pool table in a tavern a year ago in the Portuguese-American community.

Yet for some people no punishment would be harsh enough for this hideous crime.

Many rape victims, at their most despairing, advocate castration as punishment, or even castration and jail. A judge in South Carolina has become their champion.

Judge C. Victor Pyle has offered the options of surgical castration or 30 years in jail, the maximum in this case, to three young men found guilty in a rape and beating. (Some convicted rapists have consented to chemical castration, in which a female hormone is injected to stem the sex drive.)

The three, Michael Braxton, 19, Roscoe James Brown, 27, and Mark Vaughan, 21, pleaded guilty to assaulting a 24-year-old woman repeatedly and burning her with a cigarette lighter in a motel in Anderson, S.C., a year ago.

The man and victim are black and the judge white, so the sentence is being denounced as a return to the era of slavery when castration was common punishment. But the question really has nothing to do with color.

The young men have some time to contemplate their dilemma while the judge's sentence is being appealed by their attorneys; it probably will be heard near year's end. Defense attorney Theo Mitchell says the appeal seeks to declare that the judge overstepped the constitutional bounds of his authority and to remove him from the case. Judges in Ohio and Texas have since followed Pyle's example.

"When the sentence was read, everyone thought he was joking. But this is as serious as cancer," Mitchell said. "We can't even find a doctor in the state who is willing to perform the surgery. The doctors are standing by their Hippocratic oath that this is barbaric. The judge's action is not reasonable or legal."

The judge has been quoted as saying that he at least is giving the men a choice. As for the defendants, in television interviews Braxton said he is undecided, Vaughan is looking to prison and Brown said he would choose castration because "he could be destroyed either way."

But choice or no, this kind of justice is disgusting. As ghastly as the crime of rape is, mutilating people as punishment is more ghastly.

Women are human beings first; it is important to remember that, especially when others treat us inhumanely. Many women would maintain that they are more compassionate than men, because of their biological role and that assigned to them traditionally by society. There is a segment of feminist thought that holds that this gentleness is not a strength but a weakness turned against women by a male-dominated society. It makes them easy victims, emotionally and physically, in daily life; and rape is a man's ultimate means of trampling both aspects of their being.

The bulk of research on rape shows it to be more than simply the product of a sex drive out of control. Its trigger is violent, not sensual. If castration were made acceptable, even by choice of the rapist, there would simply be violence by other means.

Think of the extremes to which this type of "eye for an eye" punishment could go: the lopping off of hands of thieves, or perhaps, in what would be the male counterattack for castration, the disfiguration of female prostitutes.

Many states need tougher rape laws and fewer stipulations on the admission of evidence, especially regarding the character of victims. A new Illinois law, to take effect July 1, finally acknowledges spousal rape for the crime it is and removes from the victim the burden of proving she resisted. It also repeals eight laws on rape and other sex offenses and establishes four categories with penalties ranging from probation to 30 years in prison; gang rape warrants a fixed sentence of 30 to 60 years.

Life imprisonment, certainly upon a second offense, is not unreasonable. (The death penalty is never reasonable. Arguments against it parallel the arguments against castration: It is brutal and irreversible.)

This subject is not one to be dealt with flippantly, though it opens up any number of sick jokes. Many women polled informally on the matter were quick to condone it, and with great seriousness; most men were struck speechless.

As surely as men mentally undress women, women mentally castrate men. That is as far as it should go. ■

April 29, 1984

Jeff Fort can't
be "rewritten"

The mention of gang leader Jeff Fort conjures many images, all of them terrifying. Yet there are community leaders who find him "a man of impeccable character . . . dedicated to the good of humanity" and "a pious man with enormous respect for authority and justice." And one even thinks he has the potential of Dr. Martin Luther King Jr. or Jesus Christ.

These descriptions of Fort were in letters to a parole board to help win Fort's early release on a 13-year sentence for conspiring to distribute cocaine. Fort is in the federal penitentiary in Terre Haute, Ind., on a Mississippi conviction. He is studying for his GED diploma, said his lawyer, Charles G. Murphy. Murphy suggested the letter-writing, but said he did not solicit the letters himself.

The letter labeling Fort "impeccable" was written by an aide to State Rep. Larry Bullock on the legislator's stationery; Robert Lucas of the Kenwood-Oakland Community Organization (KOCO) can claim the "pious" tag; and businessman Noah Robinson of the Breadbasket Commercial Association was the one to elevate Fort to the stature of King or Christ.

Fourteen such letters were written on Fort's behalf by people who would not seem the type to consort with Fort. They include ministers, former Ald. William Barnett (2d) and the Concerned Mothers of Woodlawn. (I suppose there have been mothers concerned over the years about Jeff Fort—concerned about whether their children would encounter his gang members on the street and live to tell about it.)

What contacts Fort has—politicians, ministers, businessmen—are the kind any upstanding citizen would have. But having stood up for Fort, some of these people have had to account for their statements.

Robert Lucas of KOCO now says he wrote the letter on impulse, has written a second letter retracting the first and "would like to put the matter behind [him]."

Businessman Noah Robinson issued a press release to explain his letter, emphasizing that he was not recanting what he wrote. He said he formulated his opinion of Fort on the young man's civil rights work, reiterating from the letter Fort's participation in three marches: with Martin Luther King for open housing in Gage Park in 1967, in which Fort "shielded Dr. King with his own body from the sticks and stones hurled . . . by angry, violent mobs"; with Jesse Jackson in a hunger march to Springfield in 1968; and with minorities trying to break into the construction trade unions in 1969.

But the explanatory press release is hardly as persuasive as some of the letter's passages: "I want to take this opportunity to talk about Jeff Fort, not the one that the media has characterized as Mr. Notorious over the years . . . . He has been socially and community conscious since early in his life. . . .

"Jeff is a natural leader of men. He has god-given charisma. He also has a track record for standing up and fighting for the little man who is either too weak or too fearful to stand up for his own rights. And that's really a major portion of Jeff's problem. His sense of concern for others and willingness to challenge perceived injustice by those in authority have resulted in his being characterized by some as a dangerous man. . . .

"History now refers to [King and Christ] as dedicated and determined. Whatever else Jeff might be, he is also dedicated and determined. If Jeff chooses to use his talents in a positive, constructive manner, he could be a powerful force for the good of mankind in general and his community in particular."

But the point is that Fort has not chosen to use his talents positively.

Since the early 1960s, Fort has gone from two-bit to thousands, from leader of the Black P Stone Nation gang to high priest of the El Rukn sect, from hustler to real estate mogul, from menacing to malignant, although some of those years were spent in jail. The El Rukn have muscled into the drug and real estate markets nationwide with a savvy that would shame an MBA.

Their latest ploy for legitimacy is politics. They were discovered to be behind a political organization that pamphleteered for Jane Byrne, with Rep. Bullock reportedly the liaison. And this year many of them joined Nation of Islam leader Louis Farrakhan in going to the election board to register to vote for the first time, stirred by Jesse Jackson's candidacy.

Getting religion and exercising the democratic right to vote cannot cover up what the El Rukn really are. Nor can these letters remold Fort.

There is but one comparison, and every letter overlooked it—Al Capone. ■

HOME AND FAMILY

"Home" to Leanita McClain was a public housing project on Chicago's South Side. Her "family" was an African-American lineage mixed lightly with European white and native American Indian genes, a legacy of the slavery years that is not uncharacteristic of black American families. Historical differences meant profound cultural differences that set her concept of home and family apart from the mainstream American image. While families of European immigrants might call up memories of Ellis Island, McClain's family would speak of a Greyhound bus or Chicago's old 12th Street railway station. From all of this, McClain found many aspects of home and family that are the same for all of us, and she used these familiar reference points to introduce readers to her own home and family and to her views on weightier family issues like housing or abortion.

May 24, 1981

More of a home to me now . . .

While McClain was editor of the Tribune'*s Perspective section, she wrote the following essay as an introduction to a special May 24, 1981, report profiling six successful Chicago professionals who had grown up in public housing projects. Mayor Jane Byrne had just moved into the Cabrini-Green public housing projects, a controversial and, of course, quite temporary change of address that at least brought some long overdue public attention to the endless problems of public housing residents. But, as a product of the projects herself, McClain did not like the way most of the publicity surrounding Byrne's move portrayed public housing residents as little more than miserable and hopeless. With a team of reporters, she initiated a special report to give the other side of the story. Headlined "Six Success Stories from the Projects," the section might as well have been entitled "Seven Success Stories from the Projects," one of McClain's friends pointed out later, since McClain ironically had written a fascinating profile of her own years in public housing, yet had neglected to include herself in the count.*

The projects.

For many, their image is of squalid, foreboding hallways in which merciless thugs wait in ambush. They are, it is said, home to hordes of neglected children whose futures are sealed, to part-time fathers with no full-time jobs, and to pregnant young girls doomed to make the same mistake again.

Chicago's public housing projects are all these things; their woes should not be denied or underestimated. But beyond this, the projects are home to 140,000 people—a home, like any other, where families eat and sleep and share ups and downs.

Mine is one of those families.

The projects were the only alternative for my family when an expanding Michael Reese Hospital bought my grandmother's house on 29th Street and Ellis Avenue. So, when I was five weeks old, my mother, father, two sisters and I moved into Ida B. Wells Homes. It was November 1951. My parents have remained there, nearly 30 years, in the same four-room apartment, though my sisters and I left, like clockwork, when we each reached 20.

Ida B. Wells is one of the city's oldest projects, "humanistically" designed with three- and four-story walk-ups and two-story rowhouses that front on grass courtyards, though the grass doesn't seem to grow as it once did.

The original Wells (not including the Wells extension, a series of seven-story buildings built in the mid-1950s) includes more than 1,600 units. The project sits on 47 acres from 37th Street to Pershing Road (39th Street) and King Drive, formerly South Parkway, to Cottage Grove Avenue. It cost $9 million to build. At ceremonies in June of 1941, the diary of Ida B. Wells, the crusading black newspaperwoman for whom it is named, was placed in a cornerstone. A year later, a *Tribune* story recounts, "The dwellers in Wellstown are jubilant in their new homes and easily the envy of colored persons still living in the rickety houses less than 50 feet from the gleaming new buildings."

We said "projects" without hanging our heads. People in projects led lives as full of personal cheer as anyone else—birthday parties, graduation celebrations, block club parties and tearful farewells and funerals.

In those "poverty program" days, there were dance classes and sewing classes and charm classes, when we weren't roller skating or bicycling. There was a corner soda shop, Doc's, that made the best malts in our limited world.

People raised money to pay the rent by selling baked goods or chicken dinners. Every Sunday morning there was a parade of scrubbed Sunday school children, and every Sunday afternoon there were white Bible students from Wheaton who came in, without incident, to nourish our souls and broaden our horizons. Every summer, the father of one friend set up a curbside candystand that kept us amply supplied, and there was a day camp in Madden Park run by nuns. There were safe summer evenings sitting on the lakefront or on the doorstep watching the fireworks from Sox Park.

And there were fathers who were fathers to those without them, and plenty of working people, factory workers and domestics whose rush hour began long before dawn.

No, it wasn't paradise. There were purse snatchings and burglaries, regularly scheduled weekend domestic rows and gang fights that kicked up the dust in Madden Park and left bloodied noses or, at times, knife wounds. There were kids left unattended for days, a policy numbers den—though I never knew anyone who hit the jackpot—and women who worked by the light of the lamppost. But these were the exceptions. If there were drugs then, I didn't know about it.

Wells was, for me, a decent place to live, built to last an eternity, dependably heated, with abundant hot water. The projects were just right for bargain-hunters, including teachers and other professionals, or for those down on their luck, but not down and out.

Above all, the projects were a stopover. In my family, we were brought up knowing we would not have to raise our children there. Now, it is not uncommon to find three generations of a family trapped in the projects. The object was to get out, and get out we did.

By my adolescence, when everyone's world expands beyond the corner traffic light, the stigma attached to being from the projects took hold. The smoothest-talking suitors stumbled all over themselves to make a getaway once they learned my address.

But the late sixties arrived and made being lower-income—not poor—almost noble, especially for those making progress to better their lives. In college, having come from the projects was a great conversation starter. "You actually *live* in the projects? How many roaches do you own?" Carloads of white classmates shuttled in to take a look at a real, live housing project.

I may be as alien to the projects now as were those old visitors. Still, there is comfort in rounding the corner from Pershing onto Rhodes and seeing the gates of Madden Park come into view. But now I wouldn't drive in midafternoon some paths that I strolled at midnight in my reckless youth.

My parents, now retired, insist on staying, though their activity is curtailed. They have never signed a mortgage on Ida B. Wells, but it is their home as surely as if they had. Oldtimers who remember when the projects were a closeknit community, not a closed one, keep an eye on them.

What has happened to the projects? Low-rise Wells has escaped the problems of Cabrini, but it's not the Wells of my youth.

Is it the buildings or the people? That is a chicken-before-the-egg argument and the answer is, of course, that each has changed the other.

I can see that building maintenance has fallen off, ostensibly because of financial problems, and that apartments are not painted as often. Locks were put on all outside entrance doors a few years ago. Window burglar bars are everywhere. Keeping hallways lit is a constant battle because of lightbulb theft, even though fixtures requiring a special screwdriver were installed some time ago. The playground equipment in Madden Park is often broken. My parents sometimes clear incinerators of obstructions and scrub the halls to remove graffiti.

As for the people, I see more young, single mothers trying to live out their stunted childhoods along with their children. And I see more aimless, jobless young men desperate to make an easy, illegal buck.

Where there was simply poverty of the pocket, there is now also a poverty of the spirit. The projects remain more of a home to me now, even 10 years removed, than they ever will be to the present tenants. ■

November 10, 1981

Tragedy of illegal abortion

Anyone who ever held a girlfriend's hand during an illegal abortion has no choice but to be pro-choice.

In June 1970, nearing the end of her sophomore year in college, Janet became pregnant. She didn't even realize it at first, when she couldn't keep her breakfast down. She went to the doctor thinking she had stomach flu, just a bug. The rabbit proved otherwise.

There was little discussion. The thing to do was to finish school, get that degree. No one had time for babies. On that, everyone—including Janet's mother—agreed. No one had any doubts. An abortion was the only solution.

Initially, some little "magic" black pills—ugly, hard to swallow, licorice-like—were tried, to induce bleeding. They only made Janet more ill, more anxious. They had no label, no prescription, though they came in a bottle that looked like it came from a pharmacy. Perhaps they were someone's idea of a joke, at $18 a bottle.

Meanwhile the search for someone to perform an abortion continued. The friend of a friend of a friend found someone—not a quack, but a real, live practicing MD connected with one of the largest hospitals in town. Still, the abortion had to be performed in his home, in the guest bedroom, with Janet quivering and in tears.

It was a painful night for everyone. Four girlfriends stayed over, but it was no slumber party. First, cold compresses were applied, then hot, then cold again as Janet tried to keep her cries muffled from the rest of the family. Janet's every convulsion was shared. It was not a pretty sight, certainly not one that could be forgotten. When it was over, no one ever talked about it again. Janet went back to the books, graduated, and is happy and successful today—and religiously taking her birth control pills.

Abortion was legalized three years after Janet's ordeal, and anti-abortionists have been trying to reverse the decision ever since. It has become their cause in much the same way the ERA is for the feminist movement.

Having failed in several attempts to reverse the Supreme Court's Roe vs. Wade decision, which guaranteed women the constitutional right to privacy in choosing to have an abortion, anti-abortionists are trying a new tack. They are pushing a Human Life Amendment to the Constitution. Hearings are under way in the Senate. In essence, the amendment states that life exists at conception and that this "person" is deprived of due process as guaranteed by the 14th Amendment. If scientists and doctors cannot agree on when life begins, how on earth can congressmen?

Taken to its irrational extreme, this amendment would even outlaw certain birth control methods. For example, the morning-after pill, it could be argued, might have been taken after fertilization. Abortion could be made criminal in some reactionary states.

Women will never stop having abortions, but this amendment may send them searching, like Janet, for illegal ones again. It is a step backward.

Abortion is an issue with few gray areas. However, one can be pro-abortion but against the use of public funds to pay for abortions; or one can be anti-abortion except in the cases of medical emergencies or rape. Surely, abortion cannot be condoned when used repeatedly as a birth control method.

Abortion is also a war of semantics. The anti-abortionists, taking a cue from positive advertising psychology, much prefer to be called pro-lifers or right-to-lifers. Who, after all, can be against life?

The pro-abortionists, mimicking the opposition, are pro-choice. Shouldn't everyone have a choice in life?

While the issue is not as starkly black and white, good and evil, as the anti-abortionists would have one believe, the time has come for everyone to stop playing the semantic game and come out on one side or the other.

The anti-abortionists have been relentless zealots, even given polls that show 60 percent of Americans back the Supreme Court decision. But riding the Moral Majority, neoconservative, right-turn wave, they are particularly brazen these days. Many of them are the very people who would not adopt an unwanted child, who are all too quick to cluck their tongues at the frightened young girl who has made a mistake, who support cuts in social programs that affect the lives of children whose mothers cannot support them.

Anti-abortion arguments, delivered without hysteria, deserve a hearing, but so does the story of Janet writhing on the floor. ∎

February 28, 1983

A man's discovery of dignity

The following column, written for the Chicago Tribune *in February 1983, was not designed to be read right after her* Newsweek *piece ("The Middle-Class Black's Burden"), but it might as well have been.*

February, Black History Month, has been a celebration of heroes. Here is the story of one that has never been told.

Memphis has never liked to consider itself anything near the Deep South, yet in 1929 it was as segregated and devoid of conscience as any backwoods spot at the turnoff of a dusty road.

At least it wasn't Mississippi. The young black man—colored then by everyone's standard and proud of it—always reminded himself of that. He had escaped Mississippi at nine, running away from the white family in whose care his father had left him when he set out to get a good job with the railroad. Memphis had been his home ever since, but it would not be his home much longer.

The day that was to change everything for him began like any other in his time-clock existence. He had worked since he was 14, though a second-grade rural Mississippi education hadn't advanced him very far. At 26, a

job was a job, but he was always at work, always on time and always looking elsewhere. He hopped aboard the morning street car and sat in his
proper place. Then it happened.

When the street car jerked to a stop, the scrawny young conductor
said to a woman about to board, "You don't want to get into this car,
ma'am, there are too many niggers."

Nigger was a word as widely used as please and thank you, probably
more widely used. It was as much a part of the ride as the announcement
of the stops. Everyone heard it, but on this morning the young man felt it,
felt it deep inside some hidden place.

He tapped his buddy on the shoulder and gave a quizzical, mischie-
vous look. "Fred," he said aloud and almost jokingly, "you see any niggers on this car?"

Fred had heard the conductor's remark, but it wasn't Fred's day to
feel it. Fred had felt his buddy's remark, however. What, Fred thought,
has gotten into this fool?

What had gotten into the young man was not ignited by the morning's remark. It was just that time in every black man's life when he had to
feel something, feel his own dignity. Many of those who did so soon after
left widows. But what had he to lose? No wife, no family, mother long
gone. There was only his father, Old Joe, who was just an acquaintance
who popped in with tales of the promised land in Chicago where there was
no sharecropping. His instincts told him this was already a bad day.

"What'd you say, boy?" the conductor demanded, striding up to the
young man.

There was that other word that everyone used. He felt it, too, for the
first time.

The young man bolted to his feet, nose to nose with the conductor,
enough of a challenge from any black man to shave a few years from life.
Who knows who got off the first slug. Nothing was rolling except the two
bloodied men and a reluctant Fred. Finally, the young black man snatched
the metal sign identifying the street car from a window. He slammed it
over the conductor's head, not even with great force. The conductor fell
to the floor groaning.

At the police station the young man was booked, allowed a phone
call and beaten with a rubber hose. His hair was set afire. It was standard
procedure for any black bold enough or stupid enough, or both, to hit a
white person.

This young man had never been in serious trouble before, carried a
pocket knife for practical uses like skimming milk, opening packages and
trimming toenails. He was not, as the snarling police kept insisting, "one
of those trouble-making niggers." When the calls began to come inquiring

about him, from his white bosses, from his friends, from the lawyer they had contacted, it only made the police more indignant, more cruel.

"Never seen so much interest in a nigger," spat one policeman.

Freed on a lesser charge and fine, he returned to work, but his life did not return to its usual monotony. His white coworkers, in all well-meaning and solicitousness, gave him a good preaching about knowing better than to go around beating up a white man. They secretly wondered whether this was the good-natured "boy" they all liked so much.

No, he was not anymore.

When he went to pick up his paycheck that week, it was $10 short. He asked why. "Who's going to pay that white boy's doctor bill?" was the only answer he got.

Meanwhile, up North in the promised land, his father had gotten word of the trouble. Old Joe knew what he had to do. He knew the signs, the symptoms. If he didn't go to get his son, he would soon be childless. He had had enough of losing his family, to the influenza, to circumstance. His sister Fannie had gone to New York to work for a white family. For lack of knowing how to read and write, no one ever knew what became of her.

Old Joe came back to Memphis and packed up his son. The young man protested, but his father's word was law; he would go. He headed out of Memphis for the promised land and has never set foot outside of Chicago since.

This is living black history.

This is my tribute to Black History Month.

This is my tribute to my father. ■

September 11, 1983

The CHA,
my alma mater

Now that everyone has had his say about the Chicago Housing Authority, it's my turn. I just so happen to have lived in "the projects" from the ages of 5 weeks to 20 and still have relatives and friends living there who I visit just about weekly.

•**Andrew Mooney.** Remember him? He's the well-intentioned, well-spoken young former chief of the CHA. He had his problems, not the least of which was that he worked for CHA bad guy Charles Swibel in the latter's waning days.

For 20 years no one, at the local, state or federal levels, had bothered to look over Swibel's shoulder. But when Mooney was named by Mayor Jane Byrne just a year ago, everyone was looking over his shoulder—blue-ribbon oversight panels, the state legislature, the federal Department of Housing and Urban Development and the CHA board, which suddenly awakened to its responsibility. Given all of this, Mooney was doing the best he could concerning budgets, morale and image. Whether or not he was taking orders from Swibel or from Mayor Byrne, as was alleged, it appears his greatest sin at the CHA was being the wrong color. That is no more right than all of the years there were missing black faces. You don't have to be black to run the CHA, nor have grown up in the projects to have some sensitivity for them, but it could help.

Mooney deserved but never got a chance to prove himself. His replacement, Renault Robinson, was one of the factors in his demise. Yet Robinson deserves a chance, too.

•**Renault Robinson.** His image is that of a troublemaker. Thank goodness for his troublemaking through the years on the CHA board or there would have been no voice for the tenants.

People who cannot accept Robinson must separate the Afro-American Patrolmen's League and CHA crusader from the new CHA chief. Robinson himself will learn soon enough the difference between crusading and running a quasi-governmental unit. What the CHA as an agency needs is a good manager first. What tenants need is a crusader second. Robinson has the brains for the former and the stridency for the latter. He deserves the chance to discover that running the CHA is high on the Top Ten damned-if-you-do-or-don't jobs in this town, for anyone of any color.

•**Elevators.** Robinson is learning his lessons fast in the great elevator flap. Spending $40 million to replace more than 400 elevators is nonsense. That's crusading, not managing. The problem with the elevators is not the elevators but some of the people who use the elevators, specifically vandals and criminals. Robinson's ideas to tighten security and help tenants simultaneously by hiring them as operators is good management and good crusading.

As for the horror stories of the elevator repairmen, I can match, even top, those. As a reporter some years ago my purse was snatched in Taylor Homes by three fleet-footed adolescents, but that didn't color my opinion of every resident in Taylor. And by the way, I was working on my day off, not on company time. If *all* of the elevator repairmen don't want to be painted as loafers, why should they paint CHA tenants as barbarians? The minority who terrorize the laborers terrorize fellow tenants more, and the tenants deserve the greater sympathy.

•Buildings. Central to the problem of elevators is the problem of high-rises. I grew up in Ida B. Wells, a series of low-rise walk-ups no more than four stories at King Drive to Cottage Grove and 37th Street to Pershing Road. Even they lack the "home sweet homeness" of my youth. Where there were grassy courtyards, there are dirt patches. There are bars on first-floor windows, and I've only been gone 10 years.

It's time for someone to try just one grand social experiment—to come up with the money to relocate just one building of folks from Taylor or Cabrini-Green into existing low-rises or rehabbed six-flats and find some hospital, school, skill center or other organization or institution to use all or part of the empty building. If it doesn't work, at least it will have been tried.

A community worker in middle-class Chatham once was bold enough to tell me that if the people from Taylor Homes were transplanted into Chatham, you'd have Taylor Homes in single-families. If insults can't be tolerated from elevator repairmen, such thinking can't be tolerated from a black person in Chatham, which leads to my last but most important point.

•Tenants. Only days before the flap over the elevators, there was much hugging and kissing of Robinson by nice little old CHA ladies. And the *Chicago Defender* ran lovely pictures of CHA gardens, one just a clutter of containers sprouting beans, tomatoes and flowers on a porch in Cabrini. There is more to these than good PR. They are a reminder that the tenants of CHA are people. Mayor Byrne's move to Cabrini showed that, too, and it was great PR. (Robinson has dismissed such a move as "gimmicky," and he has every right to do so.)

The point is that 140,000 living, breathing, feeling people live in the CHA. Just ask me.■

October 9, 1983

You can go
homeward again

Although she had no way of knowing it at the time, the Hyde Park house that Lea bought and described in this column was to become a symbol of much that she hated about her life. She had originally hoped to fill the "nine-room prison constructed of my own hopes," as she called it in her "Generic Suicide Note," with happy babies and a husband. Instead it remained a lonely place for her, largely empty of furniture, refurbishment and family, a haunting house.

The Bridgeport neighborhood to which she refers at the end of the column was the all-white and Hispanic South Side home of the late Mayor Daley. It became a symbol of antagonism between whites and blacks as the mayor stood by idly when blacks who moved into the neighborhood were attacked and harassed into moving out. Similarly, Montclare is an all-white Northwest Side neighborhood.

When the discount store on Broadway added an "Afro hair products" shelf, I took notice.

When the Jewel at the Berwyn Avenue "L" stop sprouted bunches of fresh collard, mustard and turnip greens, I made the best home-cooked meals ever.

But when the 10-pound pails of chitterlings jutted out from the freezer at Treasure Island, the gourmet grocery, I knew it had happened.

Integration truly has come to the North Side.

Having done my part these 10 years for community relations, the time has come to move on, or rather to move back—south. Despite Thomas Wolfe's admonition, the needs of aging parents beckon me homeward to the South Side.

A decade ago, I was a stranger in a strange land on the North Side. Like any real Chicago kid, I grew up not knowing about this great beyond.

All I knew of the North Side is that that's what we passed through on the way to Riverview. Its existence wasn't verified until Christmas of 1962 when my dad and I drove to Montgomery Ward's main warehouse on Chicago Avenue to pick up my Barbie doll house. There it was spread out before me, the North Side, and it even had black people.

Only in recent years, however, has it really had black people.

Ten years ago to be black and to live north was pioneering. It was a perfect excuse to leave boring South Side parties early: "Oh, you know, they have to drive *allllllllll* the way to the North Side," someone would say with sympathy and wonderment.

And sometimes not with sympathy and wonderment, but contempt. "Up there with those white folks" was just as common a response. What a fine example of the isolationist "city of neighborhoods" mentality that afflicts all Chicagoans.

I've gone from humble North Side pioneering in a cramped one bedroom in an eight-story imitation of a four-plus-one on Wrightwood, to a dilapidated but charming two-flat graystone on Pine Grove. After saving my pennies, I became a grown-up, bought real furniture and got a mortgage on a Sheridan Road condo with "wdbg. frplc." After selling that, the next move was to a responsibility-free apartment at "3600 LSD" (Lake Shore Drive, of course). And last, an Edgewater high-rise when Lakeview's ambience and parking roulette just didn't seem worth it anymore.

In 1970, before it was certified trendy, Lakeview actually had 986 blacks, according to the census. But then came the cry, "Northward, ho!" The wagon train rolled in, and now some 6,757 blacks reside in Lakeview. There have been similar results in Rogers Park, from 763 to 5,225; and in Edgewater, from 373 to 6,514. (Interestingly, the Near North Side has lost 4,000 blacks, from 26,090 to 22,000, but the Cabrini-Green outpost is secure.)

Soon the barriers may be broken on the Northwest Side. Even Jefferson Park has five blacks and Norwood Park six where there weren't any a decade ago. Montclare and Edison Park are the only holdouts citywide, with zero, but I think the 52 in Edison Park in 1970 might have pulled up stakes to start the suburban expansion. Even on the Southwest Side, Clearing, at the city limits, has maintained five and Chicago Lawn, where Marquette Park is located, has increased from 10 to 4,782.

So with the northern territory established, I retire to Hyde Park, where integration is a little older and little more comfy, where 90-year-old brick Victorians are still affordable, where you don't have to dress up just to go to the mailbox, where people who confess to being existentialists actually know what it means and everyone white already knows about Afro hair products, greens and chitterlings.

Sorry, Bridgeport, although your black population declined from 79 to 39 during the last decade and you could use some help, I've never lived more than a mile from the lake. Besides, Hyde Park is "the new Bridgeport" with Harold Washington in residence.

So goodbye CTA, hello IC.

Goodbye indoor parking, hello street cleaner roulette.

Goodbye Belden Corned Beef, hello Ribs and Bibs.

Goodbye DePaul, hello U. of C.

Goodbye miserable Cubbies, hello winning White Sox.

If it doesn't work out, there's always Montclare. ■

December 21, 1983

High cost of out-of-wedlock births

Some 55 percent of black children are being born out of wedlock. You don't have to be moralistic and point your finger to shame anyone about that statistic to realize that it does not bode well for black families or the race as a whole.

Its effects can be seen in the infant mortality rate and in the health of the infants who survive.

Its effects have been proven on black income. The median black income actually would have increased from 1970 to 1980 except for the changes in family composition. The proliferation of poor, female-headed households, due to the rising divorce rate and births to single, primarily teenage mothers, held down the median. It would have risen from $12,674 to $14,830, but with adjustments for these families it was only $13,325.

Of course, the effect on these children as they grow is more disturbing and is not as easily quantifiable. It cannot be put dramatically in a figure, but ultimately will be more costly than any number could relate. Will these children show a pattern of underachievement in school? There already is proof of a pattern in teen mothers begetting future teen mothers.

The illegitimate birth rate can be discussed academically and blamed on failed sex education, the decline of the American family and permissiveness generally. But ultimately the blame (and "blame" is such a moralistic-sounding word in this context) must fall on those young men and women who are parenting.

It is time for black people to confront the enormity of the problem and its implications for future progress. It is time to say to the mothers and fathers: Stop and think.

Some black people can get terribly defensive on this topic. After years of hearing how useless we are and "all having babies and on welfare" from other people, it is hard to admit that there is the slightest truth in that the problem exists. But to admit to the problem does not mean to accept or to give validity to the reasoning of those malicious perpetrators of the stereotype. They can be ignored, so long as the problem is tackled.

And some people still do hold to a fear of genocide as justification for being fruitful. Being fruitful once, mistakenly, is not necessarily cause of condemnation; being overly fruitful is.

Teachers and adults who work with unwed parents are forever saying that the problem with the problem is that there is no stigma attached to teen pregnancy any longer. It is not something to be whispered about, but often to be paraded about.

At a Dallas high school a 17-year-old unwed mother was voted homecoming queen recently. Most people did not know she had a 2½-year-old daughter until the child showed up at the dance. Lots of parents protested, trying to get the girl dethroned. But many students said they did not care. They should.

The "sin" of it all is not so much in having the children as in having them without being able to provide for them. Something is terribly amiss when a young man can strut around a high school with a photo pin of offspring for whom he cannot buy milk, with whom he may never live. Young people should be made to face up to the ugliness of their neglect in bringing forth a thing of beauty.

There are so many factors at play that a single solution is impossible: Young girls needing attention, or wanting to escape home and be on their own; young unemployed men needing a way to feel some manliness and self-esteem and in control of something or someone; a simple dare or thrill-seeking. But all of these bombarding social factors eventually come down to two people. And their immaturity, chronologically or otherwise, is becoming less and less of an excuse.

The greater burden will fall on the females. Unfair as that may seem, it will be ever thus. And so the greater responsibility for preventing this problem must fall upon females. Don't count on the guys, my dear. Abstinence, I fear, is too naive a suggestion anymore. There is enough contraceptive information and enough contraceptive suppliers around to meet this requirement. Getting young girls to partake of them is something that the black community cannot afford to be shy about. ■

April 18, 1984

Hope for the troubled black family

The black family is in a woeful state, plagued by unemployment, an incredible 50 percent illegitimate birth rate and the domestic tensions that follow from these.

But at least now this ugly truth is being acknowledged, from the new conservative voices to the rock-ribbed old liberals and some even more to the left. Finally, blacks are not silencing those who point it out, and are in fact saying so themselves: What has become of values, of hope, of aspirations? Slowly, it is becoming permissible, even fashionable, to deal with the topic.

The only impediment to solving the crisis of the black family may be that the variant philosophical camps are spending too much time trying to place blame; so strident are they in defending their ideology that they may overlook the significance of having found common ground just in admitting that a crisis exists. They may also overlook a sensible joint solution that could draw from each perspective.

One school holds that the decline of black families is due to liberal do-gooder programs. President Reagan is, of course, the best-known proponent of this approach, but it is significant that there is a growing black conservative view that feels no compunction about saying so. It espouses free-market economics and "trickle downism" that will benefit everyone; this view is ridiculed by most blacks because it ignores the burden of racism.

On the other side are those who cleave to the liberal do-gooder programs but who are at last admitting that these programs need revision. They have seen the good these programs have done and lament that lending a hand to the less fortunate of whatever color is out of vogue, in the government, among corporations and in everyday American life. But even they can no longer ignore the regression that has occurred simultaneously with the progress of blacks over the last two decades. In 1960, 75 percent of black families were two-parent, now 50 percent are headed by women.

Then there are views such as those of California sociologists Nathan and Julia Hare in their new book, *The Endangered Black Family: Coping with the Unisexualization and Coming Extinction of the Black Race.* They come to the same sad conclusion about the black family but from yet another route. They rail against a genocidal conspiracy, homosexuality and even the primarily white women's liberation movement for easing black men out of the job market. But even from this radical approach, the conclusion is clear: There is trouble in black homes.

Whether any side has the ultimate understanding is not the issue; what is is that all sides find the frankness to speak out and at last agree on the problem, if not its causes or solutions.

The significance of this relationship was foreseen in an article by New York journalist Elizabeth Wright in 1982, "American Blacks and the Cultural Facts of Life" in the *Lincoln Review* quarterly. (The quarterly is a publication of the London Institute for Research and Education in Washington, which bills its work as re-examining the social policies of the sixties and has conservative leanings.)

Wright wrote that "after years of coerced silence, a weary and disillusioned band of defectors, both black and white, are ready to break ranks and speak of the formerly unspeakable . . . . too many blacks learned to use avoidance techniques to deny the evidence of deepseated negative cultural patterns within the group."

That kind of talk was once seen as traitorous, and white liberals were as quick to silence it as were blacks.

But even black leaders of the pure liberal persuasion can bite their tongues no more.

Thirty black scholars gathered under the auspices of the Joint Center for Political Studies in Washington last year to formulate a "Policy Framework for Social Justice." Law professor Eleanor Holmes Norton, former head of the Equal Employment Opportunity Commission, was its chief spokesperson. The report predictably pointed fingers at racism and denounced Reaganistic solutions, but it was unpredictable and refreshingly candid about the enormity of the crisis. Of course, it still saw government as the primary salvation, but it did say that social programs should be revamped. This is revolutionary, especially at a time when such pronouncements could be taken by the conservatives as proving their point.

Conservatives have a point in their "bootstrapism," and few know better than blacks, who start the race bootless, what that can achieve. Liberals have a point in wanting to maintain social programs, and few know better than blacks what can be achieved through these programs.

The solution lies somewhere in the mean. ■

SCHOOLS

The older she became, McClain would say, the greater regard she had for the value of education. It was education that liberated her and her sisters from the low-income life of public housing residents. Education had enabled countless European ethnics to go from near-poverty to great wealth in one generation and was helping newly arrived Asian families to do the same. Yet education was declining in quality for many of those who needed it the most. Perhaps nothing shocked her more than the deterioration of the all-female inner-city high school she and her sisters had attended only a few years earlier. In less than ten years, literacy rates at her alma mater had declined as dramatically as its teen pregnancy rate had shot up. All-girl gangs had appeared, and much of the faculty seemed to be afflicted with a growing malaise. How can future generations of inner-city youngsters ever hope to improve their condition, she asked, if they do not have the necessary intellectual tools?

The award-winning magazine article that resulted from that return to her high school is included here, as are columns she wrote on the declining state of inner-city schools and the lessons that need to be taught to children and adults for that decline to be reversed.

Chicago, *October 1981*

Who will save our schools?

Time was when teachers taught, students learned and parents took care of everything else—food, clothing, shelter and the nightly inquiry "Where's your homework?" Teachers were feared—and revered; school was a community institution with at least as much sanctity as the church; and parental concern augmented the daily lessons in the classroom. But no more. By all accounts, teachers are too busy trying to keep order to teach, high school graduates cannot fill out job applications and parents are an apathetic, elusive lot who would gladly have the schools feed their children dinner as well as breakfast and lunch.

The Chicago public schools are a public disgrace—financially, physically and spiritually. The Board of Education barely met its $1.3 billion budget this year, only after raising nearly $80 million by selling Midway Airport and obtaining federal community development funds and increased tax revenues. Next year, the nation's second-largest public school system faces a deficit of about $100 million. It must come to terms with this while trying to educate nearly half a million youngsters, increase the salaries of 23,190 teachers, and avoid firing any of its 42,450 employees. Among its other ills, as outlined in a report by school superintendent Ruth B. Love, are these:

The average reading level for eighth graders is 7.3 (seven years and three months), considerably lower than the national norm of 8.8; an average of 54,000 students are absent each day, resulting in a loss of $24 million a year in state aid; three million dollars is spent each year to repair vandalized buildings; more than 15,000 students drop out each year; and fewer than 40 percent of high school graduates enter college.

Every concerned Chicagoan is deeply troubled by the situation, but few are as saddened as those of us who came through the system. The many thousands of us, both black and white, who truly are "proud products of the Chicago public schools" remember when those words were said in earnest rather than with contempt and derision.

It wasn't that long ago that one could grow up black and poor in Chicago and still receive an education. I did. So did my two sisters, who remain in the system as elementary school teachers. We and the thousands like us did it by mastering standardized tests and the English language. We did it without free meals, busing, pupil or teacher desegregation plans or euphemisms that hid the fact that children simply weren't making it. To fail was just that. It was not a perfect education. The public schools provided a solid if unimaginative curriculum in basic reading and mathematical skills that those with initiative could develop. We can read, and write, and reason. And so we ask ourselves, perhaps more than anyone else in this city, What went wrong? When did our alma maters become war zones? When did many of the teachers whom we worshiped "burn out"? When did education stop?

These questions compelled me to return to my teachers and my schools, James R. Doolittle Elementary on the South Side and Lucy Flower Vocational High School on the West Side, to seek some answers. From September 1956 to June 1968, these two schools were my home away from home, teaching me skills that I use every day in my home and in my work as a journalist. In 1981, in visiting both schools for nearly two weeks, I learned one more lesson.

* * *

In my youth, the Doolittle School at 535 East 35th Street was made up of two three-story buildings—one of gingerbread red brick built in the past century and one of gray brick that dates from the early forties. The two buildings were connected by a passageway. In the early sixties, a third building, Doolittle West (which I never attended), was built. Today Doolittle West has nearly 1,000 students in lower grades. The gray-brick Doolittle East, the one I revisited, has 645 pupils in fifth through eighth grades. The red-brick building was torn down about four years ago, and I miss it still.

What I found at Doolittle East was encouraging, if surprising.

"Kids are still basically kids, except that some take a bath more often than others," said Zenous Morgan, one of two of my teachers who are still there. A 21-year Doolittle veteran, he was my seventh- and eighth-grade history teacher, but I remember him best for his square-dancing class. He is one of the best-known square-dance teachers in the country; he entertained at the White House for Jimmy Carter's inauguration.

Yes, he was correct; the kids are still kids at Doolittle. They giggle, form lines (boys on one side, girls on the other) and march like drunken soldiers, and the smaller boys still wait for that adolescent growth spurt that will put them a head above the girls. But teachers repeatedly said that they exhibit neither the manners nor the motivation that children once did. Some administrators wish that a dress code would be reinstated, including one for teachers.

Most important, I found that the education process still exists at Doolittle. It exists, the teachers said, in spite of, not because of, a gradeless, directionless reading curriculum called Continuous Progress that was implemented nearly ten years ago by the Board of Education. Continuous Progress, the teachers argued, allowed children to drift along at their own pace, did not acknowledge substandard performance, and left children of vastly different achievement levels in the same classroom. Some have called it "Continuous Regress." Whatever it is called, Superintendent Love is discontinuing it.

* * *

My visit to Doolittle left me unprepared for my return to my high school. Lucy Flower Vocational High School ("For Young Ladies," I once added for snob appeal) was once the only all-girl public school in the city. A few years ago boys were admitted. Last year there were 13 out of an enrollment of more than 700. Flower students train for clerical, retailing, data-programming, lab-technician, food-service, and home-economics careers.

The school, at 3545 West Fulton Boulevard, is in a four-story, sand-colored building about half a block square opposite the Garfield Park Conservatory. Students from all parts of the city can attend Flower, though most of them have always come from the surrounding West Side.

While I found the building much the same, the students are not. There is no dress code. Far worse, there is little of a moral code, and the true "young ladies" are by far outnumbered by girls who are proud of their pregnancies and so uninterested in an education that they skip class and boldly sit just outside the school door playing cards. Troublemaking young men, drawn to Flower like bees to honey, loiter outside in souped-up jalopies. An all-girl gang, the Vice Ladies—a women's auxiliary, if you will, of the Vice Lords—is another student activity.

Inside the building, budget cuts have left typing students trying to learn on machines without ribbons. The students rely on carbon paper, sandwiched between sheets of typing paper, to make the impression of the keys. Some 100 students are trying to train on three key-punch machines; and the art budget has decreased in recent years from $175 to $50 to $37.50—slightly more than 25 cents for each art student. Two of the extra niceties of high school life, the newspaper and yearbook (both of which I worked on and fondly remember), are gone. Student lack of enthusiasm and poor writing skills, I was told, killed the newspaper. Increasing costs did the same to the yearbook.

"We used to save the majority of students," one teacher said. "Now we save the minority."

Teachers at both Doolittle and Flower had similar complaints. They did not dwell on books and programs, the tangible causes for the changes in the schools. Rather, they complained of more troubling and less easily solved "people" problems that have downgraded the importance of education in general. These are:

•**Home life.** Changing American lifestyles have altered family ties for people in all economic classes. Parents simply do not have the time or the willingness to be as supportive of the schools or of their children.

•**The permissiveness of the 1960s.** When the dust settled from the social agitation of the 1960s, much of it initiated by my generation, it left the generation behind to sweep up, teachers believe. Curiously, many white and black young people now have arrived at the same aimless, undisciplined, irresponsible end through entirely different circumstances, the former by being given everything, the latter by being given barely enough.

•**Poor reading skills.** Reading scores nationwide began a 14-year decline in 1964, the year I finished Doolittle. Americans just do not read as much as they once did. College entrance scores also have declined.

•**Gangs.** Youths who lack parental support, a code of conduct, and probably reading skills find gangs a natural niche.

•**Teenage pregnancy.** The particular scourge of Flower, this is a direct result of the aforementioned factors.

* * *

What has happened since that day 25 years ago when I kissed my mother goodbye in the school yard?

When I started school, so did my mother in a way. She was active in the PTA—both at Doolittle and at Flower—even after I had gone to college. So one of my first questions last June was, "Where are the parents?" The answer most often was, "Out doing their own thing," and that obviously does not include their children.

"Everything begins at home, and it just isn't there any more," said Dorothy Williams, a business teacher at Flower for 16½ years and director of the Office Occupations program, in which students work part-time at clerical jobs.

Teachers blame the home environment for nearly everything, including why children can't read—homes without parental care and often homes without books. Teachers recognize that both parents usually have to work in today's economy, but, that aside, they say that the quality of parenting is lacking and that television is a sorry substitute.

Today's extremely young parents are sometimes almost as immature as their offspring. "I have 14-year-olds whose mothers are 28," Morgan said. "Now, you know the story there."

Indeed I do. In the Near South Side Douglas community around Doolittle, which includes the Ida B. Wells housing project where I grew up and where my parents still live, I know of a 27-year-old grandmother. She had her daughter at 13, and her daughter repeated the cycle last year.

"What kind of an example is a parent who rips out a page from a kid's brand-new dictionary, a dictionary provided by the school, to write a note to the teacher?" asked Paula Simpson, who was my sixth-grade teacher. In her 23d year at Doolittle, she is now the adjustment counselor in charge of tallying enrollments, assigning pupils to classes, and other organizational functions.

Lucille Williams, a remedial reading teacher and former coordinator of a special federally funded reading program that began at Doolittle eight years ago, said, "We have parents in, to learn reading games they can work at at home with their children. We even take parents on field trips so they can learn to bring these experiences to their children." Another Doolittle teacher has adopted the much-publicized "contract" approach to reach parents, requiring a signature nightly to verify that a child has read so many pages of a lesson.

Elisha Walker, the principal at Doolittle since 1973, said that he is blessed with a core of about ten supportive parents. But he added, "It's hard to reach the parent you really want, the one with the problem child. Getting that parent is extremely difficult. You can't reach them by telephone or note."

At Flower, the PTA is nearly invisible. If parents are invisible, then more than discipline is lacking in students' lives.

"These students are starved for you to like them," said Helen Stephenson, a typing and shorthand instructor at Flower. She said that they cannot seem to understand that when teachers exert authority or criticize them in class it is for their benefit. Stephenson, who is also a Flower alumna, returned to the school as a teacher the year before I graduated and inspired those of us who were interested in attending college.

"For many girls, this is home," said Ruth Stewart, an assistant principal at Flower for 21 years. Spend 15 minutes in her office and you will see a parade of girls coming to her with problems that range from what to wear to a party to how to get help for their babies. "We need some special counseling here," she said, pleading, her expression revealing both frustration and sympathy.

A crumpled note from one 16-year-old student, who is the mother of a three-year-old, tells the story:

> *Miss Stewart . . . I wish you were my real mother. Because I love you just like a real mother. Do you love me like a daughter? Tell me so I can. Someone say you don't even be thinking about me. is that true? Please answer today before seven period. OK. I love you mom.*
>
> *your daughter*

Stewart and other teachers might as well be the parents of these students, considering all the parental support that they provide.

Many of the reforms that were generated by the social agitation of the sixties, though desperately needed, were less than fair compensation for years of disfranchisement; but some black educators are now beginning to ask whether some of the reforms went too far. It is one thing to recognize the richness of black English, but it is another to ignore the fact that it is not the language of business. Shakespeare became irrelevant. Why could not both Shakespeare and James Baldwin be relevant?

"There hasn't been a good class at Flower since 1969," said one retired teacher, pinpointing exactly when she felt that everything fell apart. The sixties, in our human need to place blame, catches all the flak. Schools had been a solid rock until the sixties began chipping away. Because the schools had been so entrenched in tradition, they stood for a long time, but when change at last came, the foundation crumbled. Fortunately, I had moved on by then to college, taking advantage of one of the sixties' great successes, the minority scholarship.

Schools not only took on too much that was black oriented but also tried to do too much of everything, so that, as one Doolittle teacher put it, "we are the policeman, parent, and social worker." Out went dress codes and corporal punishment; in came permissiveness and students' rights. Out went the standards, the great American cookie cutter everyone was supposed to pass through. "Students now know all of their rights and none of their responsibilities," says Gladys Patrick, my high school math teacher, who has been at Flower for 23 of her 26 years as a teacher. Frustrated with the caliber of the students she now teaches, she says, "I'm mad at society for giving these kids a diploma they can't read."

"I think the pendulum just swung too far," said Morgan, who is among those black revisionists who think that, in addition to helping some blacks, many social programs also have ensured a dependent class, whose children now make up the majority on the school rolls.

"What we're up against now isn't just teaching, it's altering an entire lifestyle," said Doolittle's Simpson.

Of all the obligations the schools are bridled by, the free-meals program is the one criticized most often by teachers.

It would be hard to criticize the program in theory. Poor children could not learn because they came from home hungry, and so they were given free meals. Of the nearly 450,000 Chicago public school children, more than 284,000 are eligible for free meals, according to board figures. An average of six million free breakfasts and lunches are served monthly in the system's 497 elementary and 72 high schools and 32 specialty schools. At Doolittle, 505 of a total of 645 pupils were eligible for free meals during the 1980–81 school year; at Flower, 659 of 708. Of the remainder, most get reduced-price meals. The full price of lunch is 40 cents in elementary schools, 50 cents in high schools; breakfast is 20 cents.

There have been free lunches in the schools for about 20 years for the neediest children, the ones we used to take extra clothes to and collect canned goods for at Christmas. The expanded program began in October 1970.

"The kids get free breakfast and free lunch. Their moms get a welfare check. Everything is given to them and therefore nothing has any value,"

Morgan said. "You can stretch that to the point [with crime] that life has no value."

The waste in the lunch program is well documented. One Doolittle teacher even confessed to salvaging untouched fresh fruit to take home to her own children. A parent, when told about the waste, shot back to this teacher, "It isn't your money, is it?"

Another Doolittle teacher, asked about free meals, replied with a rhetorical question: "What do they do on Saturday and Sunday?"

"Not only are there free meals, but free tokens to ride the bus to get there, and we also have the health records—eye tests, dentist, shots, even advice for shots for their babies," said Stewart, the assistant principal at Flower.

None of these teachers is a hard-line conservative. None of them wants to take food out of a hungry child's mouth or glasses from the youngster who cannot learn to read because he or she cannot see the page. But teachers would like to see some minimal charge made to parents, to give them some stake in their own children: "Even ten cents, two cents toward the lunch," Simpson said. It is not the services that irk teachers, it is what they represent—abrogation of the parents' responsibility to the schools. Teachers realize that taking away some of these things might make teaching even more difficult, but they also know that adding all these things hasn't made it easier. What concerns them, in addition to the attendant bookkeeping that comes with everything the schools take on, is that society wants them to do all these things and teach, too.

At Flower, I looked at the free-lunch guidelines. For a family of three, the income limit was $8,580 for the 1980–81 school year. Had there been free lunches when I was in school, I would have qualified (by the time I entered high school, my two older sisters had left home). Yet I must remind myself that to be poor and to live in the projects is not the same any more, just as the schools are not the same. I can see the despair, the lost sense of self-sufficiency, when I go back to the old neighborhood. And were my family forced to live today on my father's $6,000-a-year salary, my life would be one of despair, too, I'm sure.

I asked how many of the students receiving free lunches at Flower are "truly needy"—in the words of the Reagan administration.

"There must be some because they try to get all the extra milk they can to take home to their babies," one teacher said. "But they seem to have money for other things. Many of them carry more money than I do."

Another teacher has seen students take a free lunch, then go back through the line to load up on an *à la carte* meal. No one cared to venture where they get the money. Anything is possible with gangs present, one teacher remarked.

Flower's Vice Ladies are more bossy than bloodthirsty, everyone agreed, but they do make their presence known among the other girls. One day last June, Stewart had to make one of her regular phone calls to police when a member of the Vice Lords was shot a block away at the Lake Street bus stop and the Vice Ladies dragged him into the school.

At Doolittle, the Disciples have just begun to make trouble; a few children have been intimidated, and their fearful mothers have kept them at home.

When I was in school there were bands of students, but not organized little machines of gun-packing, knife-toting con artists with secret codes. There were bad kids and we stayed away from them. Generally, school was school, and the streets were the streets.

There were also activities to channel our energies constructively. Doolittle was one of 178 schools with "social centers" after hours where we could roller skate, sing, play games, and, of course, square dance with Mr. Morgan. Teachers were paid for staying overtime; this was before they began racing out of school faster than their students. Budget cutbacks had ended social centers even before I finished Doolittle.

"Social center gave you a chance to hug a child, hold hands with them. They could feel love," Morgan said. "Even when you were on their case in class, they knew you really liked them. And there weren't any attacks on teachers' cars then, were there?"

Nor were there attacks on teachers. One teacher marks the turning point at Flower by an incident in the early seventies, when a home-economics teacher was attacked in class. The girls chopped off her hair and locked her in a closet. When someone heard the uproar and came to her rescue, she denied that the incident took place. (In the 1980–81 school year there were 512 assaults on Chicago public school teachers, according to the Board of Education.)

Such discipline problems have subsided at Flower, only to be replaced by a more vexing, uncontrollable problem—teenage pregnancy. When I attended Flower there was no sex-education program. There was also a rule that prohibited pregnant girls from attending classes. Girls who became pregnant just disappeared, left school for a year to have their babies, and then came back to finish school. It was a costly and unfair lesson, the loss of one year of a young life.

But pregnancy is so widespread now, even with sex-education programs, that no one disappears. In one morning during my visit last June, the school nurse, Eleanore Garner, counseled seven expectant mothers. Garner comes to Flower once a week but is desperately needed full-time.

"They're just babies having babies," she said. "Some are 13. I try to explain what it will mean to their futures, to the babies, but they tell me, 'You had yours, didn't you?' 'Yes,' I tell them, 'but I also had a husband.'

"I don't even ask any more if they have sex. I ask when they last had it," she said. She counseled 190 pregnant girls during the 1980–81 school year. That's more than a quarter of the 708 enrollment.

In my four years at Flower, there were perhaps 60 pregnant girls, and the enrollment was 1,700. Flower's principal, Hortense Bright, who has been at the school since 1975 and in the school system since 1956, shook her head. "The majority of our girls are sexually active," she said. "I wish I knew what we could do. There's no stigma or shame. I can't figure it for the life of me. They *want* to be pregnant."

Said another teacher, "Having a baby is almost a status symbol to these girls. It's the one thing in this world they can do right."

But, of course, they cannot really do that right. How can a young girl with a second-grade reading score (yes, some Flower students are admitted with a score that low) know what to do when a child has swallowed poison? How can she simply read her child a bedtime story, or handle any of the myriad other tasks of motherhood?

Teenage pregnancy, of course, isn't a problem just at Flower. It is a national curse. The East Garfield Park community in which Flower is located has one of the highest birthrates to teenage mothers in the city, 37.4 percent of all births, according to city Health Department figures. An estimated 13,000 teens city-wide, 554,000 nationwide, become mothers each year, according to the latest figures available. Most won't marry, and more than 60 percent will drop out of school.

Flower tries at least to keep them in school. In a home-economics class, a bulletin board full of sewing patterns encourages: MAKE IT FOR BABY.

"Our girls come here with a knowledge of sex you wouldn't believe," Stewart said. "I can be walking down the hall and get a note in my hand that says 'I just had an abortion last night and I'm still bleeding,' or 'I had my IUD in wrong; where should I go?' "

Abortions cannot be legally recommended to these girls; however, birth control information is made available. In the office of Irwin Lesinski, who has been a guidance counselor since 1968, I found birth control pamphlets that made me blush.

"Lea," he admonished me in much the same way he had when I was one of his favorite weepers, "we've got to do something."

Said Richard Dattilo, whose hair has turned a dappled gray since my school days but who is even more dapper, "Our permissive society has confused them." Dattilo runs the Cooperative Work Training Program, which sends girls out to work part-time in semi-skilled jobs.

* * *

Was I being unfair? I saw scrubbed, innocent-looking faces of girls who talked about their career plans. But I also saw hardened old women whose faces exhibited one too many assaults from a boyfriend's knuckles. Then, of course, there were the pregnant girls—both the innocents who regretted their predicament and the matrons who flaunted their new status.

"We have good girls here, girls who want to learn," said Willa Mae Hutsona, who, in 1967, became Flower's first teacher aide. "Things are sort of at a standstill now. We do have some problem children, but what can you expect? This is the ghetto." Administrators, teachers and students are issued plastic I.D. cards, and a check is made every morning of everyone who comes through the doors. The problem is one of intruders—troublemakers who would defy, even hurt, anyone who tried to toss them out of the school. They are the kind who have become such a severe problem that the shrubbery around the school has been trimmed because of a number of rapes. Some sit outside the school for hours, passing out leaflets to entice the girls to parties at cocktail lounges. One flyer read, "Top security, good stuff, no junk." Stewart offered a translation: "That means the dope will be the best." Later, she came running into the teachers' lunchroom with a policeman to point out another troublemaker, a knife-wielding character whom school authorities had been trying to apprehend for two days. They lost him again. What could school authorities do, she asked, short of having a police car sit outside all day?

All of this stress naturally has had its effect on teaching and teachers.

"Well, I'm tired," said Dorothy Williams. "It's discouraging to walk into a data-programming class with girls who don't even know the words in the manual. It's still challenging, though, because I see the need. In spite of the frustration, you keep at it."

* * *

So what has happened? A look at two schools out of a system of more than 500 hardly lends itself to a definitive analysis. Other schools are in better shape. Some are in worse. Much more than this is right with the schools, and much more is wrong. In a recent issue of *The Public Interest,* J. S. Fuerst, a professor of urban studies at Loyola University, wrote of four superior elementary schools with predominantly black enrollments. But even Fuerst conceded that most black children are not being well served by the city's school system. Busing, faculty integration, political infighting at the board level and dismal reading scores deserve further examination. The views of parents and students also require discussion. Teachers, of course, are not entirely blameless.

Much of what is wrong with the schools is what is wrong with the world—for example, the increase in violent crime and our troubled economy. It is now clear that the system was beginning to erode even when I was a student. Two years ago, when Joseph Hannon resigned as superintendent, we learned that the system's finances had been rob-Peter-to-pay-Paul for years. The problems of gang influence, lack of discipline, the decline of basic skills and teenage pregnancy are in as desperate need of remedy as is the financial situation.

But I, and many of my former teachers, believe that the ultimate answer lies in the home. "I don't want to think it's hopeless," Simpson of the Doolittle school said, "but if we can't get to the parents, we are lost." She suggested a home-visiting teacher program in which teachers actually go into the home and re-establish ties between the community and the schools. She participated in such a pilot program at Doolittle for six months many years ago. Doesn't such an idea essentially mean teaching parents to be parents, in addition to teaching their children? How many teachers would be willing to do that? How many parents?

These problems are not unique to Chicago. Public education is in a sorry state everywhere, including the white suburbs. However, for black and poor youngsters, these problems have consequences a hundred times greater. If everyone on the ladder slips two rungs, the person on the bottom is off the ladder entirely. And my innate black cynicism, the cynicism that millions of black people put on like a coat of armor every morning to get through the day, compels me to question whether there really is less concern for education in this city because roughly 80 percent of the students are members of minority groups. Which leads me to another question: Was I educated by default? Did I receive an education because most of the students in the system were white?

There is another, final reason why I made it. It has nothing to do with being black or white, or middle or lower income, or having a father or not. I made it because it was expected of me. Raise the standards for what is expected of these schoolchildren, and their hopes will rise, too. They are not beyond help, no matter how bleak some of the evidence seems. Stop experimenting, set some goals, and penalize those who do not live up to them. Set standards for administrators and teachers as well.

There are no easy answers. ■

September 14, 1983

Buddy Young's lessons for youths

Claude "Buddy" Young, the star Illini and pro football running back who first gained attention at Phillips High School here in the mid-1940s, was hailed in eulogies last week at funeral services attended by Mayor Harold Washington, National Football League Commissioner Pete Rozelle and about 1,000 other dignitaries and mourners. Young, 57, died in an auto accident near Dallas.

In his day, Buddy Young was what football was all about in terms of statistics and fame and skill. But what he was about just before his death—director of NFL player relations—carries even more important lessons for youths, particularly young black athletes, with pro stars and dollar signs in their eyes. In his NFL job, Young counseled players to help them keep in touch with reality as they balanced the stresses and temptations of life on the fast track, and he steered them through retirement to find new careers.

While giving of himself at the professional level, Young was beginning to do even more good works by reaching back to students in high school. Just a month ago he was in Chicago to kick off a program called "Mayor Harold Washington's High Hurdles for Academic Excellence." The name has double significance—the mayor was a hurdler in his days at DuSable High School and has proven himself in the hurdles of black life.

Young and the mayor were among a stellar gathering Aug. 12 at McCormick Inn that included schools Supt. Ruth Love, State Sen. Richard Newhouse (in his role as chairman of the Committee on Higher Education) and coaches Eddie Robinson of Grambling, Dennis Green of Northwestern University and Bo Schembechler of the University of Michigan. George Taliaferro, special assistant to the president of Indiana University, also was there. They met with more than 180 Chicago high school coaches and principals in an all-day seminar to talk about preparing young athletes to also be scholars in light of the National College Athletic Association's "Rule 48."

"Our concerns ranged from the demons of alcohol and substance abuse to developing rigorous academic standards to make these students strive to reap some of the benefits they work so hard for," an aide to Newhouse said. "Mr. Young felt a strong commitment to excellence—athletically, scholastically and humanistically. With his death we feel an extra commitment ourselves to carry on."

NCAA Rule 48 has raised academic standards, and it has raised howls from blacks in sports, some presidents of black colleges even charging that it is a plot to "whiten" teams. The rule, approved at the NCAA convention in San Diego in January, will take effect in 1986.

It requires high school seniors to have a score on the Scholastic Aptitude Test (SAT) for college admission of 700 out of a total 1,600, or on the American College Test (ACT) of 15 of a possible 36. It also requires students to have a high school "core curriculum" in English, math and the social and physical sciences and a grade point average of 2.0.

Students without these can be recruited by colleges but are forbidden to play or practice in their freshman year. Sports would be permitted in the sophomore year after a review of the student's progress.

Initially, black athletes will be hurt most by this new rule. But of course they were the ones most hurt by past practices that fed their brawn and ego temporarily and left their minds to waste.

Despite the "black" look of sports, blacks get fewer than one in 10 of the athletic scholarships in this country, according to Harry Edwards, a professor of sociology at the University of California at Berkeley. In an article entitled "Educating Black Athletes" in last month's *Atlantic* magazine, Edwards also noted that an estimated 25 to 35 percent of black male high school athletes qualifying for these scholarships cannot accept because of academic shortcomings.

Standards are standards. For blacks to cry foul and say black athletes cannot meet them is self-defeating. That is not to overlook the grave disadvantages blacks suffer in education and every other institution, but the line has to be drawn somewhere.

It's time to end the exploitation of athletes who draw crowds to fundraisers for alumni associations that they themselves never get to join.

Buddy Young knew that lesson of life. It should not be lost on the black kid who lives and sleeps with his basketball, baseball bat or football helmet. ■

September 18, 1983

A schools lesson unlearned

Chicago teachers deserve a raise, and it would be a shame if they actually have to strike Oct. 3 to get it. I take this position confessing that the Board of Education supports most of my family. (I have two sisters who are elementary school teachers and their husbands are a high school teacher and a board administrator.) But I would think so regardless.

If nothing else, teachers deserve the combat pay, and I say that with some understanding since one of my sisters was caught in gang crossfire and shot some years ago leaving school. But she's still at it.

Chicago Teachers' Union President Robert Healey, who usually grows fangs in the public image every year at this time, is still an admirably tough leader. He has a valid complaint that other public employees have gotten raises while teachers haven't. (Firefighters already are clamoring for 10 percent.) And his thinking isn't far off from the average taxpayer's: Where is that extra $117 million going? Do people expect "Our Miss Brooks" with starting salaries of $13,700?

There is truth in everyone's side of the school story. There are useless jobs with huge expense accounts at the board that are being protected and there are useless teachers who need to be removed.

The mess that the schools are in, just like the mess the city generally is in, has taken years to accumulate. It will take years to undo with some hard-nosed decision-making.

Teachers are aware of the imbalances in the ledger. They rallied in the campaign to "Save Our City/Save Our Schools," wrote more than 40,000 letters and helped to prod the legislature into increasing city property taxes—which many of them also pay—to shore up a budget that did not include raises for them. But they hoped anyway.

Teachers should get something, but not for nothing (and here is where I probably will be disinherited by my family union members).

Two years ago the board agreed to the pension pick-up for teachers in lieu of a seven percent raise. Teachers don't like to call that a raise, but it meant more take-home pay. It was a gimmick then to avert the annual crisis, but worse it has come to be viewed as an entitlement, a permanent feature of contract negotiations, and that is not what it was meant to be. It also is setting an unhealthy precedent for public employee negotiations. Even many private companies do not pay the full share of their employees' pensions.

Last year, the pension was picked up again. That was not a raise, just maintaining the status quo. So who could begrudge teachers a raise this year? Except this year it seems they are holding out for the pension again and a raise, too. They argue that to relinquish the pick-up but get a raise of a lesser percentage would leave them with a negative balance. All of the sympathy in the world for teachers won't balance the books to get them enough money for both demands.

Something or someone has to give, and the teachers hold the basket with the larger number of eggs: health benefits, class size, personal business and sick days. But the downtown administrators have some fat to trim, too, in consultants, lawyers, etc.

Chicago United, a business group that offers clearer thinking on school problems than anyone in the system, has suggested some sacrifices that teachers could make if they really want to get a raise.

First, Chicago United also supports a higher salary, but links it to merit pay, the latest hot issue in education and one that goes over with most teachers' unions like scratching chalk on a blackboard. Merit pay is how most of the working world works—each one according to his ability, not just seniority. Surely teachers, who recognize the varying limitations and levels of achievement just among the children in their rooms, can see the merit of merit pay; it would be like pasting up gold stars for some teachers.

Second, Chicago United proposes to reduce teacher paperwork, but they also propose that teachers take two or three more children in the classroom, that the school year and day be lengthened and that the ratio of hours of actual study to nonacademic activity be increased. They don't just pick on teachers; the report also deals with underachieving and uninvolved parents, board politics, the administrative bureaucracy and other thoughts probably far too progressive to get anywhere in this town as long as contracts and minds are made of granite.

Mayor Harold Washington should stand by his vow not to get involved, not to perform any last-minute miracles. It's time the teachers and the board learn the real art of negotiation. ■

October 19, 1983

Pathetic state of Chicago's schools

The "prevailing wage" issue comes up just about every time Chicago faces a teachers' strike, which, in recent years, is just about every autumn. The late Mayor Daley was able to win valuable political help from organized labor by compensating city workers, including school janitors and other nonacademic employees, at the same wage level as workers in the private sector. Other mayors upheld the practice until reformer Washington came along to point out that the public workers were, in effect, receiving better pay than workers in the private sector, who were subject to weather and other adverse conditions, and he planned to end the practice. McClain was appalled that all of these issues were stalling the education of Chicago youngsters for reasons that had nothing to do with education.

By now a zillion different charges of collusion have whirled about the Chicago school strike, many of them leading to the city council factionalism or race or an effort to embarrass the mayor.

Operation PUSH charged that teachers' union President Robert Healey had met secretly with Ald. Edward Vrdolyak. Many people are finding it suspicious that for the first time the trade unionists, 97 percent white, have joined with the teachers; this is seen as retribution against the mayor for his pronouncements against the prevailing wage.

Even one black veteran craftsman for the board admitted to half of that theory, but not as conspiracy: "I don't believe that stuff about Vrdolyak. It's a matter of money. The city owes me $2,000 in back pay. It doesn't matter what the teachers get, they aren't going into any schools that don't have heat. Money is the issue."

The disgruntled craftsman is all too right about money being the issue, whether for teachers or the trade unions. So much is wrapped up in money—and teachers do need more—that no one is talking about education. There is my conspiracy: the one against the mostly minority students in the system—and by minority teachers.

But there is another conflict in the school strike. It was summed up by a poster waved by teachers at a protest outside of CUE (Center for Urban Education), the hurriedly thrown together administrative offices of the schools. (The board's ineptitude at even finding itself a home is just another example of a system in disarray from top to bottom.)

The sign read: "Ruth-less Love-less."

Say what you will about the changing times, when teachers, supposedly pillars of the community, would resort to such directness, it is obvious that much of the strike is a backlash against the imported school of management of Supt. Ruth Love.

Love enjoys an astonishing good press, not undeservedly. Student test scores have recorded gains since she arrived. She is forceful, dynamic, a positive role model.

But many in the system and in the black community have looked askance at her since she and her coterie of outsiders arrived and added to an already obese bureaucracy. Her entrance was a stormy one, with many in the black community refusing to roll out a red carpet. A contingent of women traveled to Oakland to meet with Love; though the meeting supposedly was informational, the information passed on to Love was don't come to Chicago.

And Love's $120,000 salary is simply salt in the wounds of school employees.

"She's all hype," said one black activist whose organization is among the six joining Operation PUSH in a suit asking that the schools be re-opened. The person requested anonymity in the senseless climate of taboos that say one black should not speak out publicly against another.

Love's rift with Manford Byrd, the black deputy superintendent who was her chief rival for the superintendent's spot in 1981, is yet unsettled. She announced in August that she might abolish his post as head of the Office of Systemwide Reorganization, a job he had denounced as a demotion anyway.

Mayor Byrne apparently was never enamored of the independent-minded Love, who reportedly was nicknamed the "Queen of Sheba" around City Hall. Relations worsened when Love refused to make campaign commercials for Byrne, while others such as former police Supt. Richard Brzeczek consented. And relations with Mayor Harold Washington are said to be strained for much the same reason, her political neutrality.

Where does all of this innuendo lead?

It is not my job to sit in judgment of Love or the allegations of office politics.

But the nastiness in the air reminds us of one thing: That the system, from top to bottom, from the board to Love, to the most hard-bitten veteran principal, to the newest substitute, to the cook in the cafeteria, is in a pathetic state.

And those who are suffering are the children, mostly black and Hispanic.

"Four weeks of work with these kids down the drain," said my sister, an eighth grade teacher, in disgust as she headed for an early-morning picket line.

And where are the black parents? My sister noted that in the second week of classes a mother pulled a gun on a teacher because the mother felt her child had been given too much homework.

This is not an indictment of all parents or all teachers or all administrators. But there certainly is enough wrong with enough people in the system that even if the strike ends soon and everyone gets a cut in the deal, the schools will remain an ungodly mess. ■

November 30, 1983

"Renaissance" for Chicago's schools

The high school "renaissance" program announced by schools Supt. Ruth Love is a praiseworthy return to standards. The only distressing aspect of it is that the schools have fallen into such disrepair that a basic curriculum has to be announced and given a fancy name.

But if the program initially lifts only a few hundred children out of the rut of lowered expectations, "renaissance" will have brought a renaissance. Supt. Love is right in being demanding of the students, but that toughness will have to permeate the system to administrators, teachers and, perhaps most important, to parents. Everyone laments the passing of hard-and-fast standards in education, and this program just may give them a chance to stop talking about it and act.

Love's plan, which has won approval by the Board of Education, requires that children have a 7.5 reading score to graduate from elementary school, beginning in 1987. Those who do not will be retained in eighth grade for up to two years and given noncredit remedial courses.

Beginning next September high school course requirements will increase from three years combined math and science to two years of each. Where there are no requirements now, the plan will institute two years of a foreign language, one of computer education and one of typing. The current requirements of four years of English and three of social studies will remain unchanged.

The plan has been lambasted for its lack of forethought on implementation, for its unknown costs (perhaps $18 million to $20 million and as many as 600 new teachers will be needed) and for the possible embarrassment of those children who will be left behind. Would you rather see an embarrassed 12-year-old keep trying or an embarrassed and unemployed 20-year-old who quit trying at everything?

Money always will be a giant problem, but those who cry that so many children will be lost befoul the intent of "renaissance." If purpose cannot be restored to the schools, no amount of money will matter.

When detractors point out how minority children will be hurt most, they insult the intelligence of these children. Too many now are not making it because no one has ever expected that they would make it. There is no denying some children will be left behind; an estimated 7,000 pupils could not meet the 7.5 level now. But it would be better to stop coddling this percentage and put energies into the majority who ultimately might succeed, or even overachieve.

As hopeful as the program is, though, it will have an obstacle in many of the same dispirited teachers who have doomed these children so far, who collect paychecks for babysitting and little more. To that end principals will be given greater latitude to choose staff.

During the strike, teachers had a good case for higher pay, but there was an equally good case for getting more concern from some of them, more "quality time" in the fashionable parlance. The teachers got very little from the strike, but the students got even less. There was no discussion by the union of cooperating with administration to sift through its rolls. It was an unfortunate episode for everyone. The complaints on both sides— about the board's overpaid bureaucracy and teacher burnout—remain legitimate and unresolved.

As for making "renaissance" work, there is one other element that is required, the cooperation of parents. Even a spectacular teacher can do only so much for a child during the school day.

I know the argument about many young parents in particular being part of the cycle of public school failures. But that, too, has become a sorry excuse for giving up on kids before even trying. There are no courses that can make good parents.

Just for comparison's sake, I looked up the courses I took in high school here in the not-so-distant past of 1964 to 1968. (It was an easy undertaking since my mother has every report card of mine since kindergarten.)

Guess what. I passed "renaissance," only it was called "what you needed to graduate," with the subtitle, "and you better have done well." It included four years of English, two of Spanish, three of social studies, four of physical education, two of music, one of art, three of math, two of science, two of typing, plus electives of shorthand, bookkeeping, home economics and drivers ed. Only a computer course was lacking, but in those days "high tech" was being the first on the block to have a color TV.

Please give "renaissance" a try. Whatever respectability is left in the system is worth it. ■

April 4, 1984

Undermining of teachers' authority

There was a time when a stern look or even the sound of the teacher's footsteps commanded silence and respect, but not anymore. And this loss has been aided unintentionally by judicial and legislative rulings on the rights of students.

Order cannot be had in today's schools the way it is in court, with the crack of a gavel, unless the gavel is cracked across a student's noggin; and then the student likely will sue.

The area of student rights has left a long, litigious trail in recent years, while the reciprocal expectation for student responsibility has diminished.

There have been legal decisions awarding students their rights to dress; to freedom of expression, in a 1969 landmark Supreme Court case in which students were given permission to wear black armbands to protest the Vietnam War; to challenge school records, in congressional legislation in 1974 called the Family Educational Rights and Privacy Act; to protest disciplinary action, suspension, expulsion and corporal punishment, under the 14th Amendment right of due process; and to refuse searches of their persons.

These rulings were not always wrong, and school officials are not always right, but they have created conditions which are intrusive and burdensome for teachers. The courts seem to have gone to the extreme to undermine teacher authority, and at the very time that other traditional authority figures in a student's life also are declining.

The U.S. Supreme Court is now hearing arguments in a New Jersey case concerning the 1980 search of a student's purse. The search turned up drugs, and a conviction resulted. Attorneys for the student have invoked the 4th Amendment's protection from unlawful search and seizure. (Previous cases have found that searches of lockers are allowed because the lockers are considered school property; but this case involved a student's purse and person.) The National School Boards Association has intervened, asking that the 4th Amendment not be applied to schools at all.

The New Jersey courts overturned the conviction based on the ground that because the search was illegal, the evidence it turned up could not be introduced in court. The U.S. Supreme Court is being asked to review the case, specifically to determine whether evidence obtained by a school official is subject to the same legal requirements as that obtained by law enforcement agents.

The argument over excluding illegally obtained evidence—the exclusionary rule—is a many-sided and ongoing one in the legal community, but it seems to be no more than a technicality in this case. The key concerns here should be, first, that drugs were indeed found, and second, that school authorities have the right to maintain safety and security on school property.

I can just imagine the response that charges of unlawful search and seizure would have brought in Mrs. Albright's fifth grade class when she confiscated the mirror Larry was using to look under girls' dresses: swift adjudication with the back of her hand.

But the back of Mrs. Albright's hand would be impractical against a knife wielder. The threat has to be toughened in answer to the times now that schools are dealing with drugs, weapons and who knows what else, things that could cause harm to the offending student, those around him and the teacher.

Chief Justice Warren Burger has said in the New Jersey case that there is a "social cost" overlooked by the lower court's ruling, which is that drug pushers may go free. Is it really better that a student squeal about his rights, rather than on a pusher? Schools already have had to make up the balance for so many social costs—sexual permissiveness and drug use, the need for women to work and for poor children to be fed. The courts should have increased the discretionary power of school officials along with the increased demands on schools.

There must be some reasonableness in the closed society of a school. Teachers should go only so far to maintain order, and they can forget, too, the acceptable limits to which they should go. But the courts have bound schools so that they are ineffective against the very problems everyone expects them, and them alone, to solve. ■

Afterword

Leanita McClain told her readers what she thought they needed to hear, not what they wanted to hear, and her candor was not always welcome. The power of her most incisive work often was confirmed by a barrage of stinging letters and phone calls from those who held opposite opinions. An extremely—perhaps fatally—sensitive person, McClain was pained by such criticism. Yet she persevered.

McClain wanted to see people of different races, ethnic backgrounds and religions living together in harmony. But such a vision was more utopian than realistic. Paddy Bauler, a notoriously corrupt alderman, once said that "Chicago ain't ready for reform," and McClain soon found out that Chicago wasn't ready for ethnic utopia either.

Her writings about black problems were disparaged by many whites who said they had problems of their own. Her criticism of the bigotry that pervaded the 1983 Chicago mayoral campaign and that was later manifested during Harold Washington's administration, on the other hand, brought angry responses not just from bigots but from whites who felt they weren't prejudiced and didn't like having their genuine criticisms of Washington's ability to govern lumped in with those based simply on racism.

However, in making their point they missed her point. McClain did not feel Washington was above criticism. Although she usually supported him, she did not spare criticism when she thought it was appropriate. For example, in her June 25, 1983 column, "City's puzzlingly prudent pol," she noted that "the Berry incident leaves you wondering whose counsel Washington seeks if not the man he entrusted to construct the framework of his new government." She also talked about Washington's inaccessibility and his alienation from potential allies and power brokers. More pungent is her Oct. 30, 1983 column, "Washington's electrifying elocution," in which she suggested that the mayor might need to "have his mouth washed out with soap" after his temper got the best of his tongue.

McClain's attacks on the bigotry that plagued Harold Washington's political life focused on a more subtle prejudice: The thinking that Washington was not ready to govern because blacks in general were not ready to govern. Her Dec. 7, 1983 column, "The black 'quarterback syndrome,' " dealt with black quarterback Vince Evans and "this society's pathological unwillingness to accept blacks in leadership roles. His [Evans'] predicament is representative of black life in sports, in politics, in business, or whatever." McClain then noted: "Many blacks maintain that it was 'the quarterback syndrome' that defeated Los Angeles Mayor Tom Bradley in his bid to become California's first black governor. . . . The effect 'the syndrome' would have was much talked about during the election of Harold Washington, too. How many whites simply could not—cannot now—accept black leadership?"

As one of the few Chicago blacks who had access to a national audience, Leanita McClain tried in her much-talked-about *Washington Post* article to give the country a black perspective on the racial turmoil that split the city and destroyed her dream of ethnic utopia. But, perhaps predictably, a lot of people could not read past the *Post*'s overstated headline ("How Chicago Taught Me to Hate Whites"), which, in typical newspaper custom, McClain neither chose nor knew about before publication. The headline and an out-of-context reference to McClain's feeling "like machine-gunning every white face on the bus" were all that many Chicago readers knew, since few had access to the *Post*.

There were other controversies. Some Jews accused her of anti-Semitism for her defense, purely on constitutional grounds, of a local weekly's racist and anti-Semitic "personals" ads, even though she made it clear that the ads offended her too. More than a few blacks who read her criticisms of Harold Washington questioned her loyalty to her own people. Attacks by blacks increased after McClain wrote her Aug. 20, 1983 column, "Tree shaker or jelly maker?", discussing the probable presidential candidacy of Jesse Jackson and pointing out "his zero experience in public office." A later column, "Black votes and Jesse Jackson" (Nov. 6, 1983), perhaps reflecting the furor caused by the Aug. 20 column, noted that it was not treason for blacks to vote for someone other than Jackson, but nonetheless, "emotions are feverish among blacks; to express any doubt about which lever you might pull is heresy."

Leanita McClain was neither an anti-Semite nor a quisling. She believed simply that she could criticize anybody who deserved it. Of course this did not sit well with members of whichever group she challenged. Indeed, it often does not even seem to matter whether the scrutiny comes from within the same race, religion or ethnic group, especially if the critic is from a different social or economic class. Those who speak negatively about their own become suspect, damned for publicly airing communal dirty laundry.

McClain was a victim of the no-man's-land in which black journalists find themselves when they are criticized by both whites and blacks. She realized early in her career that as a nouveau middle-class black she would remain an eternal outsider. Her brilliant *Newsweek* column spoke exactly to that point: "Whites won't believe I remain culturally different; blacks won't believe I remain culturally the same," she wrote after observing that ghetto blacks accuse middle-class blacks such as herself of having sold out and become "Oreos"—black on the outside and white within.

Nonetheless, although she intellectually understood her paradoxical position, she was emotionally devastated by it. It remained a significant burden in the load that constantly pressed upon her, a weight intensified by her grief over the 1980 death of her much-loved four-year-old nephew; the failure of her marriage; her doubts about her own abilities, coupled with the increasing demands of her job and community status; and the outpouring of hatred engendered by the Chicago mayoral election.

Was McClain right about the resilience of racism in American society? Or was she naive to hope for anything more than anyone could expect? Those who knew her well, as I did, knew long before her death that although Leanita McClain was gifted in her writing and perceptive in her thinking, she was also chronically depressed. Her poetry, in which images of death, woe and self-destruction prevail, provides ample evidence of this.

Extreme pessimism and the chronic conviction that things will never improve are major characteristics of depression. McClain, who was predisposed to depression and already adversely affected by her unhappy personal life, agonized over the slow progress of human rights.

Yes, blacks have made great advances since the time American society considered them as chattel. But this is not enough consolation to one who despairs, because depression emphasizes failure over success.

At the same time we must not forget that progress has been made— and that this could not have happened without blacks who fought for their own rights, sometimes in schools, sometimes in courts, other times in the pages of such newspapers as the *Chicago Tribune*. It was individuals such as Leanita McClain who made the difference.

The difference she made was manifested in her impact upon such diverse issues as the attitudes of white racists, black political awareness and inner-city education.

Monroe Anderson, a friend of McClain's who was City Hall reporter for the *Chicago Tribune* when the *Washington Post* article ran, says that McClain "really upset white racists because she was such a lady. She fit everything they said a 'proper Negro' should be, and then she pointed a finger and highlighted their racism. There was no 'safe harbor' among blacks for their [white racists'] long held attitudes."

As for her effect on the black community, Anderson notes, "Because she spoke the truth as she saw it, she helped stimulate dialogue among blacks of differing political ideologies. I'd have people tell me what they thought of an article of hers, not knowing we were friends. One would condemn it because they thought it was too accommodating to the white power structure, while another would say that it was perceptive."

Professor Robert T. Starks, of Northeastern Illinois University's Center for Inner City Studies, sees another contribution: McClain's ability to "point out the abiding contradictions of American politics, which preaches tolerance and practices intolerance; pleads for the participation of all while excluding all but those who are basically white, middle class and American born; and tells black people they should vote on the basis of merit without regard to race or ethnicity, but at the same time votes exclusively for white ethnics."

McClain's impact on inner-city education, on the other hand, was probably more attributable to personal example than to the few powerful articles she wrote. As Starks says, her life itself had an impact upon inner-city education because she came from the inner city and still achieved the success she did. She was proud that she was a product of inner-city schools, and she pointed this out to many inner-city students.

Somebody once remarked that suicide is the most sincere form of criticism. Was Leanita McClain, who spent her career as a journalistic critic, making this ultimate criticism? I don't know. I do know that ultimately she will be judged not by her death but by her life, and by the contributions to society that she made during its too-brief span.

Charles Chi Halevi